# The Romantic

## The Vers Podcast #2

### by
### RILEY HART

Copyright © 2023 by Riley Hart
Print Edition

All rights reserved.

No part of this book may be used, reproduced, or transmitted in any form or by any means, electronic or mechanical, including photocopying, recording, or by any information storage and retrieval systems, without prior written permission of the author, except where permitted by law.

Published by:

Riley Hart

This book is a work of fiction. Names, characters, places, and incidents are products of the author's imagination or are used fictitiously. Any similarity to actual persons, living or dead, is coincidental and not intended by the author.

All products/brand names/trademarks mentioned are registered trademarks of their respective holders/companies.

Cover Image by RafaGCatala
Edited by Keren Reed Editing
Proofread by Judy's Proofreading and Lyrical Lines Proofreading

**Parker**

When it comes to *The Vers*, the queer podcast I host with my best friends, I'm The Romantic. The one who's looking for love in all the wrong places. If there's a jerk close by, I'll find him. I'm beginning to think my Mr. Right doesn't exist.

It's definitely not Elliott Delgado Weaver, the shameless flirt who keeps asking me out. We're *not* supposed to run into each other in Vegas or get drunk together. We definitely aren't supposed to wake up married...only, we do.

Before we can figure out what to do, Elliott's family finds out. He doesn't want to let them down by telling them it was a drunken mistake. My parents had the perfect marriage until my mom passed, and since I'd hate for my father to discover what I did, Elliott and I decide to pretend we're in love and stay married for six months. Better to amicably divorce later than own up to our screwup, right?

All I've ever wanted is my happily ever after, and now I live with a serial hookup artist who never planned on settling down.

But then, why is Elliott so good to me? He takes me on dates, makes me laugh, and touches me like I'm someone to cherish. He's shown me I'm a sucker for praise, and lucky for me, he loves giving it to me. Our marriage is playing tricks on my heart because suddenly I'm wishing my happy ending can be with the husband who doesn't think love is for him.

The Romantic *is a wake-up-married, opposites-attract romance with tons of praise, an unforgettable massage, found family, and sweet moments on the pier.*

# Special Thanks

**Jessica, thank you for your help with all things Cuban.**

# PROLOGUE
## *Parker*

ALL I'VE EVER wanted was to find the perfect man.

Not the perfect man in general. My rose-tinted glasses weren't that pink. Perfection didn't exist. I did want to find the perfect man for me, but for whatever reason, that motherfucker seemed to be doing everything he could to dodge me, and I ended up with bad date after bad date. Asshole after asshole. I've noticed that guys who just wanted my hole or my dick weren't too discriminatory in that department. The point was, they didn't want *me*. Not the real me. Not for longer than a date or a week or a few fucks—which yes, I was excellent at, but that was irrelevant.

What mattered was that I sucked at dating. This was proven again tonight, as I was currently sitting in a quiet bar in West Hollywood for a first date…and I'd been stood up.

Again.

Fuck my life.

To make matters worse, my ex-boyfriend showed up, saw me sitting at the bar, and was now trying to hit on me. The same boyfriend who knew I was looking for something permanent and had dumped me because he wasn't. He also thought my laugh was annoying. Who the fuck said that to someone? But Jim was known for saying the quiet parts out loud.

"We should get out of here together. I miss you," Jim said, giving me the smile I used to find sexy but now realized was smarmy and gross. I had horrible first-date vision; hindsight was, in fact, twenty/twenty.

"No. Why the hell would I want to leave with you? And you don't miss me. You just want to have sex with me. There's a difference."

Ugh. And he was really good in bed. Why were all the assholes really good in bed?

"Because I know you're sitting here waiting for someone who didn't show up," Jim replied, making my heart drop. How the fuck did he know? Did I wear a sign on my back that said *desperate and unlovable*? Or maybe one that said *take advantage of me*? "Might as well still enjoy the night," he added.

"Fuck off, and no, I'm not waiting for someone. I just felt like getting a drink." In a bar. Alone. He cocked a brow, obviously not believing me. "I have a boyfriend. He doesn't work far from here. I'm waiting for him to get off work."

I hated lying and liars, but desperate times called for desperate measures. And the last thing I wanted him to know was that I was a sad, lonely man with no life outside of my business and my friends. Which really should be enough. I wasn't an idiot. I knew I was capable on my own and that I shouldn't settle for someone who wasn't worthy of my time. I did know that. Hence the reason I was still single. But I wanted something more. I wanted to find my person, the way my parents had. They'd been each other's whole world, and then I had been too. I wanted that kind of love. Clearly, the universe didn't get the memo because it wasn't happening for me.

"You have a boyfriend, huh?"

"Yes." Jesus, why was he acting like it was so hard to

believe? I was a fucking catch, and while I didn't want to sound cocky and I wasn't a conceited guy, I also happened to know I was easy on the eyes. Apparently, my personality just sucked or I had the worst luck ever in the history of the world.

"I can't wait to meet him." Jim winked.

Fuck my life. He was going to sit there and wait to meet my fictitious boyfriend. And if I left, he would know I was lying. How ridiculous would I look then? Why was he such a dick? I couldn't figure out what I'd ever seen in him.

"Whatever you want." I shrugged and took a drink of my Sprite. I wasn't drinking because I was supposed to be meeting the man of my dreams and I hadn't wanted to be inebriated.

"Hey, babe. Sorry I'm late." I froze at the sound of the voice I didn't recognize and the hand at my back.

"Oh," Jim said as I turned to take in what was, quite literally, the most gorgeous man I had ever seen. He slid onto the stool beside me. His hair was a mocha color, just a couple of inches long and slightly messy, like it had a mind of its own and the guy was too hot to care. He had a bit more length on the top than on the sides. His eyes were a similar color, the perfect shade of brown that made them seem comforting.

His face was stubbled, but neatly so. I could tell he kept up on it, probably liking the fact that it was the ideal length to feel incredible against another man's skin. Mister Sex on Legs had a bow-shaped mouth, perfect for kissing, and mischief danced in his gaze.

"Elliott. Nice to meet you," he said, holding his hand out for Jim but looking at me like... Oh. He was making sure I knew his name.

"Jim," my ex grumbled. Yeah, what did he have to say now? My new fake boyfriend was way hotter than him.

They let go of each other's hands, and Elliott looked at me again. Christ, his skin was flawless. I heard that about my skin a lot, but his was perfect, and while mine was on the paler side, his was more golden. He definitely looked like he was part Latino.

"Sorry I kept you waiting. Did you have a long day?" His voice was smooth as honey and I was a biscuit that wanted to drown in it. Elliott reached out and brushed the back of his hand against my cheek. I trembled, because oh, he was good. My dick was also getting quite interested in my savior.

"Yeah, you know how it is, but it's better now." I smiled at him. Two could play this game. If Elliott was going to sell this shit, I wouldn't leave him to do it alone. I had no idea *why* he was doing it, but it felt good to stick it to Jim.

"Babe," Elliott said.

"Hmm?"

Elliott grinned, and I was pretty sure I'd gotten lost in his eyes. What in the fuck was it about him? "That guy is speaking to you."

"Oops." I turned to my ex, who was scowling. He clearly wasn't on team Parker and Elliott. I, however, was a fan.

"How did you guys meet?" Jim asked. I had the feeling he still didn't believe us. Fuck him. I was hot. I could totally pull Elliott in real life.

"On a blind date." Elliott rested his hand on my nape, tickling it with the tips of his fingers. "I was immediately smitten, not just because he's sexy as hell, but because he's kind, funny, and that thing he does with his tongue...fuck, it kills me."

Okay, so he was laying it on a bit thick, but I couldn't find it in myself to care. I also wasn't typically the kind of guy who wanted to be saved, but Jim was an asshole and this was fun. I was happy to let Elliott swoop in and save the day.

"I don't remember," Jim grumbled.

"Maybe you didn't give him as much to work with."

Elliott winked.

"Fuck you," Jim told him.

"You ready to get out of here?" Elliott asked me.

"Yeah, sure. I already paid."

This was the weirdest thing that had ever happened to me. I seemed to attract weird shit, so I was going with it—and at least it wasn't unlucky weird as per usual. Well, unless Elliott turned out to be a murderer. That would suck. I wasn't ready to die, and especially not at the hands of someone so beautiful.

He stood, and I did the same. When he tried to hold my hand, I pulled mine back. We didn't need to go overboard. We could walk out together. I would thank him and then be on my way.

"Good to see you again, Jim," I lied.

"Nice to meet you, man," Elliott said. "I guess I owe you a thank-you…for not knowing what you had when you had it. Your loss is my gain." Elliott smirked at him. Oh, he was cocky as fuck, and while that normally annoyed me, it was golden in this situation.

"You're an asshole," Jim told him.

"So I've been told," Elliott replied, then to me, "shall we?"

I hooked my arm through his, deciding that yes, we should add some more icing to the cake before the two of us parted ways.

But Jim was right behind us. Shit. Was he going to follow us? To my relief, the second we got outside, he went to the left, and Elliott and I to the right.

"I think he's pissed he didn't get laid tonight," Elliott whispered, amusement in his voice.

"I think you're right."

We didn't let go of each other until we made it down the block some and around the corner. Then I immediately let go of him. "Fuck yes! Thank you. That was more fun than it should be. Also, how did you know to do that? *Why* did you do that? Oh God, are you a stalker?" I hadn't even considered that Elliott could have some other motive here.

He laughed, rich and deep, the sound going straight to my groin. "I was sitting a few people away from him. Neither of you noticed. I overheard you talking. He's a dick, so I thought I'd jump in and have a little fun. What did you ever see in that guy?"

"I have no idea. But then, people rarely show their true colors until they want to."

He frowned, nodded.

It was busy out tonight, the way it usually was in WeHo. We continued down the sidewalk, passing people eating on restaurant patios and filling the streets.

"Do I get your name?" he asked.

"Parker Hansley," I replied, wondering if I'd see recognition in his face. I ran a queer podcast called *The Vers* with my three best friends. Not that we were famous, but we had a fairly big following in the queer community. It was always interesting to me when I dated someone who listened to *The Vers* because it was known that I had bad luck with guys and that I was the romantic of the group.

"Elliott Weaver." He reached out, and I shook his hand. He didn't seem to make the connection with *The Vers*. "What do you do, Parker Hansley?"

I chuckled at him using my surname as well. "I'm a baker. I own Beach Buns in Santa Monica."

"I live in Santa Monica. I haven't been there, though."

"I live there too! And it's the best bakery in Southern California if you ask me," I teased. "What about you?"

"I'm a city planner for the city of Los Angeles."

We kept walking for a few minutes, the street getting less

and less busy. Elliott talked about his job, then asked if I was born and raised here, typical questions when you were getting to know someone.

"I've lived here my whole life," Elliott said. "My mom is Cuban. She moved to Florida for college, then to California for law school. She met my dad there. Ten years after they graduated, I came along."

"They're both lawyers but you had no interest?"

"Yes, but we try not to speak about that around my father. It's a sore subject."

"Expectations can be tricky." I hesitated, then said, "My mom died when I was young. She was great." She'd been a pediatrician who loved baking and her family more than anything. "I still miss her." My dad did too. As far as I knew, he hadn't even dated since losing her. If he did, it had never been serious and he'd kept it on the down-low. He'd loved her so fucking much that he didn't know how to be happy without her.

"I'm sorry for your loss."

"Me too. Anyway, I don't want to bring the mood down. Thank you again for helping me with Jim."

"No problem." He motioned behind me. "Ice cream?"

I turned to see we were standing in front of a parlor.

"I probably shouldn't," I replied because I liked him, and when I liked people, it rarely turned out well for me. Plus, I didn't want him to get the wrong idea and think that because he'd helped me with Jim, I would be going home with him tonight.

A small frown curved his lips, and I could tell he hadn't expected that answer. Still, he said, "Okay. It was nice meeting you, Parker Hansley."

Well, shit. I figured he'd at least ask for my number. Clearly, I could ask for his, but I didn't let myself. "Nice to meet you, Elliott Weaver."

We shook hands again, and he walked away.

I regretted it the second he was gone. What if I'd just let a good man slip through my fingers? Hell, he'd jumped in to help me without knowing if he'd get anything out of it.

For a good ten minutes, I tried to talk myself out of going after him, but it didn't work. He'd gone in the direction of the bar. I would go back and see if he was there, and if he was, I'd take that as a sign that I should get his number. If not, it wasn't meant to be.

I made my way back, the bar busier than it had been when I left. I spent at least twenty minutes looking for Elliott, but he wasn't there.

"Fuck," I grumbled, then shook it off, telling myself he'd been too good to be true anyway. Something about him had felt different, though.

When I got outside, I ordered a car from my phone. While I waited for it to arrive, I paced the sidewalk. Maybe he would come to Beach Buns. Maybe we'd run into each other again. Maybe he was the world's biggest dickhead and I'd dodged a bullet. I had no way of knowing.

When I got to the corner of the street, I froze—Elliott was in the bar's parking lot, leaning against a black BMW, making out with a guy.

Ah, so that's definitely what it had been about. He'd helped with Jim to score points with me, thinking it would get him laid. It's why he hadn't asked for my number. He'd wanted to have sex, and when I didn't keep the night going, he found someone who would.

I was replaceable.

I turned around and walked away.

# CHAPTER ONE
## *Elliott*

*January*

I SAT AT the bar, trying to force myself not to look at Parker. What were the odds I would run into him in Las Vegas?

I'd been a little obsessed with the guy for close to a year now. Okay, *obsessed* was too strong a word. I didn't generally get that wrapped up in anyone or anything, but I'd been intrigued by him since I'd met him at a bar in West Hollywood. He'd snagged my attention from the start because how could he not? Parker was long and lean, with short black hair and a smooth face without the hint of stubble. He had strong, angular features, but not overly so—his face and jawline looked like they'd been carved to perfection, yet at the same time, it was also a bit of a baby face. I didn't know how he managed to pull it off. What really killed me about him, though, was his eyes. They were so damn blue. Every time they met mine, I felt like I was lost at sea and didn't want to be found. It might sound dramatic, but it was true.

It hadn't taken me long to realize the asshole sitting next to him was his ex and that the guy was a real piece of work. When I heard Parker tell him he had a boyfriend, it was clear his story was a lie. I'd almost walked away but found I couldn't. I was curious about him, and when something interested me, I wanted to learn more about it. I liked to follow my urges—though I couldn't pretend that hadn't gotten me in trouble a time or ten.

So I went over and acted like we were boyfriends, hoping like hell Parker wouldn't think I was a psycho.

The verdict was still out about that, but he'd taken my helping hand and then we'd gone for a walk. The way he intrigued me grew, so I was disappointed when he turned down my suggestion to go get ice cream with me. But he did, so I'd returned to the bar to do what I'd started out the night wanting to do—get laid.

I'd figured that would be the end of it. That *should* have been the end of it, but then *poof*, I found myself at his bakery a few days later. I mean, why wouldn't I want to try a new spot? I liked sugar and bread and coffee. It had nothing to do with him. Supporting small businesses like Beach Buns was important, and I was a good guy like that.

He'd smiled when he'd seen me before schooling his features, which surprised me. It became this game between us where I flirted and asked him out and Parker told me no and pretended not to like me. If I thought he really didn't enjoy it, I'd back away. I always made it clear that if he asked me to stop or not come to Beach Buns anymore, I would, but he never asked. And sometimes he flirted and bantered right back before turning surly again the moment he seemed to realize what he was doing, as if he had to remind himself he wasn't supposed to enjoy our game.

And for whatever reason, I kept going back for more. I joked about having a crush on him, but the truth was I did. There was nothing wrong with a harmless crush.

And now he was here in Vegas the same day I was. That was a big-ass coincidence if you asked me.

His gaze met mine. Even with the distance between us, I

could see his eyes go wide. He was with a few friends, a couple of them I'd seen at Beach Buns with him. I swallowed the rest of the liquor in my glass, set it on the bar, and walked over. Was he…trying to hide under the table? What the fuck? I grinned as I heard, "Ouch. Motherfucker. I hate him."

"I'm assuming you're talking about me, but I'm not sure what I did wrong." That's what I couldn't understand. The walls went up after the night we met, and while we bantered, sometimes he seemed…angry, though for the life of me, I couldn't figure out why.

"Exist?" he said.

I rubbed a hand over my left pec. "I should be the one saying ouch. You've made it your life's goal to break my heart, haven't you?"

Parker rolled his eyes. "Please. Like you really care about anyone but yourself."

Well, that barb hit its target. I glanced away, trying to cover up that his words bothered me. "I just came to say hello. You have to admit, it's a huge coincidence we'd run into each other here."

"Hello. Nice to see you. No, I'm not going out with you." Parker crossed his arms as if proud of himself.

"I wasn't going to ask." I winked, and his pride deflated, but it was more than that—disappointment made those blue eyes of his storm. That's what kept me around. Though he was different from the night we met, Parker liked this game we played. I saw him at the grocery store once, and when I didn't approach him, it was Parker who came up to me.

"Oh. Good. Here with someone?" he asked, his voice tight.

Bingo. Parker didn't like that idea. "Wouldn't you like to know?" I teased, before cupping his face. "Have a good night, beautiful." He trembled, his breathing picking up. I dropped my hand and returned to the bar.

*Don't turn around, don't turn around, don't turn around.* It was silly that I had to talk myself out of seeing if he was watching me. Parker shook my usual confidence and somehow always got me coming back for more.

I found a seat and ordered another drink. Every once in a while, I would look his way and catch Parker staring at me.

"Who's the twink?" my friend Vaughn asked, plopping down beside me. He was sweaty from shaking his ass on the dance floor.

"Hmm?"

"The twink you're staring at who keeps looking at you when you're not watching."

*I knew it!*

"He does?" I turned to look before sobering. "Of course he does."

Vaughn dropped his head back and laughed. "You're not smooth. You were shocked he's paying attention to you, and you like it. Wait—is that your baker?"

The fact that Vaughn called him that with so little backstory said something. I'd told him about Parker at some point. How I flirted with him and how he liked to bust my balls, which he hadn't done that first night, thank you very much. "He's not *my* baker, and I don't want him to be, but yeah, that's him."

"Holy shit. Your baker is in Vegas at the same bar as you? That's fucking nuts."

I didn't call him out for calling Parker mine again.

"Go talk to him," Vaughn said. "I'm good on my own. I might go home with these two guys."

"I already tried. He said he hated me." Vaughn laughed again. "Has anyone ever told you you're a shitty friend?"

"I can't help it. You're totally feelin' this guy, and he

won't give you the time of day. That never happens. Who are the men with him?"

"His friends."

"Holy shit, is that—"

"Yes, he's friends with Sebastian Cole." Sebastian Cole was a famous movie star. I wasn't much of a movie person, and I didn't pay attention to celebrity news, but I did recognize him. I couldn't pretend I wasn't jealous the first and only other time I'd seen them together. Watching them tonight, though, it was clear he was dating Parker's friend.

Vaughn's mouth dropped open. "What the fuck, El! You didn't tell me your baker is one of *The Vers* guys!"

"The what? There are a lot of vers guys in the queer community. And how would you even know that?"

He rolled his eyes. "For someone so social, it amazes me that you never know what's going on. *The Vers* is a queer podcast. You've never listened to it?" I shook my head. "I'm not a faithful listener, but I've heard it. They talk about everything. Hell, half the time all they do is argue. It's addictive as shit. It was a huge thing when people found out Sebastian and Declan are dating. Declan's the loner and—"

"Wait. The loner? What are you talking about?"

"Try and keep up, would you? They each have a personality on the show. Declan is The Loner, and then suddenly he's dating Sebastian Cole and there's all this fucking drama, people thinking Sebastian was cheating on his ex with Declan and so on. They sorted it out on their show, and it all seems to have died down—how did you not know this?"

"Because I don't care how other people live their lives?" Well, except Parker. I cared about him in a want-to-get-to-know-you way. "So they each have a nickname-slash-personality?"

"Yeah. Declan is The Loner and God, he has great hair.

Then the tall guy with dark skin, that's Marcus. He's The Realist. He's hot as fuck and clearly very toppy. The really pretty one who is fairer is Corbin. He's The Charmer, and he has a popular Instagram page, but you probably wouldn't know about that either."

"And Parker?" I asked, because how could I not?

Vaughn frowned. "He's The Romantic, the guy who's looking for his happily ever after but happens to have the shittiest luck when it comes to guys. His dating stories are *crazy*. If they're true, I feel bad for him."

I really, really needed to start paying more attention to things going on around me. I'd been flirting with Parker for months and had no idea he was part of a well-known podcast. More importantly, was that why he gave me shit for being a flirt and dating so much? I felt guilty for how I acted but also thought that was a little judgy. Maybe I was looking for *the one* too. I wasn't, but he didn't know that, and how did you find said guy if you didn't date?

Still, the ball of discomfort in my chest grew. Should I apologize to him? Never see him again? Stop flirting? Hell, I didn't know.

"You good?" Vaughn put an arm around me.

"Yeah, I'm fine." When I glanced up, Parker was watching us. He whipped his head around so fast, I wouldn't be surprised if he'd pulled something.

"Good. So then you're cool if I head out? I really wanna have this threesome."

I laughed. "Go for it, man." So much for a weekend away with my friend. "Have fun."

He waggled his brows. "I will."

Vaughn disappeared, and when I looked again, Parker and his friends were dancing. I watched them for a moment, saw how carefree he was with them. I'd seen glimpses of it before, but it was amazing to see it tonight.

Parker was The Romantic...on a podcast I'd never listened to. I sure as shit planned to change that tonight.

I left the bar and went to my hotel room, where I searched for *The Vers* and started listening. While I did that, I browsed social media for *The Vers*, Beach Buns, and Parker Hansley. He was in town for a baking event, but it was also Corbin's—The Charmer's—birthday. His group seemed extremely close, especially Parker and Declan. That much had been clear when I saw them together. Declan tried to protect Parker, which I was sure he didn't need. But Vaughn had been right: Parker had *really* bad luck. The more I researched, the more I understood why he was so gun-shy—bad dates, getting stood up, getting used for sex, cheating. If it was bad and it could happen, it seemed to have happened to Parker. Still, he was The Romantic. He wanted more. He loved romance. Even though settling down or having more with someone had never appealed to me, all this knowledge did was make me more interested in him.

# CHAPTER TWO
## *Parker*

I FROWNED WHEN I saw a private Instagram message from Elliott Weaver. It definitely wasn't what I wanted to see first thing in the morning. Was he finished with the man he'd been with last night and now wanted to try and get me to go out with him again? I almost didn't let myself open it, but I didn't have it in me. I was one of those people who couldn't let anything go. I clicked the message.

**Hey. Hope you're having a good time with your friends. I just wanted to apologize if my flirting and asking you out really bothers you. You seemed interested the first night, and afterward, it felt like a game we were both into. But if I misread things, I'm sorry. I'll respect your boundaries from now on.**

Wait. What? I reread the message, trying to make sense of it. There was a voice in my head telling me this was a good thing and I shouldn't be annoyed, but what the fuck? Was he suddenly not interested? Was I not worthy of his flirting?

*This shouldn't be upsetting. You don't like Elliott. You want different things.*

Well, yes, all that was true, but I also liked being flirted with by a hot guy. Sue me. And if anyone was going to call an end to this, I thought it was supposed to be me. He said if I told him not to come around anymore, he wouldn't, and I didn't, and... God, I was ridiculous. Why did I care about this?

I didn't.

I sent a message to our *Vers* group chat: **You guys up?**

When no one responded right away, I got up, made coffee, then checked my phone again. The guys hadn't messaged, and yep, Elliott's note hadn't magically changed either.

I had no idea what to even say to him.

I drank my coffee, then showered before the first reply came through.

***Declan:* Yeah, I'm up. Bastian and I are going to do some sightseeing today.**

Oh. That made sense.

***Corbin:* Ended up meeting a guy last night. I'm not finished with him yet. I'll be free by tonight.** He signed it with a winky-face emoji.

***Marcus:* I'm actually meeting up with a seller about some property here.**

Everyone had made plans without me? What was I supposed to do today? They'd be leaving tomorrow. I'd expected us to spend more time together because...well, because that's just what we did, and I was maybe a little needy, but that had always worked with us. Plus, we were here for Corbin's birthday, and yeah, we'd hung out last night and only came here to celebrate it because I had my event, but still.

***Declan:* Come with me and Sebastian.**

"Ugh!" I tossed my phone to the bed. Now I was getting sympathy-asked to hang out with my best friend. I knew things would change after Declan fell in love with Sebastian, and I couldn't be more stoked for him. Declan meant the world to me, and nothing was more important than his happiness. He deserved someone like Sebastian, but sometimes I was lonelier now—if we'd come to Vegas before they got together, Dec and I would have automatically spent all our time together. Hell, I'd be rooming with him now rather than on my own.

And since I'd decided months earlier to take a break from men and stop dating and hooking up, that meant I couldn't even go find someone on my own to spend time with, so I was just…alone.

I picked up my phone again and saw two more messages—Marcus asking if I wanted to go to his meeting with him, and Corbin offering to kick his sex buddy out and go to breakfast with me. Their responses didn't surprise me. It's how we were with each other. It's how we'd been from the start, but I also wasn't going to make them change their plans around for me. I wasn't *that* needy. I could handle shit on my own.

**Me: Nah, it's okay. I need to get a few things for my class tomorrow and stuff like that.**

Lies, lies, lies. I had absolutely nothing to do, but I was in Las Vegas. It wasn't as if I couldn't keep myself busy.

They all replied to call them if I changed my mind, which I absolutely wasn't going to do.

I finished getting ready and headed out to find somewhere to eat breakfast. I found a restaurant I could walk to, which gave me plenty of time to read Elliott's message again, still expecting it to magically be different.

I really shouldn't respond, but that was rude, and I wasn't a rude kind of guy. Something about him tended to bring that out in me, but I was stronger than my Elliott-induced urges.

**Why are you apologizing for asking me out? That's weird.**

His answer came through quickly.

***Elliott:* Because you said you hate me?**

Oh. Well, that was a good reason. Not that I really hated

him, he just…wasn't my type. We wanted different things, and I didn't see any reason to pretend otherwise. I'd seen him with numerous guys since the night we met, and he'd also told me he wasn't looking for more.

**I've said that before**, I replied, because I had. What was it about Elliott that turned me into a giant asshole?

*Elliott:* **Are you saying you want me to keep flirting with you? Because I have to admit, you're throwing me some mixed signals here.**

**No. I'm not. I don't know… Just don't apologize for it. Like seriously, Elliott, WTF?**

*Elliott:* **Holy shit. You're *offended*. You think I don't want you anymore…which means you want me to want you…but you also keep wanting to turn me down.**

When he said it like that, it sounded really fucking bad. Like *I* was the kind of guy who would go out with me and treat me like shit. That clearly wasn't what I was going for.

**No.**

*Elliott:* **Then what are you saying?**

"Argh!" I grumbled too loudly, and the woman walking beside me gave me the evil eye. The truth was, I had no fucking clue what I was saying. "Sorry. Man trouble."

She grinned and said, "I hear ya," and kept walking.

The thing was, it shouldn't be man trouble at all. No part of me should care about what Elliott said.

**I don't know what I'm saying. Call it temporary insanity. I'm going to have breakfast now.**

I turned my phone off so I couldn't torture myself wondering if Elliott messaged back. I wasn't supposed to be thinking about guys at all. I wasn't supposed to give a crap, so that's what I was going to do.

I had breakfast, which was delicious. Then I did some exploring around Vegas and didn't make it back to the hotel until early evening. The day hadn't been too bad except the times when I'd wanted to share something with Declan, show something to Corbin, or listen to Marcus explain how something worked, which he was known to do.

The guys had messaged while my phone was off, so we talked and made plans for dinner.

What would it hurt to log on to my Instagram page and see if Elliott had messaged back? I *had* left him hanging earlier.

***Elliott:*** **How much longer are you here for?**
**Why?**
***Elliott:*** **Because I'm going to kidnap you and wanted to see how much time I had to prepare.**
**Ha-ha.** Before I thought about it too much, I added, **You?**
***Elliott:*** **Three days. I was just making conversation.**

A knock came from my door, so I closed the app and shoved my cell into my pocket.

Corbin stood there looking sexy and bright-eyed, the way he always did, his black hair styled nicely, his blue eyes a lighter, icier shade than mine. "Wanna head down with me early?"

"Sure." I shrugged. "Did the guy wear you out?" I grabbed my key card and followed him.

"Do guys ever wear me out?"

"You know there's more to you than how gorgeous you are, Corb. That's not where your worth lies."

He stumbled, not having expected that. Corbin had been teased really badly as a kid. He'd been heavy, had acne problems, and was clumsy. Eventually he grew into his looks, and became obsessed with working out. He'd gotten some work done too. Corbin had always been beautiful to me, and now everyone saw it. But ever since, he acted…superficial, which I knew he wasn't.

"Yeah, that and my cock," he teased. When I quirked a brow at him, he sighed. "Not all of us can be completely comfortable in who we are and what we want like you, Park."

I frowned. "I'm not—like, at all."

Were any of us, really? I didn't just mean the four of us, but everyone. We were all fucking messes.

Corbin's brows pinched together. "What's wrong?"

"Nothing." Jesus, was something wrong? I was a little weird about my whole back-and-forth with Elliott today, but that was it.

He hooked his arm through mine and pulled me close. "A guy would be lucky to have you, and it'll happen. When it does, all I know is he better treat you right, or he's gonna have Marcus to deal with."

I barked out a loud laugh. "Volunteering him to beat people up for me?"

Corbin winked. "Of course. What are friends for."

We went into the elevator, and I dropped my head onto his shoulder. I was all up in my feels today, and I couldn't understand why. "I love you."

"I love you too. You know it's because of you that we all even have each other, right?" I shook my head. I wasn't so sure about that. "When we were kids, you wouldn't take no for an answer until Declan became your friend. Then you talked him into coming to find me when I needed someone." In middle school, there'd been a marching-band accident when Corbin and his trombone had gone tumbling. He'd run away upset, and I'd talked Declan into going to find him. "That very night you asked me to be your friend, and you never left my side. You got Dec to open up to me, and though Marcus and I had been talking online, we likely wouldn't have made the move to meet in person if I hadn't told you about him. You put it all together. You're the heart of us, Park, and one day someone else is going to love you for that heart just like we do."

I wiped the lone tear that leaked from my eye, annoyed that it had set itself free. "Can you find him and tell him to hurry?" I joked, earning a laugh from my friend.

"Who knows, maybe he's in Vegas right now. Maybe you'll see each other and everything will fall into place. This will be the beginning of your romance."

Now it was my turn to chuckle. "I think you're forgetting my horrible luck with men." No way would my romance to end all romances happen in Vegas. Corbin was out of his mind.

We had a drink downstairs while we waited for the guys. Marcus arrived first, followed by Declan and Sebastian, and we spent the evening enjoying each other's company the way we always did.

After dinner, we were walking back to the hotel, Declan with his arm around me while Sebastian was talking to Marcus and Corbin.

"What did you do today?" Declan asked.

I shrugged. "Just hung out. Elliott messaged to apologize for flirting with me and asking me out so much."

"Good. I don't trust him."

I didn't either, but at this point, I didn't trust many people anymore. "It was nice of him, though," I replied, surprising myself.

"Parker…"

"What?" When he just looked at me, I groaned. "I don't like him. I don't even know him. I mean, he's fucking hot, but dating hot guys hasn't gotten me anywhere. I'm just saying it was nice of him. Nothing more." He opened his mouth to respond, but I said, "Let's not talk about me. You and Bastian still look deliriously happy."

He tossed a look over his shoulder at his boyfriend. "Still can't believe he chose me."

"He'd have to be an idiot not to choose you."

"It's going to be hectic this summer. He'll be gone, promoting his movie, and like, what the fuck am I supposed to do? Go with him to events? Red carpets? I don't know how to do that shit."

"But you will. For him." It was hard for Dec sometimes. People would take photos of them together at the beach or out to lunch and post them online. He wasn't comfortable with that kind of thing. Still, he nodded. We both knew he would. And I loved seeing Dec like this. Loved knowing he would never be alone, even if Marcus, Corbin, and I weren't around.

But a small part of me couldn't help being jealous because I wanted that too.

"You'll do fine," I added, and he would.

We'd just made it into our hotel's bar area when Sebastian was spotted.

"Holy shit. Are you Sebastian Cole? And that's your boyfriend, right? The podcast guy. Can I get a photo with you both?"

One person became two, then three and four. The second there was a break, Sebastian and Declan sneaked away to their room. I understood. They couldn't get any peace.

At that point, we ended up all saying our goodbyes and heading up to our rooms.

I still didn't respond to Elliott.

The next morning, the guys showed up in my room for coffee and pastries before they headed back to Southern California, and then I was alone.

# CHAPTER THREE
## Elliott

I DIDN'T TRY to get ahold of Parker again. I'd said my piece, made conversation, so now it was up to him. There was no reason for us to continue speaking anyway. We weren't friends. He clearly didn't want to go out with me, and I wasn't sure anymore if it was a good idea for me to go out with him. I was having fun at this point in my life and couldn't see myself settling down anytime soon. Parker was hoping for that. While I was looking to enjoy a few nights with someone, he was looking for the person he would spend the rest of his life with, and I just wasn't there yet and didn't know if I ever would be. I wasn't anti-relationship, but it had to be someone really fucking special for me to want to change things up. I'd never been the guy to get attached romantically. I loved sex and dating. I liked men and having fun. But I'd never been in love, never craved a commitment from anyone.

Vaughn and I spent most of the day together. At three we went back to our hotel to relax a little before the evening. We had plans for dinner tonight, but I wasn't sure what was going on after that. I sat on the bed in my room, feet up, checking my email, when a text came through. I didn't recognize the phone number, so I almost ignored it, but then instead, I exited my inbox and clicked.

**Hey...**

That wasn't much to go on, but I knew it was him.

**It's Parker**, he added before I could ask.

I smiled. I hadn't expected him to message. He had the uncanny ability to turn me down when most people didn't.

**Hey, gorgeous**, I replied. "Shit." I'd slipped into flirt mode without thinking. *Don't flirt with Parker, don't flirt with Parker, don't flirt with Parker.*

**Have a date or ten tonight?**

I rolled my eyes. Instead of texting back, I called him.

"What the fuck are you doing, Elliott? No one talks on the phone anymore. It's the absolute worst," he said instead of hello, and I couldn't help but laugh.

"Sorry, not sorry?"

"You're definitely not sorry. I can't believe you call people. I knew there was something wrong with you."

"I've been told my voice sounds sexy. I thought about doing the phone-sex thing when I was nineteen but never gave it a try."

"Eh, I couldn't say it's any sexier than your voice in person."

I grinned again. "Parker...did you just call my voice sexy?"

There was a long pause. "That's not what I meant."

"Yes it is."

"No it's not, and oh my God, why do you bring out the ten-year-old in me? I messaged to ask what you're doing tonight. That's it. I'm sure you have a date or hookup to get to, but on the off chance you don't, I was bored and thought I'd toss you a bone, but now I'm really regretting my decision." I opened my mouth to make a joke about his bone comment when he added, "And my choice of words—regretting that too. You don't get my bone. That's not what I meant."

"But you made it so easy to tease you."

"Do you have plans or not?"

"Are you this sunshiny with everyone, or am I just lucky?" It shouldn't make me feel fortunate, but for some reason it did.

"Have a good evening—"

"Wait," I rushed out before he ended the call. "I'm free." Or at least I would be when I called Vaughn and canceled. He would understand.

"As I said, I'm bored. All my friends left. This isn't a date. I just don't feel like sitting in my room all night."

"Not a date. Got it. But it kinda feels like you just asked me out on one." Why couldn't I stop flirting with him? It was an addiction.

"Elliott…"

"*Parker*…" At the loud silence on his end, I added quickly, "I'm just giving you shit. I'll be good, I promise. Where are you taking me on our date—I mean, our hangout since you're bored? You know, a lesser man would be offended by that."

"I think your confidence can take the hit."

"Gee, thanks."

"I don't want anything fancy. I just want to drink and eat so I can go back to my room and pass out."

We decided to hit up a bar that served food and wasn't far from where either of us was staying. It was on the Strip, so we could both walk there. "Perfect…and wait. How did you get my number?"

"You gave it to me a couple of months ago. Oh my God! You don't even remember."

Shit. I didn't. That was probably a bad sign. "I was kidding. I remember. See you soon!" I ended the call before he could change his mind, then hit Vaughn's name in my address book. "I have to cancel for tonight."

"Okay." He yawned. "I'm tired anyway. Meet someone?"

"I'm going out to dinner with Parker."

"Jesus Christ, did you not listen to his podcast?"

"It's not a date! I don't want to fuck him." When he answered with a *pfft*, I amended, "Of course I want to fuck him, but I know that's not happening. He's bored."

"Wow, that's a ringing endorsement for wanting to spend time with you."

"Yeah, it's strange. It's throwing me for a loop. Most people can't resist me." I wasn't trying to sound cocky, but it was true.

Vaughn laughed and told me to have a good night.

I showered, then tugged on a pair of slacks, a white V-neck T-shirt, and a black button-up over it, left open. It was a great look for me.

I ran a hand through my hair a few times, which was as good as it got, brushed my teeth, tugged on my jacket, and headed out to meet Parker.

It was a short walk to the bar. When I arrived, Parker was already outside. He looked adorable in his coat and a beanie.

"You're early," I said when I approached.

"I'm on time."

"No, I'm on time."

"If you're not five minutes early, you're late." He gave me a cute, smug look before turning for the door. I chuckled and followed him in.

The place was fairly busy, but the bar counter was open, so Parker and I went for the end. Once we removed our layers and sat down, Parker said, "I want a shot. We should do a shot."

"Okay…"

He frowned. "What?"

"Nothing." I just hadn't expected that.

When the bartender arrived, Parker asked me, "Jägerbomb okay?"

"Works for me." It wouldn't have been my first choice, but I was fine with it.

"Two Jägerbombs, coming up." The bartender poured them for us. "Want to start a tab?"

"Yes, please," Parker replied, pulling out his card.

"No, no. My treat."

"Not a date, Elliott."

"Didn't say it was," I countered.

"Wow, the sexual tension between you two is *thick*," our bartender chimed in.

"Right? He hates me, though, but I think we'd be explosive together."

"I don't hate you."

We both handed over our cards.

"I'll split them," the bartender said, sliding our drinks to us, then walking away.

"Wasn't that a surprise. You don't hate me." I held up my shot glass. "To friendship."

"Well, I don't know if I'd go that far." His answer was accompanied by a grin before we clinked our glasses together. The alcohol burned my throat—not a huge Jäger fan—but I took it like a champ. Parker said, "Whew. That was good. Let's eat. I need to eat."

Something was different about Parker tonight, but I couldn't put my finger on what it was. He'd been fun and playful the first night I'd met him, and I saw it often when he interacted with customers at Beach Buns or his friends. He hadn't been like that in a while with me, so I was waiting for the other shoe to drop.

We ordered burgers and fries, along with another shot. The conversation flowed easily. We were about halfway through our meal when he asked, "So...what made you all of a sudden apologize for asking me out?"

I shrugged, going for honesty. "I didn't know about *The Vers*. I found out at the club that night...about all the romantic stuff, and how you're looking for something serious. It made me feel like a dick because I want the exact opposite. I've never been serious about anyone, never been in love. Not even sure if I have it in me. I enjoy my life just as it is, and why shouldn't I? So I pulled back."

"Oh my God!" He swatted my arm.

"Ouch. You don't have to hit me. I was trying to be nice."

"That didn't hurt, and what? You thought I'd fall madly in love with you and you'd have to break my heart?" He took a drink of the vodka tonic he'd ordered. "I can handle your flirting without falling in love with you."

"I'm pretty irresistible."

"I can resist you."

"Not if I gave it my all, you couldn't, but I won't because I'm a nice guy and we want different things."

"Yes, we do. But you also need to keep flirting with me."

This was getting good. I couldn't deny the somersault feeling in my gut while talking to him. Parker was fun. "I do? Hmmm. You want me to ask you out. You like it." It felt good when someone was interested in you. I understood that.

"Ugh. Gross. No, I don't. I just don't want you to stop doing it because you think my delicate heart can't handle it. Totally wouldn't fall for you...or have sex with you, FYI, even if I wasn't on a sex sabbatical."

A laugh jumped out of my mouth. When the bartender looked my way, I pointed toward Parker's drink so he knew I wanted one too. "A sex sabbatical. Why on earth would you do that? Sex is fucking awesome."

"I knooooow." He dropped his head back. He had a long,

pretty throat I wanted to kiss and suck. "I love sex. And I'm very, very good at it, if I do say so myself. I've had zero complaints. But men are trouble, and I've decided I'm not dating or hooking up for the foreseeable future. If you listened to any of *The Vers*, you'd know I have the worst luck with men."

"I heard that. You do seem to attract assholes." Some of the stories had been pretty bad. "Not me, of course. I'm not an asshole, and I'm honest with the people I fuck."

"Honest in that you're just looking for a good time?"

I shrugged because it was true.

The bartender brought us both new drinks.

"You sound like Corbin. For him it comes from somewhere different, though. But he has one of the biggest hearts of anyone I know." He spoke with a softness and so much love in his voice, it was clear how much Corbin meant to him.

"How do you know mine doesn't come from somewhere else too?" I took a few sips as he seemed to consider that.

"Does it?"

I didn't really want to get into it, so I changed the subject. "Tell me about you, Parker. Do you have family around? Other than your friends, of course."

He grinned, which I assumed was about the guys, but then sadness seemed to envelop him, a heaviness I wasn't sure he knew he showed. "My grandparents and some cousins. My dad lives in LA, and we're close. Like I said, my mom passed away when I was ten, but she was great. I loved her so much." He took a couple of large swallows.

Fuck. He'd told me about losing her that first night, but it was obvious how much he still missed her. "I'm sorry."

"It's okay. We were lucky to have her, and I'm lucky to have him. He didn't really know how to relate to me. He didn't expect to be a single father, and was a little thrown by the whole 'gay son' thing, but he tried hard. He always had my back. It's tough, though. I know he wants more for me, to see me happy with someone the way he was happy with Mom."

Even if I didn't know it already, the hope-laced melancholy in Parker's voice told me he wanted the same thing for himself.

"You'll find your Prince Charming."

"How do you know?" he asked seriously.

"You're too sweet not to. And also, hot as fuck."

Parker laughed, which I'd hoped he would. He'd been lonely tonight. He missed his friends, and he wasn't home. He didn't want to hook up or go out with anyone, so he was using me to stave off his loneliness. I was okay with that. I liked spending time with him, liked being around him, and hoped we would be friends after this.

"What about you?" Parker asked.

"I'm also hot as fuck."

He rolled his eyes but grinned too. "I meant your family."

"They're both here and close. Both are lawyers, like I mentioned before, and my dad is actually one of our representatives now—California house district thirty-three, to be exact."

"Holy shit. No way."

"Yep, he is. It's hard sometimes because they're both so accomplished."

"You're accomplished. You're a city planner. You do good things for our community. That's nothing to sneeze at."

"Thanks, and yeah, I know. They do too. I just...well, I know they both wish I'd followed in their footsteps and that things were different for me. Both my parents are really smart. School was a lot more of a struggle for me. They loved it. I hated it. Plus, I've always had a bit of a wild streak in me. I like to test the limits and do new things. If there's trouble, I used to find it. I'm much better now, but..."

"Like how? What kind of trouble?"

I couldn't believe I was sharing this with him. It wasn't something I typically talked about. Some of it he would know if he looked me or my dad up online, but still, it wasn't something I shared easily. "For starters, I almost didn't graduate from high school. I was too busy having fun. And for education-minded parents who'd always been focused on carving out a future for themselves, that was hard to understand. There's also being gay. They're liberal and affirming and supportive, but again, it was something they hadn't expected.

"Then in college, I felt bad getting money from them—and I didn't get scholarships, of course. So I ended up doing jerk-off videos online. I didn't show my face, but I got found out. My father was a DA at the time and had political aspirations, so that made things difficult for him. I think I was resentful because of the pressure to succeed and then being in the public eye that way. I wanted to experiment and be free, but it often came back on them. I feel terrible about that, but no matter what, they always supported me. Sometimes that makes it harder..."

I didn't look at him as I took a drink, before continuing, "I feel like I was always letting them down, never being who they wanted me to be, and I was so fucking lucky—to have them and to be in the position in life we were in. My mom came from nothing, and she's so smart and successful and does so much good. I hate that I've disappointed them, and that even though they would never say it, they wish I was less me and more them."

Holy fuck. I couldn't believe I said all that to him. I'd never spoken those words to anyone before. Most of the time,

I tried to pretend they weren't there at all.

"You're not a disappointment to them," Parker said. "And thank you...for sharing that with me."

I forced myself to make eye contact with him, and I could see the compassion in his gaze. I didn't want him to feel down tonight. I wanted him to have a good time. I wanted to make him feel better, so I said, "No more heavy shit. We're going to turn Vegas out tonight. You with me?"

Parker's lips stretched into a wide grin. "I'm with you. Let's do something fun and new!"

I couldn't wait.

# CHAPTER FOUR
## *Parker*

I'D HAD A bit of a bad day before calling Elliott. If something could go wrong, it did. One of the instructors hadn't shown up. I'd been asked to teach a lesson, and don't ask me how it happened, but fire extinguishers ended up being involved—through no fault of mine, of course.

When I'd messaged the guys, all of them had been busy. I hadn't told them what was going on. If they knew I needed to talk, they would have made it happen, but I didn't want to be that guy. Just because I was all up in my feels, acknowledging that I was almost thirty-four years old and still single, didn't mean they had to drop whatever they were doing and console me.

But now? Now I was having the best fucking time *ever*. And not totally because of all the alcohol I'd consumed, but I'd had *a lot* of it, and drunk Parker thought drunk Elliott was fun as fuck. Seriously, why did sober me get so annoyed by him? I couldn't for the life of me figure it out right now as we danced on a bar countertop together at... "Where are we?" I yelled. I knew we'd left the first place we'd met up at, and that was like two or three bars ago.

"I don't know!" Elliott replied, and we both started laughing so hard, we almost tumbled off the counter. We caught each other and then just laughed more.

My conscience was there somewhere, telling me I would regret this and maybe wish I was dead in the morning, but I would worry about that when the time came.

"Let's find the next place!" Elliott said, jumping down, then taking my hand and helping me. Two drinks waited for us on the bar. Well, I was pretty sure they were ours, but if not, they were now. We grabbed them and downed them before stumbling out the door in a fit of giggles—and I didn't think either of us was typically a giggler.

"Oh my God, Elliott. This is so fun! What are we gonna do next? We should do something wild and crazy! Something I've never done before!"

Wild and crazy wasn't usually my jam, but again, tonight, drunk Parker didn't give a fuuuuuck.

"Ooh, let's get in the sprinkler!" Elliott pointed.

"That's not a sprinkler! It's a fountain, and it's cold." I glanced around. "Shit. Where's my jacket?"

He shrugged. "Probably wherever mine is."

I busted up. Holy fuck. Why was he suddenly so funny?

"What do you want to do?" I asked. "No fountain swimming."

"You're not the boss of me." Elliott ran for the fountain, but I caught his wrist and held him back. We laughed, tripping over each other and falling to the pavement. People walked by us and around us like we weren't there. This was Las Vegas, after all, and I was sure they'd seen much worse.

The ground was softer than expected. When it moved, I almost screamed earthquake, but then I realized I was lying on top of Elliott.

"I thought you were an earthquake."

"What?" He chuckled, his breath against my face. It was probably cold outside, but my drunkenness took care of that.

"Jesus, you really are beautiful," he said, which made my

pulse flutter and the temperature go up a few hundred degrees. I mean, who didn't like to get told they're pretty? Compliments were fucking fabulous.

"So are you," I told him because he was and I was drunk, and…if there were more reasons, I couldn't remember them.

"What are you doing on the ground?" a woman asked, leaning over us. Her eyes were red, and she looked like maybe she'd drunk her weight in liquor too.

"I don't remember." I laughed.

"Oh my God! I love you! You're the best." She grabbed me and pulled me up.

"You're the best tooooooo." I didn't know her, but I loved her. I wanted to be best friends with her forever.

"We're getting married!" She pointed to the woman beside her.

"Shut up!" I replied. "They're getting married," I said to Elliott, who was still on the ground.

"I heard. Is no one going to help me up?"

My new friend and I both took one of his hands and pulled him to his feet.

"I'm Wendy, and this is my best friend, Larissa. We just admitted we love each other, and now we're going to get married! Do you guys want to come?"

"I fucking love weddings! Come on, El! Let's go." I dragged him with me as we followed Wendy and Larissa down the Strip and to a small white chapel at the end. "Oh my God. It's so cute. Why is it so cute?"

"Me?" Elliott asked.

"You're cute, but I'm not talking about you."

Larissa and Wendy had an appointment. I didn't understand how that worked if they'd just admitted they loved each other, but I probably shouldn't have been responsible for my brain right then anyway.

Thankfully, it wasn't an Elvis impersonator marrying them, but a guy in jeans and a Taylor Swift T-shirt. Whatever. It worked.

They were picking out flowers and looking at rings when Larissa said, "But those are ugly."

To which Wendy replied, "Wait. What? They're way better than the ones you picked."

"Uh-oh," Elliott said. "Looks like there's trouble in paradise."

"We always have to do what you want!" Larissa shouted. "Our friendship is so one-sided. I didn't even want to come to Vegas."

"I didn't even want to get married!" Wendy countered.

"You're the one who asked me!"

Elliott and I looked at each other wide-eyed and unsure what to do. The two of them stormed out, and the first thing that fell out of my mouth was, "She didn't even say goodbye to me. I thought we were friends." Which did nothing except inspire more laughter from Elliott and me. My stomach hurt; I'd cracked up so much.

"Fuck, now I'm out three hundred and fifty bucks," Taylor Swift Wedding Guy said. "You guys wanna get married?"

That was the best idea ever! How fucking cool would that be!

"Whoa. What if we got married?" Elliott said. "That's wild and crazy!"

"Dude. I was thinking the same thing!" That quiet conscience voice came back, reminding me first that *dude* wasn't something I usually said, and second, that this was a bad idea. But I was drunk, and this was fun, and when did I ever do anything unexpected like this? When did I ever throw caution to the wind and get *married*? I mean, I'd always wanted to get married, so why didn't I just do it? "Do you wanna?"

"I do if you do," Elliott replied. "We did say we wanted to do something we've never done before."

"Good point."

"You guys aren't drunk, right?" Taylor Swift Wedding Guy asked.

We both sobered. "Absolutely not. We take this very seriously." Elliott bit his cheek.

"We're totally in love…like, so in love, it's not even funny."

"I tried to get him to date me forever, and I finally won him over."

"It wasn't that long, dear," I joked. "But long enough that we want this," I told Taylor Swift Wedding Guy.

He shrugged. "Cool, let's do it."

We picked out our bouquet, which I sure as shit was going to hold, and silver bands that would likely rot our fingers off, all the while laughing and poking and teasing each other.

Taylor Swift Wedding Guy took our info…our names… "His dad is part of the House of Representatives in California! Isn't that crazy?"

"Shh. You're not supposed to tell anyone." Elliott crossed his lips and pretended to throw away the key.

"Your secret is safe with me," Taylor Swift Wedding Guy said. I knew I liked him.

"Thank you!" I hugged him.

It was a blur after that, but I was smiling so big when I said "I do," my face hurt. I couldn't stop smiling.

The chapel had a car service that drove newlyweds to a marriage bureau office if needed, which I thought was so nice of them. We filed our official license, and then they took us back to the chapel, where they registered it for us. When we walked out, they assured us we were legally married.

Weddings were fun!

★ ★ ★

My head was fucking pounding. Was someone beating on my skull? It felt like someone was beating on my skull, which was pretty rude if you asked me. My whole body was dead weight, like I'd gained a hundred pounds overnight. I tried to move but couldn't. Panic flared in my gut, making my eyes jerk open. *Argh!* I closed them quickly as the light flooding in from the window made them sting. I felt breath on my neck, and a moment later realized that the reason I couldn't move was because of the leg and arm thrown over me.

Oh no. God fucking damn it! I'd slept with Elliott! After months of being good, going cold turkey on sex and dating, I'd caved and had what was clearly unmemorable sex with Datey McDaterson.

I groaned. Loudly.

"God. Make it stop," Elliott said, his voice husky, sounding like he spoke through a mouth full of cotton. "You're moaning so loud, it's giving me a headache."

"That's the hangover, and if you weren't attached to me like a suckerfish, then maybe it wouldn't bother you so much."

He peeked at me, only opening one eye. "Does that make you algae?"

"That makes me annoyed. I can't believe I had sex with you."

He rolled off me, and I sat up, but…oh…I was wearing clothes. Why would I have put on clothes after fucking?

One glance at Elliott showed he was dressed too. We were both wearing the same thing we'd had on last night, including shoes.

"We didn't have sex." He grabbed his head. "I'm dying. I can't believe you made me drink that much."

"I didn't make you drink anything, and how do you know we didn't have sex?"

"Because you'd be thanking me instead of being annoyed with me, and I definitely would have remembered making you come over and over again."

I rolled my eyes, which actually hurt. "Because of course you think you're the King of Orgasms."

"It's Your Majesty to you."

I tried not to laugh. It was frustrating that he was funny. "I'd argue with you, but I have to pee."

I stumbled out of the bed. Well, at least we were in my room. My feet tangled in each other, and I almost fell as I made my way to the bathroom. I didn't have the energy to close the door. I swayed when I undid my pants and pulled my dick out, moaning in ecstasy as I began to relieve my bladder. "Is there anything as good as a piss after drinking your weight in alcohol?"

"Sounds like the other men you've been with definitely weren't the King of Orgasms."

It wasn't until I was standing at the sink, washing my hands, that I noticed the band on my finger...the silver band on my *wedding finger.* "What the fuck?" I said, looking at it as I went back into the room. Elliott was still lying on his back, but his hand was in front of his face, and he was looking at... "What's that?" My heart dropped to my feet, my breathing suddenly coming out in short pants.

"A ring I didn't have last night."

My gaze shot to my hand, taking it in. Elliott looked at me, wide-eyed and panicky as he realized I had a matching band.

"Oh God, Elliott. I'm gonna throw up." I ran to the

bathroom as he jolted out of bed.

"This can't be what I think it is. It can't be. They don't really marry drunk people, do they?"

I'd already collapsed on the floor by the toilet, dry-heaving. "Busy puking over here!" When nothing came up, I tried pulling the offending piece of cheap material off my finger, but it was stuck, because of course it fucking was. "This is a joke. Please tell me this is a joke." I leaned against the wall, still sitting on the bathroom floor. "They're just rings. They don't mean anything."

"No, but this does." Elliott stood in the doorway, holding up our paperwork.

"Holy shit, Elliott!" I shoved to my feet. "I was supposed to get married on the beach…a small ceremony, just close friends and family. It was supposed to be intimate and the man with me someone who'd swept me off my feet. He'd make me cry when he read the vows he wrote for me, and he'd do the same when I read the ones I wrote for him. My dad would be there, so fucking happy that I found a love like he and Mom had. Declan, Marcus, and Corbin would be by my side, and my husband totally wouldn't care that tying himself to me was also tying himself to them."

I paced the room, my vision blurring, little spots dancing in front of me. Dizziness swept me up, and I couldn't breathe. I couldn't fucking breathe.

"Hey, it's fine. We'll figure it out. If this is legit, we can get it annulled." Elliott wrapped his arms around me, and damned if I didn't let him. "Plus, I didn't make you come like crazy, so does that mean this isn't real? Is that a thing?"

"Are you really consoling me while also bragging about how good you think you are in bed?" I said, amused despite the circumstances.

"How good I am. There's no *think* about it."

I ignored him.

But he was right. No one knew. We could get this taken care of, and then I could forget it ever happened, but…but it had. I'd wanted to only get married once in my life. I'd wanted it to be real, my fairy tale, but unlike Mom and Dad, we would get our happily ever after.

"You good?" Elliott asked, hand rubbing up and down my back, and strangely, I was. This felt nice. Elliott wasn't half bad at consoling people. He hooked his finger beneath my chin and angled my head up. "You're too pretty to look so worried. We'll figure it out."

My knees went weak. Stupid fucking legs. And why was my pulse going so fast?

He gave me a cocky grin like he could tell what I was thinking, and I jerked out of his hold. "You're so annoying."

"I have you figured out, Parker Hansley."

I didn't even want to know what that meant.

His phone rang. Elliott took long strides to the nightstand to grab it while I was still trying to catch my breath.

"Fuck. It's my dad," he said, silencing the call. A minute later it rang again.

"Is this normal?" I hoped nothing was wrong. And that had to be the case because no way could anyone know about us.

"Jesus…" Elliott said, his voice sending shivers down my spine. I'd never heard him sound so serious.

"What?"

"How the fuck do they know?"

"Wait. Who? How?"

"My dad is texting me. He's asking what's going on, says there are reports I got married…"

The dizziness hit me again. When Elliott collapsed onto the edge of the bed, I managed to make my way over too. I grabbed my phone and sat beside him. Mine was on silent, but I had five missed calls from Marcus and texts as well.

Elliott cursed again, holding his phone out so I could see.

> ELLIOTT WEAVER, SON OF HOUSE MEMBER MALCOLM WEAVER, MARRIES MYSTERY MAN IN LAS VEGAS!
>
> ELLIOTT WEAVER UP TO HIS OLD STUNTS
>
> ELLIOTT WEAVER EMBARRASSMENT TO MALCOLM AND CATALINA WEAVER
>
> FIRST STOP SEX ONLINE, SECOND STOP LAS VEGAS WEDDING

This time, I really thought I was going to be sick. How could they have found out so quickly? Or at all.

"Excuse me for a moment." Elliott stood, went to the bathroom, and closed the door. I heard the lock click in place behind him.

# CHAPTER FIVE
## *Elliott*

I HATED LETTING people down. I wanted to be liked and do the right thing and...I hadn't...so many times. Like I'd told Parker last night—like I'd told my *husband* last night—I was so fucking lucky I had parents who loved me so much, who stuck by my side and always had my back no matter how many times I'd screwed up or embarrassed them. And this was how I repaid them? By getting drunk-married in Las Vegas?

I'd embarrassed my parents again—embarrassed myself. What in the hell had we been thinking?

More than that, I knew I'd disappointed them. Relationships and marriage were big to my mom. When you married someone, you married their family. In her eyes, she should know and meet and be close to anyone I had those feelings for, and I knew this would hurt her.

I looked up the articles again, this time clicking on headlines, and there we were...Parker and I dancing, laughing. There was a photo of him throwing his bouquet and jumping into my arms and...well, shit, that looked like one hell of a kiss.

I didn't remember the ceremony, but from the photos, people had been there. The officiant also gave an interview, not mentioning our inebriation, maybe because he could have gotten in trouble for it, but talking about the ceremony and how well we got along. Pfft, that wasn't the case at all, but looking at the photos, you'd never know it. Probably because getting married was Parker's dream, only in that dream I wasn't his husband and clearly he already had the whole thing planned out and Vegas wasn't it.

My phone buzzed with another text. This one was from my mom.

**Are you okay? Whatever it is, we'll figure it out.**

Christ, they were the fucking best. The thing was, I knew they would defend me in this. They would make excuses for my behavior, but I didn't want them to have to. I hated that I'd fucked up again.

Parker knocked on the door. "Elliott...are you okay?"

I cleared my throat. "I'll be right out." After throwing some water on my face, I walked out. He was sitting in the middle of the bed, legs crossed, looking at his phone, his body heavy with sadness.

"I look happy. I can't believe it. I guess just because that's what I always wanted? And in my drunken state, I didn't realize it was to the last person I should be marrying."

Ouch, that hurt. Not that I wanted to be married to him either, but I didn't think he was the last person I should have said I do with.

"Oh God, Elliott. You don't think I did this on purpose, do you? That I trapped you into a marriage because I'm a crazy romantic who doesn't know how to be on his own."

"What?" I sat beside him. "No. I don't think that. First, you know how to be on your own just fine. Second, we were both there. We both drank like crazy, and we both made the decision to get married. It's not your fault." I rubbed a hand over my face, feeling the wedding ring there.

"My dad is going to hate this. He and my mom, they loved each other so much that it's like...I don't know, it feels like mocking love in a way. Like I don't have respect for it or marriage. I also know that most of his sadness will be for me…because he wants me to have what they had."

"I'm sorry." I awkwardly patted his thigh. How did one comfort their husband? I didn't know how to do this. "I feel like I'm putting another scandal on my parents. Especially as a gay man. Straight people can and do fuck up marriage every single day, but we had to fight for this right, and it just feels really gross that we didn't take it seriously…"

"Fuck." Parker fell backward, lying down. I did the same.

"We can always fake it. We looked happy in those photos," I said jokingly, trying to break the quiet. Parker froze beside me. "I was kidding. Relax. You won't be tied to me for long." But really, it wasn't a half bad idea. The possibility began to form in my head…

"Why do I feel like you're actually considering this?"

Maybe he'd said that because he was too. "It could work… I don't want to let my parents down. You don't want to let your dad down. You don't want to date or sleep with anyone anyway, so it's not like I'd be a roadblock in your happily-ever-after quest."

"What are you talking about? We can't pretend to be married." Parker shoved off the bed and resumed pacing. "Why would I do that? Why would *you* do that?"

"To avoid the annoying truth that we got so drunk, we stumbled into a chapel because *Oooh! Weddings are fun* and we wanted to do something different."

Parker stopped. "You remember?"

"Bits and pieces are coming back to me."

He began pacing again. "That's stupid. We can't do that. We'd drive each other crazy."

"Um…welcome to marriage?"

"No." He shook his head. "I can't do that. When I get

married, I want it to be for love."

I didn't remind him that he'd already gotten married, and it was, in fact, not for love.

"God, I'm gonna get crucified on *The Vers*. The Romantic tricked a guy into marrying him in Vegas."

I didn't know where he got the tricked part, but yes, people would likely talk shit. No one wanted to take a look at their own lives, but they loved pointing out others' shortcomings, especially on the internet.

"I would lose my mind pretending to be married to you," he said.

"Seems like you're thinking about it awfully hard over there." I'd mostly suggested it as a joke, but it could work.

"How would we do it?"

"I don't know…tell people we'd been dating secretly, fell for each other, threw caution to the wind, and decided to cement our love. My parents would be hurt they weren't there, especially Mom, and that they didn't know about you, but I think it would be better than getting an annulment and chalking it up to a bad decision."

"I think…God, I think my dad would consider it romantic." That made me smile for some reason. It sounded like he and Parker were more similar than he thought. "I can't stay married to you forever."

"No shit." I rolled my eyes. "We'd agree on a certain amount of time—like six months. Until the summer. Then we make a joint statement that we grew apart. Straight people divorce all the time." What the fuck? Why were we even pretending this was an option?

My phone rang again. It was my dad.

"How would you survive not having sex with all your admirers?"

He thought I had admirers? Parker paid more attention to

me than he wanted to admit. "I can keep from having sex if I want. I just don't typically want to because why should I? I love fucking. Gay sex is something we were taught to be ashamed of. In the past we were told it was something that would kill us. If I'm safe and protected, why the fuck shouldn't I enjoy sleeping with whomever I want as long as they want the same? I'm proud of who I am."

"I'm proud of who I am too."

"I didn't say you weren't. You're the one who judges me. I don't judge you, beautiful."

He blushed and looked away. "God, why am I even considering this? Are you serious? I mean, like you said, I don't want to date or hook up, so this actually helps, and…"

And he was embarrassed about what we'd done. He was ashamed. I understood that. We both had people we would let down.

"Declan, Marcus, and Corbin will know the truth."

"As long as they can keep your secret, I don't care. So will Vaughn."

"Who's that?"

"My best friend you were jealous of and thought I was sleeping with."

He cocked a brow. "Have you slept with him?"

"Not the point."

"It kinda is, but I don't care about it much right now. How long have we been together? What's our story? Oh my God. How am I going to handle being fake married to you?"

"Real married, sweetheart." I winked, holding up my hand. Things were clearer now, and I remembered filing the license and the chapel registering the marriage.

"You're such a flirt."

"Why shouldn't I flirt with my husband?" I was being playful, but really, I wanted a fix to this situation. I didn't like the idea of staying married to Parker, but he was gorgeous and could be a good time when he let go. It was a better alternative than the truth and all the stories that would follow. "We can work out all those details."

"I won't have sex with you."

"Good. I won't have sex with you either," I countered. "But you're moving in with me. I love my house."

His eyes got cartoonishly big. "We have to live together?"

"Husbands typically do…"

"Why not my apartment?"

"I called it first."

"Rock, paper, scissors?" Parker asked.

I stood and walked over to him. He looked at me, unsure and cutely annoyed. "Best two out of three, but I'm warning you, I'm a rock, paper, scissors champion."

He didn't comment, and we went the first round—I was rock, he was scissors. "Damn it!" Parker cursed. Round two went to me as well. "I hate you."

"So I've heard. Does that mean we're doing this?"

He covered his face with his hands and screamed into them. "Sorry. I had to get that out. We have ground rules. And…"

"And we'll figure all that out later. Looks like what happens in Vegas doesn't stay here at all."

"Fuck my life," Parker replied.

Yeah, I heard him there. Fuck mine too.

But a part of me that was maybe as irresponsible as I tried to pretend I wasn't, that part thought this would be fun.

# CHAPTER SIX
## *Parker*

E LLIOTT AND I sat down and came up with a story. I took notes. He didn't. Somehow that didn't surprise me, but I was trying to trust him on this. We were going to say we'd met a year ago—truth. Dated for a few weeks—not true, but the reasoning behind that was my ex. We'd said we were dating back then, and if he caught wind of our romance, we didn't want any loose ends.

So we'd broken up but stayed friends—also not true, clearly. But during our friendship, feelings grew, blah, blah, blah. All the things I'd hoped would really happen to me—meeting someone, getting close to them without realizing we were falling for each other until *poof*, we were in love. Elliott had amazingly been celibate the last couple of months, and while Declan, Sebastian, Marcus, and Corbin knew I'd been on a no-date/no-sex journey, I'd never mentioned it on *The Vers* or to anyone else.

We came to Vegas together, realized we were in love and wanted to be together forever but didn't want a huge wedding, and now we were husband and husband.

He'd called his parents and told them yes, he was married, then lied his lying face off by saying he was head over heels in love with me and that he would bring me over to meet them.

Which I hadn't thought of…the fact that I had to meet

the parents, but of course I would meet the parents. I'd never done that before, and now, the first time I did, it would be a sham.

I was trying not to dwell on that.

My dad didn't pay much attention to the internet, so I figured he hadn't heard and likely wouldn't until I told him, but the first thing I had to do was tell the guys. That, I wasn't looking forward to.

I sent them a group text, telling them I was leaving Vegas and we needed to meet at Marcus's as soon as I got back, gave them a time, then put my phone on Do Not Disturb.

Elliott had left a little over thirty minutes before, and I was already in my car, heading back to Santa Monica.

My eyes were continually drawn to the ring on my finger—which was fucking horrid, by the way. I was a married man. The official marriage certificate would arrive at Elliott's house in two to three weeks. Apparently, even drunk us decided his house was where we'd live.

This was supposed to be one of the happiest times of my life, but really, all I could feel was like a fraud...a liar...and sad. But I was also the type to make the best of a bad situation, so that's what I was going to try to do.

It took me four and a half hours to drive to Marcus's house. I was tired, hungover, and wanted nothing more than to be surrounded by my friends. I also wanted to hit the gas pedal and drive out of there and not talk to them until this was over.

I wasn't surprised to see everyone's cars already in front of Marcus's house when I arrived. The second I hit the porch step, the door pulled open and three people stood there staring at me. "You could have brought Sebastian," I said. I didn't want him to feel left out. He'd taught my best friend how to accept love from someone other than us, and I would always be grateful for that.

"Babe...what happened?" Declan asked instead of answering me. I closed my eyes, and before I knew it, I was pulled into Declan's arms. "I'm going to kill him."

"It's not just his fault. We were both there."

"Doesn't mean we can't kill him," Marcus added.

"Please don't make me a widower," I said, trying to make light of the situation. "Murder him *after* the divorce, at least."

"So should I call off the hit? My guys are literally en route right now." Corbin gave me a supportive smile, making us all chuckle. God, I loved them. I needed them.

"Let's go inside," Marcus said when Declan pulled away.

We went straight for the living room. Declan and Corbin sat on either side of me, Marcus across from us on a chair.

"I saw it first," Marcus said. "I tried to get ahold of you before Dec got wind of it."

"We thought our boy was going to head to Vegas. Marcus tried to talk some sense into him, but I think it was my sweet charm that eventually did the trick," Corbin teased. He was good at reminding us to laugh, providing the levity we needed.

"What happened?" Declan asked.

I started at the beginning, telling them how Elliott and I originally met, and how after parting ways, I saw him with another man in like thirty seconds. About his flirting and trying to get me to go out with him.

Fast-forward to Vegas and how I was feeling lonely and he was there, then the drinking...all the drinking...and ending with this morning—though I didn't tell them yet that we planned to stay married.

"So he continued to hit on you, knowing he doesn't want love but that you do?" Marcus asked.

"No. I never told him that. It's not typically my conversation starter. And he didn't even know about *The Vers* until this weekend. When he found out, he messaged, apologizing because he felt bad."

Marcus and Declan grumbled. It still didn't endear Elliott to them. God, they were going to lose it when I told them the rest.

"I feel like shit that we left you in Vegas," Dec said.

"You know I would have found a way to stay with you if you were having a hard time," Corbin added.

"I wasn't. I mean, yes and no, but that's not your responsibility. I'm an adult. I don't need you guys to handle my heart for me."

"Did you fuck him?" Marcus asked, getting back on topic.

"No."

He nodded. "What's the plan from here? An annulment? I'll speak to my attorney to make sure your ass is covered in any way you might need. We can—"

"We're staying married." Ripping off the Band-Aid seemed like the best way to deal with this.

"Excuse me, what? I thought you said you're staying married?" Dec stared at me in confusion.

"We decided it makes sense. You guys saw how fast the news got out. Elliott's dad is a member of Congress. He's a good guy trying to do good work. Elliott feels like… Well, I don't want to share too much of his business, but he cares about his dad and feels he's let him down enough."

"I looked him up. Elliott, that is. There's porn. He's packing," Corbin informed me.

"Thanks, Corb."

"There's nothing wrong with sex work. It's real work," he clarified.

"I know, and I agree, but not everyone does. And his dad has taken a lot of shit for decisions Elliott's made. He may be a ridiculous flirt who plans to fuck his way through life, but he's not a bad person. And I've made the decision not to date or have sex for the foreseeable future, so it should be a piece of cake. We stay married so we don't look like idiots. Then, after a specific amount of time, we announce our divorce and that we're still good friends. Yada, yada. You know the spiel."

The room was quiet for a moment before it erupted into questions and shouts of outrage. I'd expected this, and I couldn't say I blamed them. If the situation were reversed, I'd feel the same. All we ever wanted was to protect each other, and I could see why they would worry about me here, but… "Stop!"

They did, except Declan. "I don't get why you're doing this for him." He crossed his arms, clearly upset.

"I'm not," I admitted. "Maybe part of me is, but I'm doing it for me too. For my dad. He raised me and loves me and knows I wanted nothing more than to find my person. He'd be crushed to find out I drunk-married someone I'm not in love with. I don't want to do that to him. I want him to believe this is real, that I fell for someone and we tried to make it work. Maybe that doesn't make sense to anyone except me, but that's how I feel. Right now, what I really need is all of you. I can't do this without you."

It was Marcus who stood first. He walked over, held his hand out for me, pulled me to my feet, and wrapped his arms around me. Beneath that tough barrier he put up sometimes, he was more of a softy than any of us. He liked to pretend he wasn't, but Marcus was all heart and our biggest supporter.

Corbin stood next and snuggled in close. "Aww, I love hugs. We should do this all the time. End every day with a Beach Bum hug." Beach Bums was the nickname we'd given ourselves when we were young. We'd spend our days at the beach, checking out the asses of all the cute guys. The name of my bakery, Beach Buns, was a play on that.

I looked over my shoulder at Declan, who was watching me. He was worried. I knew that, but I needed him. A second later he stood and joined us. "We got your back. Whatever you need. I hate him, though," he said.

"You hate most people," Marcus pointed out.

Leave it to Corbin to ask, "Does this mean we're not allowed to look up his old sex videos? Since he's your husband and all?"

I was actually a little curious myself, but I would never admit that. "No looking at my naked husband."

"That's so weird to hear," Marcus said.

"Will *you* be looking at your naked husband?" Corbin questioned.

"Nope. We agreed no sex. This is a business arrangement of sorts." That's how I looked at it and how I was determined to continue seeing it. Maybe Elliott and I would become friends before this was over, but we would never be anything more.

★ ★ ★

I WAS EXHAUSTED, but I went straight from Marcus's to Dad's. I wanted to tell him before he saw it online. Unlike Elliott, who wanted me with him when he went to talk to his parents, I preferred to do this alone. In fact, if there was a way I could make it so Dad never met Elliott at all, I would. I wasn't a fool, though. I knew that wouldn't work.

When Dad opened the door, a huge smile spread across his face. He was always so happy to see me, the same way I was him. Life was so busy that we didn't do it as often as we should.

"Parker. This is a surprise."

Guilt already gnawed at my bones. I hated that I would be lying to him today.

"I missed you," I said as we went into the house. I knew I needed to rip off the Band-Aid and just tell him, but this was hard for me. When I got married, it was supposed to have been for love.

"I always miss you. What's new? How are the boys?" Dad always called them the boys. It didn't matter how old we got.

I sat in the living room with him, and we talked. Last I'd seen him was at Christmas, so it had been a while. He told me about work and neighbors, both of us comfortable, but in some ways, we didn't talk to each other like father and son. It was hard to explain, but he'd often simply trusted me to do my own thing, even when I was young.

Well, except when he found me blowing boys in my bedroom. That was a no-go.

I didn't want to carry this on longer than I needed to, so I said, "I have to tell you something."

Dad frowned. "Is everything okay?"

"Yes. Everything is actually great. It's good news, only I feel bad for not telling you sooner."

He nodded, clearly unsure but waiting for me to continue.

"I met this guy…Elliott…about a year ago. We dated for a bit and then broke up, but we stayed good friends. We've been talking a lot and recently got back together. He's really nice, successful. His mom is a lawyer, and his dad is a congressman." All those things were more or less true. "I have fun with him. He's…different." Those things were true too. I'd enjoyed talking with Elliott that first night, and on the night of the wedding we'd had a blast together. And he did feel different. Something about him got under my skin. "Anyway…we were in Vegas this weekend."

"I thought you were there for a work thing."

"I was, but Elliott came too. I know it sounds out of character for me, and I know it's going to be a shock, but we got married. I'll bring him so you can meet him soon."

Dad sat there for a moment, rocking in his La-Z-Boy, watching me. I could see him trying to sort all this out in his head, to make sense of it all. I shifted uncomfortably, not sure what to say.

"He's really funny. And he thinks I'm beautiful," I added because he said it often, even if it was just him being flirtatious or trying to get into my pants.

"Why didn't you tell me about him?" Dad asked softly, the hurt clear in his voice.

"The marriage was last minute," I admitted. "I didn't go there planning it, but it felt right." And I guessed in a way it had that night, even if it only felt right because it sounded fun. "He loves his family so much. He's a city planner. He feels guilty for not following in his parents' footsteps." I tried to think of anything I could say to endear Elliott to Dad, to tell him anything I could about my husband, but the sad fact was that I didn't know a great deal about him. "His mom is Cuban. He says she's his best friend."

"What do the boys think?"

I loved that he asked, that he trusted them and knew how important they were to me. "They're happy for me. They support me."

"Do you love him?" Dad's question was a knife straight through my heart.

A knot formed in my throat. It was hard to speak around it, but I forced myself to. "Yeah, Dad. Of course." The pain in my chest grew, splintered through me like his question was a pebble and my heart a windshield, now filled with cracks.

I didn't love Elliott, and I'd wanted that so, so much. But

it wasn't what happened, so I'd have to make it work.

"Then I'm happy for you, son. And I can't wait to meet him."

We stood, and Dad hugged me. I felt like the biggest liar in the world.

# CHAPTER SEVEN
## *Elliott*

"DO YOU LIVE in the kitchen?" I asked Parker while packing his apartment. I'd put off lunch with my parents, telling them I wanted to give Parker a little more time, that he was nervous they wouldn't like him after how the wedding had gone down. It was true—he wasn't looking forward to meeting them—but I also just wanted to buy us some time. This was the craziest thing I'd ever done, and I still couldn't wrap my head around it. If it felt like this to me, I couldn't imagine how it felt to Parker, someone who'd dreamed about getting married to a man he loved.

"I'm a baker."

"And they live in their kitchens?"

"Why are you asking me if I live here?" He huffed, annoyed. He was like that with me often. That probably shouldn't be fun, but for some reason, it was.

"Because you literally haven't grabbed any toiletries, clothes, or anything like that. Every single thing we're boxing up is from your kitchen."

We'd gotten back from Vegas yesterday. We'd both worked earlier today. It was now evening, and we'd decided there was no reason to stall. Well, Parker had decided, which surprised me, but I was easy and went with the flow.

"I'll take my clothes."

"I mean, I don't care if you're naked."

He rolled his eyes. "I'm sure you don't."

"Hey, all you have to do is exchange the *n* in *naked* with a *b*, and you have *baked*."

"But I'm a baker…not baked."

"Well, we can get naker if you'd rather."

His dark brows drew together. "Naker? You're so weird."

I shrugged. "I thought it was kinda cool."

We were both quiet for a moment, but I didn't do too well with keeping my mouth shut. "Is it a comfort for you?" I asked while taping up a box. "Having this stuff with you?" He gave me this adorable half-frown, half-pout look. I laughed. "Oh my God, it is, and you're annoyed I figured that out."

"Am not."

"It's okay, husband. I pay attention. Isn't that supposed to be a good thing? Shit, I'm killing this already."

"We're almost done in here," he said, clearly ignoring that. "I'll grab clothes and bathroom stuff. That should be enough for now."

I followed Parker to his bedroom and…holy fuck. Had a tornado gone through here? There were clothes *everywhere*. I was a little shocked, and trying not to comment on it. This was one of those moments when a husband should keep his thoughts to himself. "Does your dad want to meet me?"

"Yes, but we're going to put that off as long as possible."

His response stung. Sure, I was putting off him meeting my parents as well, but it wasn't because I didn't think Parker was good enough for me, and I had a feeling he felt that way about me. "I'm not going to embarrass you in front of your dad." I crossed my arms and leaned against the doorjamb.

"I didn't say that." He began placing clothes into a suitcase. Evidently, he understood the mess that was his bedroom, even if I didn't. "I'll take enough for a few days and then come back for the rest. I'm going to miss my apartment."

My chest got tight. "We can move in here if you really want. I don't want to take your home away from you." This whole thing was already going to be tougher on Parker than it was on me, and I couldn't help feeling responsible for it all. I shouldn't have done any of this. I should have come to my senses. What if I'd married him because a part of me just really wanted to fuck him? I didn't think that was the case, but I wondered about things like that.

His face scrunched up, something I'd noticed he did when I surprised him. It was cute. I wanted to kiss the tip of his nose, but I figured he might punch me.

"You would do that?"

"Yes. I'm a nice guy."

"You are?" The playfulness in his voice enticed a laugh out of me.

"Always breaking my heart, beautiful."

The same look he always got when I called him pretty washed over his face. Like it lit a fire inside him and made him want to swoon. More than that, it was almost as if he didn't believe me, as if he couldn't understand why I would say that about him, which was insane. How could someone who looked like Parker not know how irresistible he was? How could he not see it? It was interesting and would likely make me continue to use the endearment. Maybe that was something that could come out of this. I could make Parker see himself the way I did.

"I decided I'd rather stay at your place," Parker said. "After we're done, I want to be able to come home and go back to my life as if none of this happened. It would be weird to have you in my space, considering the circumstances."

An annoyed twitch vibrated through my chest. "Wow...you really don't like me."

"That's not true." When I cocked a brow, he groaned. "It's not. I know I say that, but I don't hate you. We're just different. We want different things and don't understand each other. It's just not the same for me as it is for you. I feel like I lost something. I don't say that to hurt your feelings. It's not your fault, but…"

"Fuck," I cursed. "We can still call this off. I know you still lost something, but we don't have to do this. I can deal with the repercussions of my actions."

He shook his head. "No, there's no going back now."

"That sounds ominous. Like we're in one of those end-of-the-world movies and we've made a decision to go on but we're not sure if it's the right one."

He smiled. "You got that out of what I just said?"

Eh, not really, but I wanted to lighten the mood. "You didn't?"

"I can see it. Maybe we're on a journey and now the terrain is getting rougher and more dangerous. We have to like…I don't know…walk through something really scary, like a giant-spiders habitat."

I laughed. "Giant spiders is what you came up with?"

"I don't know. Zombies, then. Or hell, people are worse than everyone else. People who want what we have. I suck at this. You try."

As we finished packing, we created our end-of-the-world journey and all the obstacles we were going to conquer together. It was surprisingly fun.

We loaded both our vehicles, and I gave Parker my address. I waited outside my place for him, Parker pulling into the driveway about five minutes after me.

I lived in a three-bedroom, two-story house in a residential area. There were palm trees in my front yard, as well as rosebushes and morning glories similar to those decorating

Parker's apartment complex. I wondered what he thought of my place, if he would hate it here, and again, how in the fuck we'd gotten ourselves in this situation.

Parker closed the door of his Honda and eyed my house. "Home sweet home."

"I'll try not to make it suck too bad." I winked.

Parker grabbed two suitcases, I picked up a box, and we headed for the door. I pressed the code to unlock it. "We can set up a separate one for you. I can round up a key if you want, but this is easier."

"I'm fine with a code." He followed me inside, tentative, taking a look around. The front door led directly into the living room, which was open concept with the kitchen and dining area. My house was decorated in mostly black and white, with photography on the walls. Modern but homey.

"Wow…"

"Wow what?"

"I expected more of a bachelor pad, and holy shit! Your kitchen is great." He let go of the bags and went straight for it. "Double oven and so much counter space. God, I would die for all this in my apartment. I love where I live, but if I could afford to…or I guess if I owned it and I could afford to, I would gut the space and remodel."

I set the box on the counter. "You're welcome to use it as much as you want while you're here."

"Marcus has a great kitchen too. I'm so jealous."

"You're all incredibly close." He sure did mention them a lot.

"They're my people."

"Sounds nice," I replied honestly. Vaughn and I were close, and I had other friends, of course, but the relationship between the four of them felt like more. I didn't know them and I could tell that.

"It is. Sometimes I tell myself that's why I've never got the dream, ya know? The husband and all. You can't have everything, and I feel so lucky to have them. Maybe I'm asking for too much."

"Not possible. You'll find what you're looking for. You deserve it." That was something I truly believed. Parker was sexy and sweet. The man for him was out there.

"You don't know my dating history." He winked.

"I drew a few conclusions from *The Vers*." I reached over and held his waist, not really thinking about my actions other than wanting to comfort him. But Parker sucked in a sharp breath and stepped back. "Sorry. I wasn't trying to get in your pants. I've heard sex doesn't happen after marriage anyway," I teased. "I was just going to tell you I'm serious. I might not want the same things you do…or even understand it on an emotional level, but you'll find the guy for you. It would be too big a tragedy for you not to."

His eyes turned stormy again. They did that sometimes when he was thinking. "That was…sweet."

"You keep talking to me like that, and you're gonna make my crush on you grow."

He rolled his eyes, but it was clearly done teasingly. "You don't have a crush on me. Stop saying that."

"How do you know?"

"You said yourself you've never felt a romantic connection."

"Does that mean I can't have a crush? Crushes aren't based in true emotions. They're interest and sexual attraction. Curiosity. I can see a beautiful man across a crowded bar, watch him lick his lips, and wonder what they taste like. See him stare off into space like he has a million things on his mind and wonder what he's thinking. I can be attracted to him, wonder how his brain works, and want to put the pieces of him together. That's a crush to me. I've been crushing on you since the first night we met."

His breathing came faster, his chest rising and falling in short, rapid pulls. "Stop trying to seduce me." He swatted my arm, and I laughed.

"Ouch. You're violent, and I wasn't. It's not my fault you're attracted to me too. All I'm saying is, a crush is different from whatever it is that makes people fall in love. Hell, maybe I'm just broken that way." I shrugged.

He frowned. "You're not broken."

"Thanks, beautiful." I grinned.

"Are you going to keep calling me that?"

"Unless you ask me to stop."

He looked away. "It's getting late. We should bring the rest of my things in, and then maybe you can show me my room."

"Whatever you say, beautiful." I added the endearment again because he hadn't asked me to stop.

# CHAPTER EIGHT
## *Parker*

THIS WAS THE first time I'd ever been nervous to record an episode of *The Vers*. It was the first one after coming back from Las Vegas, and I was going to have to talk about my marriage...and pretend to be madly in love with Elliott. The lying was hard for me, but more than that, it made me feel lonely...planning to say things I *wanted* to feel, that I *should* feel about my husband, but one drunken mistake had taken that away from me.

It had been an interesting couple of days staying with Elliott...well, I guess I should say living with my new husband because that was the situation. He'd been on his best behavior, and I'd been baking up a storm and spending extra hours at Beach Buns, but so far, so good. We stayed out of each other's way and were polite—like roommates. I was roommates with my husband. Fuck my life.

"How you doing, sweetheart?" Marcus asked. We recorded in a studio at his place. Marcus's parents were wealthy as hell, and he was too. He'd made a lot of money in real estate while they had made theirs by becoming one of the most sought-after architecture firms in the state.

"As good as can be expected," I replied.

"Don't get your feelings involved."

Ouch. "Way to cut to the point."

"It's true. I know you, and I don't want you hurt. I can't pretend to understand why the two of you are doing this, but you need to protect yourself, Park. You know you. You know your heart. It pulls people in. That's how we're all who we are to each other, but that big heart of yours, that need for love, it also makes you vulnerable."

His words were similar to what Corbin had said to me—about me being the reason our friend group was together. I didn't know about that, but he was right about me being vulnerable. When we needed someone to sit us down and tell it like it is, Marcus was the one we went to. He didn't have a fake bone in his body, and while sometimes I didn't want to hear what he had to say, it came from him loving us and wanting what was best for us.

"I'll be careful. Elliott is hot, but I know what this is."

He nodded, then pulled me in for a quick kiss to the temple just as Declan and Corbin walked in.

"What? I missed a hug? That's not fair," Corbin said.

"What's wrong?" Declan asked.

"Nothing's wrong. You know how Marcus is. He's always playing the mother hen."

"I am not," he grumbled.

"Do you know you?" Corbin asked.

"They have a point," Declan added, and I let out a sigh of relief. I didn't want to get into this again with all of them. I'd told them I wanted their support, and they'd said yes. I wanted it to stop right there.

"Make up your mind. One minute I'm an asshole, the next a mother hen," Marcus replied.

"You're both," I said. "But come on, Marcus, you know you try to take care of all of us. You say I'm the heart of us, but you're the backbone—our protector." And he was. When I'd wanted to know what it was like to kiss a boy, Marcus had been my first. Corbin's too. He hadn't done it because he wanted us, but because he wanted to make us happy. We'd congregated at his home a lot as kids, and then later on he'd helped us with our businesses. We recorded at his place and spent most of our time here. Marcus was our glue, even though he would never see it.

"You guys are crazy." He rolled his eyes, and we let it go.

We chatted for a few minutes, getting comfortable. I always sat next to Declan—and Marcus and Corbin beside each other. We prepared the equipment and got everything ready, testing our mics.

"We gonna talk about how we're doing this or just go for it?" Marcus asked.

"Just go for it. I don't want it to sound too rehearsed, and we play off each other well."

Declan looked at me with a kind smile. "You got this."

I reached over and squeezed his hand.

Three…two…one…the timer counted down in the background.

"Hello, queer people and allies," Corbin began. "Welcome to *The Vers*, where four best friends who rarely agree on anything give their versatile opinions about everything. I'm Corbin Erickson, The Charmer."

"Parker Hansley, The Romantic."

"Marcus Alston, The Realist—and I can't believe Corb didn't add something about how much better he is than the rest of us."

"Because this week isn't about me, and unlike you, I understand that," Corbin joked.

"Pfft, you understand it my ass," Marcus countered.

"Yes, you are an ass. I totally agree." Corbin smirked.

We always spent half our time on *The Vers* nitpicking at each other, but for some reason, people loved it. Maybe because we were just us, because the bond between us could be felt in every word, and we kept it real. The way we acted on *The Vers* was how we acted in real life as well.

"Can I introduce myself now, or do you guys plan to keep this going?" Declan interrupted Marcus and Corbin's banter.

"I was thinking we'd keep it going," Corbin replied.

Marcus shook his head at him. "Didn't you just say you know when something isn't about you?"

Finally, Dec cut them off, or they'd never stop. "I'm Declan Burns, The Loner."

"Who isn't a loner anymore because he has a super-hot movie-star boyfriend. But enough about everyone except Parker now." Corbin winked at Declan.

I mustered all the courage I could and plastered my happy face on to get myself in the mood. "Yes, let's talk about me now. Declan's old news. I have something exciting to share." I was surprised how real that sounded. If I didn't know myself, I'd think I was truly stoked to share about getting married.

"You're in love with me?" Corbin asked.

"No."

"You're having Marcus's baby, then?"

"Do you ever shut up?" I teased my friend. He pretended to wipe tears from his eyes.

"I'll be a good boy now." Corbin turned to Marcus. "I promise, Daddy M."

I rolled my eyes, but what he was doing helped. The lighter and sillier Corbin made this, the more it eased the thunder of anxiety sounding off in my head.

"Really, though...I've been keeping a secret from you, *Vers* listeners. There's a guy...and he's a good one. No surprise threesomes, or getting stood up, or showing up for our date dressed like a chicken... Do you guys remember that?" I chuckled.

"Yeah, I mean, what the fuck?" Marcus replied. "Do we even know why he did that?"

"Nope. I took one look at him and walked out. He chased me down the street. Clucking." There was a round of laughter in response.

"What is it about you that attracts such assholes and weirdos?" Declan asked.

"I don't know, but the good news is that I don't have to worry about that anymore because of *The Guy*. We've been dating for a while now, but because of my bad luck, we decided to keep it quiet. We were in Las Vegas and had…well, a great night. I can't remember the last time I laughed so hard or had so much fun, and we decided to just do it—we got married! It's been a whirlwind since, but I wanted to share the good news with you all. You've been such a support to me over the years." And I was lying to them. Ugh. This was harder than I'd thought it would be. "So thank you for everything. The Romantic has finally found his Prince Charming."

Nausea from the guilt formed a storm in my gut. But it had nothing on how strange those words felt in my mouth, putting into the universe that thing I'd always hoped would happen, only now it was a farce.

Declan squeezed my hand. "We couldn't be happier for him. No one deserves it more than our Parker. But, Elliott, if you're listening…if you hurt our boy…"

"No threats on air," Corbin cut him off. "But seriously, what Declan said."

"If he doesn't hurt Parker, he has nothing to worry about," Marcus added. "But we don't have to stress about that because Parker is happy and Elliott knows how lucky he is to have him."

"Let's hope he can handle my messiness," I said, just to

make everyone laugh.

"Oh God, Elliott, we're sorry you have to deal with this," Marcus said. "Parker had to stay at my house for a month years ago. I nearly strangled him with a pair of underwear I found on a lamp. How does your underwear get on a lamp?"

I wished I could say Marcus was exaggerating. The only defense I had was: "My kitchen is always clean!" Which really wasn't a defense at all.

"Well, at least there's that." Declan winked before Marcus spoke again.

"Anyway, that's enough about the happy husbands. I'm sure Parker will be rambling about Elliott more on other days. How about we jump into QHF, which is where we share a random queer historical fact, and then go on with the show?"

Marcus launched into a story about a person who was arrested in 1394 in London for having sex with a man in an alley. "They lived part of the time as a man, part of the time as a woman, having sex with both men and women."

"People like to think so much of this is new," Corbin said, "but look at this—here's proof of someone being and living gender fluid in the 1300s. We've always been here."

"And we're not going anywhere," Declan piped in.

The show went on for about an hour after that. I tried to stay involved, to laugh and joke and be the Parker they knew, but I wasn't sure I pulled it off.

# CHAPTER NINE
## *Elliott*

"HE'S AN ABSOLUTE mess. His apartment was a little wild when I was there—that should've been a clue. Still, I assumed he would be tidier while living with someone else, but no, I can now say he's not. I don't understand how he can find anything. His clothes are everywhere, including the bathroom floor, which would be fine if that wasn't also a hallway bathroom—there isn't one in his room. The sink countertop looks like a tornado ripped through his toiletries. How does one man need so many face, hair, body, who the fuck knows, products? He's beautiful, but it can't take that much work to be so beautiful, can it?" I grumbled to Vaughn, who was sitting across from me at the restaurant. We'd met for lunch so I could vent to him about my new husband. It had been about two weeks since Parker moved in, and it was…interesting, to say the least. I considered burning all his clothes just to keep them off the floor but figured that wasn't the best start to our marriage. "And the part that really gets to me? If I leave *one* freaking plate in the kitchen sink, he acts like I'm a heathen! So he can turn the bathroom counter into a beauty shop and the floor into his laundry basket, but I can't leave a plate in the sink?"

I waited for Vaughn to agree with me, but all he did was bust up laughing.

"What's so funny?"

He lowered his voice and said, "I thought this marriage wasn't real? You sound like legit husbands to me."

"You're not nearly as compassionate to me as you should be. I thought we were friends?"

That just made Vaughn laugh harder. "I'm sorry. It's just funny seeing you live with someone. I'm sure it's not as bad as you're making it sound."

"That's because you don't live with a husband you know nothing about," I replied in a hushed tone. I might have been exaggerating a bit, but it was weird having someone in my space all the time. Parker sang in the shower, which yes, was cute even though he didn't have a great voice, but I wasn't used to having someone there, all the time, making messes and singing and…okay, I couldn't complain about the baking. I enjoyed that part. My house consistently smelled like sugar now, which was nice. "It's not terrible. It just takes some getting used to."

"Welcome to marriage."

"Says the guy who's never been married. Why are you trying to sound like an expert?"

Vaughn winked. "I'm an expert on everything, baby." I rolled my eyes before he asked, "Seriously, though. You okay? He okay? How's it going?"

"My parents are freaking out to meet him. Dad's publicly congratulated us on his social media, saying how happy he is I found my person, but they're also confused as to why they never met him pre-wedding and haven't since. I just…what if they get attached to him? What if he gets attached to them? There's so much shit we didn't think about, and now that it's put into play, we can't change our minds." It was all I'd been thinking about.

"It'll be okay. The two of you will figure it out. And the

thing is, people get attached all the time and divorces happen all the time. So if you and Parker end up going your separate ways, they'll deal with the same thing anyone else does in a divorce."

"Yeah, but most people get married and plan on it working out. We know it won't—wait, what do you mean *if* we go our separate ways? I'm not staying married to him. I'm not in love with him."

"Maybe you will be by the end."

I huffed. "Nope. I can't see that happening."

He shrugged. "I never said it would. Just maybe."

"Okay, but what would make you say that at all?" I didn't know why I was obsessing about this, and clearly from the way Vaughn looked at me, he didn't either.

"I don't know, man. Forget I said it. Can we eat now, or are you going to obsessively talk about your husband?"

Well, when he put it like that... I definitely wasn't going to talk about Parker anymore.

A couple of minutes later, I asked, "Have you ever been to his bakery?" Thankfully, Vaughn wasn't in my head to realize I'd sworn off discussing Parker yet hadn't stopped thinking about him the whole time.

★ ★ ★

I'D JUST LEFT Vaughn and had climbed into my car when my cell rang. I groaned when *Mom* flashed on the screen, but I knew better than not to answer it. I'd played that game in Vegas, and it didn't typically fly. Plus, I was home now and she could be anywhere, showing up at any moment. It didn't matter how old you were, moms were like that. At least mine was.

"Hello," I said, and was immediately interrupted.

"Elliott Delgado Weaver, I've been patient enough. If you don't bring that husband of yours to the house, I'm going to show up at your place and meet him myself. Your father has been pretending to know his son-in-law when he hasn't spoken a word to the man. Do you know how many times he's been asked about your marriage? Too many to count, and he's supporting you and saying how happy we are for you—which we are if this is real the way you say it is, but I don't understand why we haven't met him. I'm not going to accept it anymore!"

Shit. She was right. Not for the first time, I was reminded how lucky I was to have them. That was part of the reason I didn't want them to meet Parker. I felt too guilty about this whole thing. "I know, Mama. I'm sorry. You middle-named me and everything. I know how serious this is." My parents had wanted me to have part of my Cuban heritage in my name, so they'd given me my mom's maiden name as my middle one.

"Why don't you want us to meet him?"

"That's not how it is. I promise. We just didn't expect the news to get out. I know it doesn't make much sense, but once we made the decision to get married, we thought we would be able to slowly work everyone into it because we know it's fast and that people might have concerns."

She sighed. "I guess, but...you're mi niño. I was supposed to meet him first. That's how it works. You know how I am. Dating is a family experience for me, and I didn't get that."

I closed my eyes, trying not to spill the truth right then. It wasn't fair to Parker. We'd made a plan, and I owed it to him to stick to it. "I know, Mama." Fuck, I hated this. "I'll talk to Parker about his work schedule to see if we can come this weekend. Dad will be home?" Sometimes he had to go to DC for work.

"Yeah, he'll be home. I'll see you this weekend."

"See you then. I love you."

"I love you too."

We ended the call, and I banged my head against the steering wheel a few times as if that would make it so none of this had happened.

Spoiler alert: it didn't work.

I drove over to Beach Buns rather than waiting to see Parker at home tonight because he lived with me and he was my husband so that was a thing that happened.

He went in at the ass-crack of dawn every day, so he usually got off around two or three in the afternoon, though often he worked late. If there was one thing I learned about Parker in the short time we'd been married—Jesus, that was so fucking crazy to think—it was how much he truly loved baking and his bakery.

He was behind the counter, talking to a customer, and I couldn't help watching him for a second. He smiled that sweet, bashful smile of his. His eyes sparkled as he listened to the customer, and the thing was, I knew it was real. He wasn't pretending to care about what the person said—he truly did.

Damn, he really was pretty. If he wasn't so beautiful, then maybe we wouldn't have been in this position in the first place, but the second I'd seen him, I hadn't been able to take my eyes off him.

His gaze flashed to me, and immediately a small scowl furrowed his lips. It shouldn't be cute, but it was, and actually prompted me to smile, which only made his grumbly face turn more serious. He wanted to be more annoyed by me than he was. I didn't know why that was so fun; clearly, I was an emotional masochist.

He continued to talk while trying to ignore me, but his eyes kept flickering in my direction. When I cocked a brow at him, as if to ask *what?* a small grin replaced his look of annoyance before he quickly wiped it away.

The woman turned to look at me. "Oh! Is this him?"

"Yes," Parker said, his scowl returning. "This is Elliott, my husband." The word sounded sticky in his mouth, like he hadn't wanted to set it free.

"Guilty as charged." I walked over. She looked in her sixties and held a Beach Buns box in one arm. "And who is this beauty?" I held my hand out for her.

She fanned herself. "Well, aren't you a charmer. He's a charmer, Parker."

We shook. "Guilty as charged," I said again and winked. One quick glance at Parker confirmed he was rolling his eyes at me.

Well, at least someone appreciated me, since he didn't.

"You have no idea how surprised we all were to hear about you! But we're so happy. Our Parker deserves the world, and I'm so happy he finally found his person." She turned to Parker. "Though I'm still upset we didn't get to go to the wedding. You always wanted to get married at the beach, but I guess when you fall, none of that matters as much. Just that you get to tie yourself to them."

Fuckity, fuck, fuck. "That was my fault. I just…couldn't wait to call him mine. I'm lucky Parker puts up with me."

"There will come the days when he wonders too!" She grinned. "And you about him. That's just the way marriage goes. Anyway, it's so nice to meet you, Elliott. I've been coming here since Beach Buns first opened. You got yourself a good one."

"I know I do," I said, which was true, even if he was filthy. "I just wish he didn't leave his dirty clothes on the bathroom floor."

She laughed.

"It's not *that* bad," Parker cut in.

"Oh no. I assure you, it is."

"He snores," Parker fibbed. He'd slept in bed with me exactly one night in Vegas, and we were both too drunk to notice something like that.

"Lies!"

"He does. And he's a terrible cook." He crossed his arms, clearly proud of himself.

"Aren't you two the cutest? I better be on my way." She waved goodbye and left.

As soon as the door closed, he said, "Why did you tell her I'm messy?"

"Because, beautiful, it's true."

I'd said it enough that the compliment shouldn't throw him off his game, but I could tell he struggled with how to reply, which made me laugh and him grumble how much he hated me.

There were a few other customers in Beach Buns, and two other workers, but no one was paying much attention to us. With a lowered voice, I asked, "Are you okay?" because I figured pretending he was happy and in love had to be hard for him.

He appeared shocked by my question—because he was surprised I cared, or that I noticed?

"Yeah, I'm fine. I'm just getting used to it."

And I was going to make it worse. "Are you almost done here? I thought we could take a walk."

Worry creased Parker's brow. "Is everything okay?"

"Yeah, same ole thing. Married-life stuff."

Thankfully, he relaxed some. Had he thought I was going to call this off? I wouldn't have expected him to hate that idea so much.

"Yeah, actually, I'm about done here. I'll meet you outside in a few minutes."

# CHAPTER TEN
## *Parker*

I WAS STRESSING, trying to figure out why Elliott had come to Beach Buns. Sure, he used to come in every now and again to flirt with me, but he hadn't been there at all since we'd gotten married. It seemed like something was on his mind, though, and that made me nervous. What if something went wrong?

After taking a few deep breaths, I forced myself to chill out. I touched base with my employees about a few things I wanted to make sure were done today, then went outside.

Elliott was kneeling next to a little girl. Her eyes were red, streaks of old tears on her cheeks. A woman I assumed was her mom was picking up funnel cake from the sidewalk, while Elliott was talking to the little girl and...was he doing a magic trick?

"Where did it go?" the little girl asked, now smiling brightly. She didn't seem to care about her treat anymore and was just interested in Elliott.

"I don't know. It's magic." He shrugged.

"Do it again!" she pleaded.

The mom joined them, and I watched as Elliott made another quarter vanish into thin air. His audience clapped and cheered, and he stood and gave a bow.

His gaze caught mine and he winked, my face flushing at

being caught watching them. I walked over just as the little girl asked him, "What's your name?"

"Samantha," her mom warned.

"It's okay. I'm Elliott, and this is my husband, Parker."

I tripped over my own two feet at hearing him introduce me that way. It sounded so…natural, like he'd been saying it for years. There was no real reason for him to do that, so I wondered why he did.

"Hi, Samantha," I said.

"Your husband is magic!" she replied.

"I'm seeing that." I nudged him, hoping it wasn't obvious I'd just learned this tidbit about my husband myself. I gave my attention to her mom. "I own the bakery. If it's okay, she can go in and pick out a free treat to make up for the one she dropped."

"Oh, wow. Thank you! That's so nice. Tell Parker and Elliott thank you, Samantha."

She did, and I went with them to the door, sticking my head through to let my employees know Samantha could pick something on the house.

"Bye, Elliott! Bye, Parker!" Samantha waved, then pressed her face against the glass cases to choose what she wanted.

Elliott motioned toward the sidewalk, and I followed him. I pushed my hands into my pockets, trying to figure out what he was going to say and why it made my heart punch against my chest. Also…thinking about seeing him with Samantha, how sweet he'd been. Doing magic tricks for a little girl he didn't know made my heart soften—something I needed to keep from happening. Been there, done that. I didn't need a broken heart yet again. "So…are you going to tell me what's going on?"

"Hmm?"

Seeing the mischievous smile on his lips, I pulled my hand

free and swatted him playfully. "You know exactly what I'm talking about."

"Oh. That. It's nothing. If you're free this weekend, we have to go meet my parents. How was work?"

My feet stuck to the ground like I'd stepped into wet cement. "Already?"

"Yes, dear. Come along." He hooked his arm through mine and began to walk again. I had no choice but to go with him.

"*Yes, dear?*"

"You're right. I forgot you like it when I call you beautiful." He winked, and butterflies played chase in my belly.

Ugh. I *did* like it. Why did I like it so much?

"My mom threatened a surprise visit to the house to ambush you if we didn't come over. She doesn't make idle threats. If you try to hide from her, she will find you."

My chuckle wouldn't be held back, so I just let it free-fall from my lips before I thought about my own mom. "I wonder what my mom would do right now if she were still around."

He continued to hold my arm as we walked. "I'm sorry you lost her. You deserve for her to be here...for her to see you get married for real and know your husband."

I did deserve that, and so did she, but that wasn't the case. "The world doesn't work on what we deserve or not. There are millions of people who should have the same thing but don't."

"No, I guess not. It sucks, though."

"It does."

"Can I ask how she died?"

I hadn't told him? But then, that made sense. It wasn't something I talked about often. "It was a freak accident—like something from a movie, to be honest. A driver had a heart attack, swerved toward a child. Mom, being who she was, pushed her out of the way and was hit."

"Jesus. She's a hero."

His reply was absolutely perfect, filling my chest with the best kind of warmth. "She is. Thank you for saying that."

Elliott let go of me and cleared his throat. He glanced my way as if unsure what to say. "You'll like my mom, and she'll adore you. If you really can't do this weekend, I can figure something out, though she won't let it go for long."

I sighed. "No reason to keep stalling. We'll have to do this sooner or later, so I might as well do it now. I'll make it work." The reality of the situation hit me, and I let out a laugh that scared me a little. "I can't believe I'm going to meet my in-laws for the first time when I'm already married, and oh—my husband isn't in love with me."

"Let's not forget you're not in love with your husband either."

"Nope. He's totally not my type." He was so very much my type. A heartbreaker disguised by a sexy face and a great body, who I'd also noticed was sweet and kind.

"I've heard great things about him," Elliott teased.

I smiled. "Like what?"

"Well, for starters, he cleans up after himself."

I rolled my eyes. "So overrated."

"He's hot."

"Cocky."

"Yes, he has a big dick too."

This time my eyes nearly fell out of my skull when I rolled them. "You know what they say when a man is preoccupied with the size of his dick…"

"That he's honest and a really good fuck?" Elliott did this cute little nose-wrinkle thing that said he was being playful. "What is your type, though, really?"

That was both a hard question and not. "I don't care what

they look like, not really. Though I won't pretend I haven't been distracted by a pretty face more times than I care to share."

"It happens to the best of us."

"I want someone kind and compassionate, not just nice. Nice is good, but kindness comes from the heart. I want someone who cares about others. Also, it doesn't matter if he's successful, but I'd like him to have a job."

"The nerve!" We were still walking, our arms bumping against each other's every once in a while. Heat radiated off him and wrapped around me as he asked, "What else?"

"I want someone who makes me laugh and likes to spend time with me. Someone who wants to cuddle on the couch at night and taste the things I bake, who shares the things he loves with me too. I want him to tell me his hopes and dreams, and what's hurt him, and what's made him who he is. I want someone who looks at me like I made their whole day when I bring them coffee and a homemade muffin in bed for breakfast. I want someone who does the same for me." I wanted a man who would see something or hear a joke and it would make him think of me, so he would send me a photo or make sure he told me when he came home at night. "I want someone I love and who loves me in return." Apparently, that was too much to ask.

Elliott stopped walking and turned to look at me. His stare was intense, a caress against my skin.

"What?" I asked.

"Nothing. It just doesn't sound so scary when you describe it."

"Is it something *you* want?"

He shook his head, and we started walking again. "It's not something I don't want either. It's hard to explain. My thoughts and desires just don't seem to work that way. Do I believe love exists? Yes. I've seen it in my parents and others. Is it something I have this deep need for? No. And I've never felt it. I've liked people, sure, and I like sex and dating, but again, I've never had that craving for more. It's never been deeper than that, and it's hard to wrap my head around feeling those things."

"It's hard to wrap my head around not wanting or having feelings like that."

"Different strokes," he replied.

We were definitely opposites that way. It was that knowledge that would keep me safe from falling for him.

Elliott said, "Let's hang out today."

"We are hanging out."

"You know what I mean." When I frowned, he chuckled. "You look surprised I'm asking."

"I am!" Though I couldn't say why.

"I mean, we're husbands. We should at least become friends, learn more about each other in case my parents quiz us."

"Oh God, don't remind me." I joined him in his laughter, before shocking myself by saying, "Sure."

Santa Monica was very eco-friendly and had great green public transportation, so we took a bus to the pier instead of our cars. It was about four by now, the weather a cool sixty, so definitely not a beach day. Still, shops were open and people were browsing, eating, and riding the Ferris wheel.

"You hungry? Want to grab an early dinner?" Elliott asked, and I agreed.

We went to a Mexican restaurant, where they seated us at one of the window booths so we could look out at the ocean.

"Do you want a drink?" Elliott handed me the menu.

"That's what got us into trouble."

"You're such a good boy." Elliott winked, and my stomach got fluttery. He cocked his head slightly, as if realizing his words did something to me, and I looked away. That was…weird.

"Can I get you guys a drink?" the waiter asked.

Elliott looked at me.

"I'll take a diet Coke."

"The same," he said.

"Where did you go to college?" I asked him.

"UCLA. You?"

"I did the Pastry and Baking Arts and Management program at the Institute of Culinary Education."

"How long is a program like that?"

We talked about school, then continued getting to know each other, only slowing down to order our tacos.

Eventually, Elliott said, "I love sunsets over the ocean."

I looked out the window, the sky painted with pinks and oranges where it met the blue of the water. Wow. We'd been talking for a while.

"It really is beautiful here. Crazy expensive to the point that sometimes I wonder why I stay, but I couldn't leave Declan, Marcus, and Corbin."

He frowned. "Are you struggling?"

"No more than anyone else. Marcus is all about investments, so he's helped, and *The Vers* is a good revenue stream for us. Sometimes I just hate it that you have to make so much money to live in a place that's this beautiful. I wish it was more accessible for others."

He smiled. "You'll like my dad. I know what people say about politicians, and I agree with a lot of them, but having grown up with him, I know how much he really does want to help people, and how much he's tried. Equity is important to both him and Mom. I've been donating time and money for as long as I can remember. We work food kitchens every

Christmas and have my whole life."

I thought that would be surprising to me, but it wasn't. I could see Elliott trying to help those less fortunate than himself.

"My mom also runs a large fundraising event for victims of domestic violence every year. It's in a few months."

"That sounds amazing."

We watched the sunset, ate our tacos, and shared random bits of information about ourselves and our families, but on a more conversational level than before. Earlier it had felt more like a checklist when we were trying to get our story straight. Now we were two men out to dinner, just talking, the way we had been when we'd gotten really fucking drunk and gotten married.

"I'd like to buy your dinner," I told Elliott when the check arrived. I could see in his eyes that he'd wanted to do it, but he nodded in agreement and let me.

Afterward, we strolled along the small pier I was sure both of us had been down a thousand times over the years. It got cooler, and at one point Elliott started rubbing his hands up and down my arms. "What are you doing?"

"Trying to warm you up. I'd think that's obvious."

"I know, but we're not… This isn't…"

"Would you argue if one of your podcast guys did it?"

"Well, no."

"Then shut up."

I laughed. "You're such a brat." But I really was cold as fuck, so I wasn't going to argue with him.

Elliott said, "I wish there was a Cuban place close by. I'd take you for Cuban desserts. They're my favorite. Have you eaten many? I don't know if that's something you make."

"I don't. I made some in school, but not much since."

"You're missing out." He led me to the side of the pier,

and we leaned against the wooden railing.

"I love the beach. When we were kids, Declan, Marcus, Corbin, and I used to spend all our summers at the water. We called ourselves Beach Bums—like saying we were bumming around, but really, we were checking out hot guys."

Elliott laughed. "Your friendship is pretty amazing. When did you come out?"

"Middle school. I never hid it well. Declan tried to fight people who gave me shit." I got lost in the memories.

"I'm glad you had them."

"Thank you. Me too. So...know what I love to ride?" I asked. He opened his mouth, and I pressed my hand to it to shush him. "Don't even think about saying your cock."

"Holy shit. We really are married. You can read my mind."

I rolled my eyes.

"You have to admit you left yourself open for that one," he said, and yeah, I had.

"The Ferris wheel."

"Oh, cool. It's right over there. Have fun...though I also don't want to be a widower, so you should keep your feet on the ground."

"What? Are you afraid of heights?"

"No. I just don't like them."

I chuckled. "Me big man. Not afraid."

"Exactly." He pulled back.

"What? I thought you were fun. Ride the Ferris wheel with me." It was silly, wanting to do this with him, but I did.

"I thought *you* were fun. Why would you want to ride the death trap?"

I shook my head. "Fine. Whatever. I don't really want to make you do something if you're scared. Maybe we can find a merry-go-round."

I didn't know what came over me, why I was suddenly being so playful with Elliott. When he didn't say anything, I poked my bottom lip out dramatically and crossed my arms.

"Shut the fuck up. You're so spoiled. Let's go." Elliott grabbed my wrist and began tugging me toward the line. "*Elliott, save me from an asshole ex-boyfriend… Elliott, have a crush on me… Elliott, want to have sex with me and risk your life and limb on a ride that's not even fun?*" His words had been spoken in a high-pitched, teasing voice.

"I asked you for none of that except the last one."

"Lies!"

We got in line, and he immediately started rubbing his hands up and down my arms again, generating a spark of heat that seemed to flicker inward and ignite there. He was just being nice. We needed to get close to each other, to become friends, if we were going to really sell this whole in-love-with-each-other thing. "You don't have to, Elliott. If it's a fear of yours, I don't want to push you."

"Now he says so." Elliott gave me a dramatic eye roll. "You're too pretty not to get your way, and you know it."

Actually, I didn't, but I couldn't pretend it wasn't nice to hear, even though I knew he just wanted in my pants and that's all it was.

It was our turn, and before I could, Elliott paid for our ride. We climbed in. The second we started moving, he closed his eyes, and guilt swamped me. "Are you really scared? We'll be okay. I'll protect you," I teased, which got him to open them again. We'd been the last ones let on, so at least we didn't have to stop every two seconds to let someone else in. I took his hand, and Elliott let me.

"A kiss would distract me…"

"Keep dreaming, husband." I hadn't expected to use the moniker, but it had rolled off my lips anyway.

"Can't blame a guy for trying." We were quiet for a moment before he added, "It's mostly the getting on. Somehow, I'm okay now. I guess it's hard not to be when you have this view and such a beautiful man beside you."

Heat rushed to my groin, which was concerning. Um…no erections for Elliott. *Bad, bad, bad dick. Get down.* "You never give up."

"I'm just speaking the truth." He leaned close, his mouth next to my ear. "And you like it."

"Who doesn't like compliments?" Why the fuck was my voice so raspy?

Elliott laughed.

"We're attracted to each other. That's nothing new." And maybe I had this weird thing where I seemed to like it when Elliott called me beautiful. No big deal.

When the ride was over, he jumped out of his seat the second he could. "I never thought I would touch the ground again."

"You're an idiot."

He pumped his brows. "Race you to the beach."

"Huh?"

"Go!" he said and bolted.

It took me a second to realize what was happening, and then I was running too. It was silly, and I couldn't figure out why I was doing it. Some people looked at us like we'd lost it, and others were clearly unhappy about us running on the pier, but I kept going, chasing after Elliott, laughter bubbling in my chest and dancing from my lips with cold puffs of air.

He won because he cheated. I bent over, trying to catch my breath, and then…I was laughing again. For whatever reason, I couldn't stop. Elliott was laughing too, and a group of people made a wide circle around us as if unsure if we were stable, which only made me keep going even harder. It felt like our evening in Vegas, only sober.

"That was strangely fun," I said when I could speak again. I didn't know why exactly, but the whole night had been.

"You bring out the sixteen-year-old boy in me."

"I'm not sure that's a compliment."

He winked. "It is."

We watched each other. Elliott's brown eyes were slightly glassy from the cold air and running. Mine were probably the same. Fuck, he really was handsome. His dark hair was thick, and I wondered how it would feel between my fingers. He kept a short, stubbled beard that would feel a-fucking-mazing against my inner thighs—totally not what I should be thinking.

His forehead wrinkled as if he was asking a silent question which was probably, *Why the fuck are you staring at me like you want to jump my bones*, so I looked away. "I should go."

"We."

"Huh?"

"We should go. We live together, remember?"

"Oh yeah." Because he was my husband. "I have to be up early for work." Which *duh*, he knew because I was always up early.

"Declan meeting you tomorrow?" he asked, making conversation.

"Yes. Not at opening, though. We have breakfast a few times a week."

We took the bus back to Beach Buns, where we'd left our cars. And then I drove to his house—our house?—the whole way trying to convince myself this hadn't been a date...and that I certainly hadn't enjoyed it.

# CHAPTER ELEVEN
## *Elliott*

DAD HAD TO go away for work that weekend after all, so we hadn't met my parents yet. But the relief was short-lived, as this weekend there was no escaping it. I woke up that morning to the sound of a vacuum, which at first threw me because I'd been sleeping hard and had forgotten I didn't live alone. Once that piece of truth made its way into my head again, I remembered I lived with Parker, who hadn't cleaned much of anything other than the kitchen since he'd moved in.

Maybe this was a dream? If so, he would walk in any moment in a French maid uniform and suck my cock. When I blinked a few times and that didn't happen, I also realized I smelled lemon and bleach in the air, which meant yep, he was, in fact, cleaning.

I took a quick piss in the en-suite bathroom, grumbling as I made my way into the hallway, where I found Parker, minus the maid uniform, frantically vacuuming. He had his back to me and his earbuds in, so he didn't notice I was standing there. I crossed my arms, leaning against the doorjamb while he danced, shaking his ass. It was a great ass, but more than that, the dancing was just adorable.

He got low along the arm of the vacuum, like it was a man, before his ass poked out and he sexily rose to his feet again. My dick throbbed beneath my boxer briefs while a chuckle fell from my lips. Still dancing, Parker spun around, and the second he saw me, his pupils went wide and he jumped backward, tugging the earbuds out. "Holy shit. You scared the fuck out of me."

"First time in my life I've ever been jealous of a vacuum."

He dropped his head back, showing me the long, pretty column of his throat while groaning. "I was trying to distract myself and forgot you were here." He looked at me, his eyes making a journey down my body before landing on my groin. "Oh, hello there. You have an erection."

"Try being me and not having one right now."

"I was cleaning!"

"Yes, there's a first time for everything, and it was also hot. A guy handling a Dyson is my kink."

Parker flipped me off. "You get horny easily. This isn't the first time I've cleaned. I hope you realize your kitchen has never been as sparkling as it has since I moved in, and please put some clothes on."

"Why do I have to put clothes on?"

"Because you're naked?"

"I'm wearing underwear."

"Your cock is trying to poke me in the eye."

"You'd have to get low again for that to be the case. It's more in line with your ass, but fine, if you're too distracted by my dick, I'll put him away." I looked down and rubbed my groin. "Sorry, big guy, you're gonna have to wait until the shower to bust a nut. I need coffee first."

Parker shook his head, but I could tell he was trying to bite back a smile.

"Because of course you would talk to your penis."

"Penis? No one uses that word except the doctor." I yawned, going for the stairs. When I hit the top one, I added, "Stop looking at my ass."

"I'm not looking at your ass! And you're still not putting clothes on," Parker countered.

"Sure you weren't."

As I headed downstairs, I heard his footsteps behind me. "I wasn't. I'm noticing it now, but it's a little flat. Just not enough to draw my attention."

"I have a great ass, you liar." The stairs led to the living room, which I crossed to the kitchen. I'd had a normal coffeepot before, but Parker had brought some fancy thing, which I had to admit made excellent coffee, even if I didn't tell him that.

"How are you not freaking out right now?" he asked, sitting on a barstool at the counter while I put a pod in to make my drink.

"Because it's not gonna change anything, but at least now I know where the early morning vacuuming came from."

He frowned. "Sorry. I didn't mean to wake you."

I waved off his concern. "It's fine. I still get up at a decent time on Saturdays. I didn't mean to make you feel bad."

His frown deepened, small lines forming on his forehead. "I'm going to fuck this day up so bad! I know it. These are things I should know about my husband." Parker wrung his hands, fidgeting in the seat before standing. He headed to my side of the counter, clearly just trying to keep himself busy by pulling my coffee cup from the machine.

"Hey." I reached for him, turned Parker so he was facing me. When he tried to look away, I gently held his chin and angled his head in my direction again, which he allowed. "You'll do fine. My parents won't quiz you on me, and if they did, the last thing they would ask is what time I wake up on weekends." I didn't mention that he would know if he didn't leave the house before dawn every single day.

"This is going to be a disaster. You know what's not fun?

Waking up married…or being in a fake relationship. It happens in all the books I read, and it's cute and silly, but I'm telling you, in real life, it's not all it's cracked up to be. Authors are liars who lie."

I chuckled. He was so fucking adorable. "What kind of books do you read?"

"Romance."

Why didn't that surprise me? "You'll do great," I said, and a spark ignited in his blue eyes. I wasn't sure Parker even realized it, which made me want to test my theory. "They're going to love you…how can they not? You're sweet, funny, beautiful, and smart. You're going to have them wrapped around your pretty little finger." I felt his body relax, felt the air in the room shift as the worry left him. "You're going to be perfect, and they're gonna wonder how I landed you."

Parker was closer, but I hadn't moved. His breath puffed against my cheek, my words having loosened his body to the point that he was leaning into me, letting me help hold him in place. Oh yes, I was right. Parker was definitely a little praise slut, and damn, knowing this did unexpected things to me too. Made my dick throb even harder, yeah, but more than that, it made me feel like I was on top of the fucking world.

"You're such a good boy."

Parker sucked in a sharp breath, then jerked back. Fuck. I'd pushed too hard, too fast. Not that I'd wanted anything from him in that moment except getting him out of his head and making him feel better.

He took a step back, then another, like he was snapping himself out of a trance, his mask slipping into place. "*Good boy?* So ridiculous."

I cocked a brow, challenging him. I liked challenging Parker.

"I'm gonna go…upstairs…and finish what I was doing…vacuuming…because I do, in fact, clean," he rambled. "How long until we leave?"

"Hours still."

"Oh. Okay. Of course. It's early. I forgot."

I fought not to laugh at his short, nervous sentences. Was it because he was thinking about how it felt when I called him a good boy? It wasn't something I'd played around with when it came to my lovers—not that Parker was that—but it felt right with him. "Okay. I'll be here. Drinking coffee." I spoke the same way he had, which seemed to snap him out of it even more, and he flipped me off. "There's my boy," I teased.

"I hate you." But he smiled.

He didn't hate me at all. I was thankful as hell about that.

Parker went for the stairs. I kept my eyes on him the entire time.

"Stop looking at my ass," he said, humor in his voice.

Unlike him, I didn't even deny it. "But it's such a nice ass."

"I can't believe you're my husband," he said in a voice low enough that I was surprised I'd heard it, and even more surprised at how amused he'd sounded when he said it.

★ ★ ★

OKAY, SO I definitely understood why Parker had been freaking the fuck out earlier.

It took a while for it to hit me, but now, as we were driving to my parents' house where I was going to introduce them to my husband, I was afraid I might throw up.

"Do you think we can run away to Mexico?" Parker asked from the passenger seat.

"You don't know my mom. She would always find us."

He groaned, then knocked his head against the window a

couple of times.

"Please don't give yourself a concussion."

"Oooh! A concussion. That's a good way out of this!"

I chuckled, which helped calm me down a little. I wasn't the type to stress out about things. I went with the flow and worked well on the fly. Overthinking things wasn't my usual MO, but then, when had I introduced my parents to my husband before? "It won't be that bad."

"It won't be that bad? What happened to *You're going to be perfect, Parker. It'll be great. They'll love you. You're such a good boy*, blah, blah, blah."

"I knew you liked it when I praise you!"

He sighed dramatically. "I don't like it."

"Yes you do, beautiful. You fucking love it, and it's actually really hot to me, but now's not the time to get into all that. I *do* believe it'll be okay and you'll do great. It's just not every day this happens."

"No, it's not. We should just rip the Band-Aid off and plan on you meeting my dad next weekend."

"We can do that if you want." I turned onto my parents' road, the ocean in the distance. They lived in a large, white beach house that was my mom's baby. It was one of the dreams she had fought so hard to achieve.

"I'll call him," Parker replied as I pulled into the driveway. The second I did, the front door opened. "Oh God," he said. "Let's do this."

When Parker reached for the door, I touched his arm. "Hey."

"Yeah?"

"You *are* my good boy. The best."

He blushed and couldn't hold back his smile.

# CHAPTER TWELVE
## *Parker*

OH MY GOD. Why did I like it when Elliott praised me? I'd been about to burst out of my skin, but something about what he said made me nearly melt into a pile of goo instead. Stupid, sexy men. They were my weakness.

Now wasn't the time to think about that, though. Elliott's parents walked down the porch steps, holding hands. As soon as I saw them, it was immediately clear where Elliott had gotten his looks. They were both gorgeous, his dad fairer skinned than his mom. They both had brown hair like Elliott's, his mom's long and shiny. The closer they got, I could tell he also had his mom's brown eyes, his dad's wide smile, Elliott's golden skin tone a mixture of theirs. "Do I have to get out?" I asked.

"It would be nice," Elliott mumbled, before adding, "you got this," as he climbed out of the car.

I took a deep breath, knowing I couldn't delay this any longer.

"Mom, Dad...this is my husband, Parker Hansley. Parker, these are my parents, Catalina and Malcolm Weaver."

*Husband, husband, husband.* I was still hyperfixated on that word. "Hi! It's so nice to finally meet you both! Elliott has talked about you so much!" God, was I shouting at them? Why was I shouting at them?

"Unfortunately, he didn't grant us the same privilege about you," his dad replied, making my back stiffen.

Uh-oh.

"Dad..."

Catalina said, "We don't mean any offense to you, Parker. We just wish we'd known the man who stole our son's heart *before* we found out you were married *from the internet*."

"I know," Elliott said. "I'm sorry. I already admitted the wedding wasn't planned the way it should have been. I just...got caught up in the moment. We had the perfect night, and I..." Elliott reached over, placing his hand at my nape, tickling me with his fingertips. "I got swept away in him."

The beat of my pulse shot up and sped out of control. That had sounded so fucking real, like something about me had entranced him, and...it was *fake, fake, fake*. I couldn't let myself get wrapped up in this story, let myself believe it was the thing I'd always dreamed of. I didn't like Elliott *that way*, and I couldn't allow myself to let go of that truth. Otherwise, I would only end up getting hurt.

"Yeah, um...me too. I have so much fun with Elliott, and I didn't want it to end..." Ugh. Why did I have to enjoy him? That part was true.

"Ever," Elliott added. "I know it wasn't how you imagined my marriage would start. I hate that you had to find out the way you did, but we're here now. You're going to love him, but don't tell Parker I said that."

I rolled my eyes because that had been a little cute. "He gives me too much credit. And you should hear him at home. All he does is complain about how messy I am."

"You're a disaster."

"He's exaggerating."

"He's lying."

"You sound just like the two of us." Catalina grinned.

"Also, he gets that from his father. Always makes a mountain out of a molehill."

"I do not!" Malcolm countered.

"Yes you do."

"No I don't—holy shit. They do sound like us."

"And I'm always right." Catalina patted him on the shoulder.

I loved them already.

She reached for me next, hugging me before Malcolm did the same. I froze a bit, not having expected it, but Catalina didn't seem to notice, hooking her arm through mine. "Come on, Parker. I want to know everything about my son-in-law."

*She sounds like such a mom.* The thought was absurd. She sounded like one because she was one, but Christ, did it make me miss my own, make me wish she could be here. Would she be as accepting of Elliott as Catalina was of me?

I knew she would, and again, I needed to remind myself that this wasn't real.

"I noticed Elliott introduced you as Parker Hansley," she said as we made our way into the house. "Does that mean you decided to keep your own last names? Or has my son not told me yet that he's changing his last name—which is fine, by the way. Whatever is right for the two of you."

Holy shit. How had we not thought about last names? How the fuck was I supposed to answer this? "We're still discussing it. For now, we're going to keep our own," I rambled, hoping I sounded believable.

"I thought about doing the same when Malcolm and I got married. I didn't want to lose my culture from my name. But things were different back then, and while I love being a Weaver, I wish I was at least a Delgado-Weaver. That's why we gave Elliott my surname as his middle."

"That makes sense. While I like the thought of taking my

husband's name, I don't think I'd want to lose Hansley. Would that bother Mr. Weaver?" Whoever my future *real* husband turned out to be, I wanted to keep that tie to my mom. To both my parents.

"Please, call him Malcolm, and you can call me Cat. And no, he would be supportive."

I watched as Elliott and his dad continued on into the living room. I stopped when I noticed childhood photos of Elliott on the walls. Family photos, beach photos, Elliott riding bikes and playing sports and laughing. They'd lived a happy life. You could tell by each and every picture, emphasized by the mischievous glint in Elliott's eyes in most of them. He still had that glint.

"He was such a handful as a kid—well, as an adult too but not as much in recent years. He was always causing trouble—not terrible things, but Elliott has always needed to test the boundaries. He's always had this curiosity in him, this ease and go-with-the-flow nature I've always admired, but he has also made me sick with worry."

I could see that, see Elliott making her feel that way, and some of what she said was what he'd described to me. "I respect that he's always known who he is and that he's not afraid to seek answers." That's what he felt like to me, at least.

"That's a perfect way to put it. He was never satisfied just being told not to do something or what something is like. He has to learn it for himself. And he never wanted to just be who he thought he should be...or who we were. While Malcolm is proud of him and will always support him, I know he wanted Elliott to follow in his footsteps—military, law school, government. They love each other fiercely, but they've bumped heads quite a bit over the years. Where Malcolm has always toed the line, Elliott has always pushed against it. They've met in the middle, though, and I love how close they are." She patted my hand. "Anyway, I'm sure I'm not telling you anything Elliott hasn't talked to you about."

Yes and no. "I like hearing it from you too."

I looked up at the sound of footsteps coming from the living room, where Elliott and Malcolm had gone on without us. "Mom, are you trying to kidnap my husband?"

"Nope. Just talking to my son-in-law." She beamed.

*Which is true... I am her son-in-law. It's not a lie...* "It smells good in here," I said, changing the subject.

"I hope you're hungry because we're making *a lot* of food," Cat replied.

"Are you kidding? I'm dying to eat. Elliott raved about your cooking, and it's all I've been thinking about ever since. I'll admit I haven't had much Cuban food." Which Elliott had said she would likely make. "I just wish I'd brought a dessert." Why hadn't I thought of that? That was my thing, and it just showed how worried I'd been about coming here that I hadn't even thought about it.

"Next time." She grinned.

I liked that. The thought of next time.

"Once you've eaten Cat's food, nothing else will compare," Malcolm told me. "I hope you're ready to learn from the best."

"Learn?"

Elliott said, "Cooking is a family affair around here. She would have done the prep before we arrived, but now it'll be all of us." Elliott rested his hand on my nape again, brushing his thumb through the hair, along my neck. "Can you handle it, beautiful?"

I trembled. Goddamn him for making me so fucking weak in the knees...and goddamn him for having this. Because the thought of being in the kitchen with family, making food and sharing stories, filled me with a comforting warmth that felt more real than it was supposed to; these were the kinds of things I'd dreamed about. "I want to say I was born ready, but that feels too much like a cheesy movie line."

They all laughed, and it made me feel mushy inside. I already liked his parents so much, and though Elliott and I weren't in love and knew this would end in divorce, I wanted them to like me too.

"You'll love it." I was surprised when Elliott took my hand, pulling me toward the kitchen with his mom and dad on our heels. "I'm making the fried plantains."

"They're his favorite, but I'm sure you know that. I planned on making them a side dish, but El will argue to make them first and pick at them the whole time we cook."

No, I didn't know that about her son, but it fit him. "I can see that. He's impatient and always ready for the next thing, wanting it all and wanting it now."

Cat and Malcolm laughed.

"I'm feeling very attacked here," Elliott complained.

"Welcome to marriage," Malcolm joked.

"You did not just say that, Malcolm Weaver." Cat crossed her arms, and Malcolm wrapped his arms around her. He nuzzled her throat, whispering and kissing it before she succumbed to the laughter she so clearly tried to hold back. They were absolutely perfect together. They were how I remembered my parents. How could Elliott look at them and not crave finding what they had? How could he not want to fall in love? "I hate him," Catalina said when she pulled away.

"Hey, Parker says that about me all the time."

"You deserve it." Because he did. He was a spoiled brat, and he knew it.

"That's how you know it's real." Cat smiled, and in that moment I didn't want to focus on the fact that this wasn't real. That I didn't love Elliott and he didn't love me. I just wanted to enjoy this, wanted to play this game because we were already involved, so why shouldn't we enjoy it? Why shouldn't we let go and make the best of this time before we walked away? I didn't want to be miserable until Elliott and I separated. I wanted them to feel like their son made a good choice, that he was loved, and when it ended, that it was just one of those things that didn't work out.

"Eh, he's all right," I said because I knew they would appreciate the joke. The three of them laughed, and I could see why Elliott hadn't wanted to let them down, why he hadn't wanted them to know he'd drunkenly married someone he didn't love, because I'd only known them less than an hour and I didn't want to let them down either.

"Come on, gorgeous. I'll teach you how to make them," Elliott said, and I went easily. We all washed our hands, then began pulling food out of the fridge.

The plantains were ripe. They could be cooked either way, but Elliott said ripe were his favorite. We sliced them up while his mom and dad were busy with the main dish.

"We're having arroz con pollo," Cat said.

"I'm looking forward to it," I replied.

Elliott and I made the fried plantains together, which according to him, would be perfection. Just like his mom said, he began to pick at them as soon as they were done.

"Have you ever tried it?" Elliott asked after chewing his piece. I shook my head, then frowned when he picked one up and held it out for me to bite from his fingers. When I didn't move right away, he shook his head with a teasing smile. After a glance toward his parents, who had their backs to us, he whispered, "Be a good boy and eat it."

Damned if my stupid, annoying mouth didn't open up and do what he said. I mean, I'd just decided to enjoy this and have fun, right? Who didn't want to eat out of a sexy man's hand?

Flavors burst on my tongue as soon as I bit into the banana-like fruit. I moaned. "Oh my God."

"Good, right?" Elliott grabbed another, and I let him feed me again.

"I think I'm in love." I meant with the food, but then freaked out slightly because I was supposed to be very much in love with the man standing in front of me, who had a horrid ring on his finger that matched mine.

When Cat began speaking in Spanish, I worried I'd done something wrong, but then she said, "Sorry. They both speak Spanish, so I forget."

"She just said we're cute together." Elliott winked. "And she's right. Mama, did I tell you how much I had to woo him? I tried for months to get him to date me."

"Elliott!" My cheeks flamed.

"That's because you're like your mama, and when you want something, you fight for it. I had to do the same thing with your father. He wanted to focus on school and his career, not a relationship, but there was no reason he couldn't do both."

"And she was right. I thank God every day." Malcolm kissed her cheek.

God. They were great.

As we cooked, they talked about their relationship and how they'd started dating. We had the fried plantains, along with the arroz con pollo, which was marinated chicken with yellow rice and vegetables, as well as a side of black beans and avocado salad. They laughed and talked together in this way I was in awe of. It reminded me of how I was with my Beach Bums. I didn't have this with family, not after my mom passed away, and it was amazing to see.

Sometimes I would lose myself in watching them, but Cat or Malcolm always tried to engage with me, and while we ate, I would feel Elliott's hand on my thigh or arm in support. I didn't get how he was able to read me so well. It was disconcerting.

"I'm stuffed. That was so good." I leaned back in the chair with a hand on my stomach.

"That's the way we like it around here," Malcolm replied.

We all cleaned the kitchen together before heading into the living room, where the conversation continued.

"Do your parents live locally?" Cat asked.

"My dad is in Echo Park. My mom passed away when I was ten." As soon as the words left my mouth, Elliott reached over and squeezed my hand in support.

"I'm so sorry for your loss," Malcolm said.

"She was great. I miss her so much. The two of you remind me of my parents…so happy and in love. Even as a kid I could see it." I shook my head, a little embarrassed when I felt myself tearing up.

"Hey." Elliott scooted closer to me on the couch, our hands still entwined and our legs resting against one another. He was a tactile person, I'd noticed, and a part of me I hadn't even known was there wanted to soak that up. "You good?" he asked softly.

"Yep." I cleared my throat. "Thank you." Christ, he was really, really sexy. The stubble along his jaw was a little thicker than usual, his lips full and wet from his tongue. None of this would have ever happened if I wasn't so damn attracted to him, which had gotten me into trouble more times than I could count.

There was a knot in my throat I couldn't seem to work

out. I tried to breathe around it, to swallow it down. Elliott gave me a knowing half-grin and a wink.

When Malcolm gave what was clearly a fake cough, I snapped out of my Elliott-induced lust, and the motherfucker laughed.

"Elliott Delgado Weaver. You be nice to your husband," Cat said, making it obvious she too knew I'd gotten a little caught up in him and that he was teasing me about it.

"He's very cocky," I said because why ignore the elephant in the room?

"You're supposed to look at each other like that. Just not around us," Cat teased. "Do you dance?"

"Um…depends on what kind of dancing you're talking about."

"He was dancing with the vacuum this morning," Elliott teased.

"Oh my God. I hate you!"

His mom got up and turned on some music…salsa, maybe? It was Latin with fast beats and numerous instruments.

"I can't believe Elliott hasn't taught you to dance. We started when he was young."

She called him to his feet. The living room was large, with a lot of open space. Elliott didn't look embarrassed or nervous at all as he and his mother began dancing together, synchronized in choreographed movements. He was good, really fucking good, the two of them dancing and laughing together. When the song ended, Cat held her hand out for Malcolm, who took it, and then the two of them were dancing, much closer than she and Elliott had been.

When my gaze found his, he held out his hand and crooked his finger for me to go to him.

"I can't do that."

"I'll teach you."

"No." I shook my head.

"Come here, beautiful, and dance with me."

Damned if I could stop myself from pushing to my feet.

# CHAPTER THIRTEEN
## Elliott

"I DON'T KNOW how to do this," Parker said, stopping in front of me.

"You forget I've seen you dance."

He rolled his eyes. "I don't mean with a vacuum. Is this salsa? Mambo? I don't even know, but I can't do it."

"I've seen you dance in a club too. You definitely have moves, beautiful. I couldn't keep my eyes off you in Vegas." It was honest, so why not tell him? The truth was, the main reason I said it was because of the way trembles ran through him, the way his lips parted, his breaths quicker and needier. I liked teasing those reactions from Parker. It was different from flirting with other men. It made my pulse beat harder and a strange joy fill my chest. "I got you. Come here."

I held his waist and tugged him closer. Parker came easily, his arms wrapping around my neck.

"There's a lot of hip movement, so follow the beat…and me. We'll start there, purely for reasons that aren't selfish, I swear."

Parker shook his head. He didn't want to like my teasing and flirting, but I could tell he did. And I enjoyed making him smile or blush, even liked being the one to make him roll his eyes.

I moved against him, holding his hips. Parker did the

same, with a little more sway and less smoothly than me, but it was enough to make my dick take notice. *Down, boy.* As much as I wanted him, in the living room with my parents wasn't the place for it.

"There you go. Just like that. Mmm, check you out. You're a natural." That made him do better, work harder, circle his hips more and thrust against me in a way the dancing didn't call for but I liked. I dropped my head so my mouth was close to his ear. "Good boys get their husband's dick hard, but maybe wait till later for that…"

He tensed, gritting out, "I'm not trying to. I'm in the same boat here. You're the one who started this."

I chuckled, brushing my thumb against his waist, wishing I could slip it under his shirt and feel his skin. "Let's move some more. I'll tell you what to do, and you be good and listen."

"I…okay."

I nearly forgot my parents were in the room with us while we danced. I told Parker what to do, step back or forward, and with which foot. It was a bit of a mess, the two of us stepping on each other and tripping over each other, but damn, it was fun.

"Ouch!" he said when he didn't move and I crushed his toe.

"I told you to step back. You suck at this."

I was surprised when he leaned forward and bit my pec. I dropped my head back and laughed.

"What's going on over there?" Mom asked.

"Your son is being mean and making fun of me," Parker teased.

"Elliott, be nice to your husband."

"He bit me! Why am I the one in trouble?"

It kept going like that, song after song. We laughed and

teased and let our bodies learn each other. This wasn't what I'd expected today to be like. At all. My parents adored him. That wasn't a shock. What surprised me was how natural everything felt. Cooking and dancing with him, letting Parker into this part of my life, something I'd never done with someone I was dating. It felt good in a way I hadn't seen coming, and I was still trying to wrap my head around it.

When I thought about the first night we met, then Vegas and the pier, and now here, the one common thread was how much I laughed, how much fun I had with Parker. We had this burgeoning friendship and an obvious connection, one that had never developed this effortlessly with other men I dated.

"Oh my God. That's enough for now. I suck at this." Parker pulled away when the song ended.

"The main point is to have fun." Mom hugged him.

"I took a secret dance class and didn't tell Cat," Dad admitted. "Then one day we went out, and I wowed her with my moves. If she hadn't already been in love with me, that would have done the trick."

"You guys are so beautiful together," Parker said in unison with my playful, "Gag. You're my parents. It's so gross."

"Ignore him." Parker placed a hand on my mouth. "I think it's sweet."

I wondered if he realized he'd done that instinctively, if he realized that we were, in fact, friends now.

I licked his hand, and Parker ripped it back. "Ew."

"You like my tongue." I winked, and his eyes popped out of his head.

"Elliott Delgado Weaver. None of that around us," Dad joked.

I laughed, reached for Parker, and pulled him close. It took me a moment to even realize I'd done it, that I held him, arm wrapped around him, and he let me. "We should probably head out. This one is usually off Sundays, but he's going in tomorrow to bake a cake and then has to go to his friend's house for their podcast."

Something about what I'd just said snapped Parker out of this fairy tale we were pretending to be in. His back stiffened slightly, and he stepped away from me. "I had a wonderful day. Thank you so much for having me."

Mom said, "I did too. And you're family now. I was nervous Elliott didn't bring you around because he knew I wouldn't approve. No one is good enough for my son, you know, but you are, and I adore you." Mom hugged him, and goddamn, her words twisted me up inside. But this had to be better than the other option—for them to know this was fake, and the hoopla that would follow.

"I adore you too," Parker told her, not making eye contact with any of us when they pulled away.

"We need to exchange phone numbers," Mom said, and they did.

"Welcome to the family, son. This had me worried with how it started, but I'm happy for the two of you. It's what we've always wanted for Elliott—to settle down and be happy with a good person."

He had? Dad had never told me that before, and suddenly, I was so thankful to have given him that, to have made him proud and happy. It was something I'd been too selfish to care about when I was younger, but yearned for now.

"I... Thank you, Malcolm." Parker raised his arm and chewed his nail, something I'd never seen him do before.

"Thanks, Dad," I said.

He gave me a smile, then asked Parker about the cake he would be working on the next day—one made with Kahlua, apparently.

Mom hugged me. "He's incredible, mi niño," she said softly, just for me.

"I know he is." It was the truth, even if this marriage wasn't one for love. "Thank you for accepting him…and me."

"Always. I'm a mom. Loving our kids is what we do." She gave me another squeeze.

★ ★ ★

WE DIDN'T TALK much in the car. I drove and Parker texted—one of his friends, I assumed. I wondered what they thought of me. Well, everyone except Declan. I knew what he thought of me. The guy wanted me to die a fiery death, but the others didn't seem as bad.

The air around us was stifling with tension, this heat in the air that filled my senses and felt like it wrapped a hand around my throat. What was Parker thinking about? The dancing? Something else? How most of the time he too wished I would die a fiery death?

"Well, that was quite the day," I said to Parker when we stepped into the house.

"I really like them." He pulled his jacket off and laid it over the back of an armchair. I didn't mention that there were hooks for that, which was where my coat went. "Your parents are both gorgeous, and so kind. And I can't get over all the food! Next time, I'm definitely bringing dessert. What do they like? I want to make something special."

My fingers wrapped around his wrist, and I gently tugged Parker closer. "Shh. You're rambling. You did so good today, Park." I went off my instinct with that, this strange feeling inside me that said Parker needed to be validated. The way he relaxed against me some, I knew I was right.

"Do you really think they like me?"

"I know they do…maybe better than me. My parents don't bullshit. I would have at least fifteen texts from Mom by now if they weren't sure." I tugged my phone out, and there was just one. I clicked on it and held the screen up for him.

**Mom: I really do like him, El. You did good.**

"See? You have them fooled. Should I tell them the truth now? That you never shower, that you pick your nose and keep me awake with your snoring?"

"I don't snore."

I cocked a brow. "But you do those other things?"

"Do they know how mean you are?"

"Oh, I'm going to tell her how mean you are to me…in Morse code. That I couldn't admit how awful you are and I'm here because you're blackmailing me."

I pretended to type on my phone. Parker played along, trying to wrestle the cell from my hand. When I went backward, he moved forward, our feet somehow tangling, similarly to how they'd done while we were dancing, only this time, we were moving too fast and laughing too hard to catch ourselves.

I fell backward onto the couch, Parker half on top of me and half on the cushion, his face close to mine, our chests vibrating together with our chuckling.

My dick took notice of the fact that there was a beautiful man on top of me, so close that I could see flecks of what looked like sunshine in his blue eyes. Our laughter stopped, and neither of us moved. My arms were around him. It was like fighting the toughest battle of my life to keep from sliding my hand down to his ass, down his pants, to feel and touch him the way I'd wanted to for a fucking year now.

"Elliott…" Parker's voice was husky with lust, shooting heat straight to my groin as his mouth slammed down on mine.

*Finally,* echoed through my head as I pushed my tongue into his mouth to taste him. We kissed like we were starving for it, like we couldn't breathe without our lips attached to each other's.

Parker climbed onto my lap, straddling me, my hands finding their home on his tight little ass, even if it was over his jeans. He held my face, took over the kiss, and I let him. Our teeth clanked together, and we laughed into each other's mouths, making out like this was our one and only chance to have each other and we both intended to take advantage.

He ripped his mouth away from mine, and immediately went for my shirt, tugging it up. "God, I hate that I want you so much. This is such a fucking mistake." I lifted my arms so he could easily remove my tee. Parker threw it, and I grabbed the back of his head and plunged my tongue between his lips again.

My hands traveled under his shirt, lifting it as I went. His skin was soft and hot, and just touching him made my cock throb even more. We pulled apart again so I could free him from the top I now had slightly tangled around his head.

"Oh my God, Elliott. Take it off."

"I'm trying," I said, laughing.

"Aren't you supposed to be better at this?"

"I never thought it would happen. Cut me some slack." Eventually, I got the damn thing free, then leaned in to flick my tongue over one of his pebbled nipples.

"Fuuuuck." He trembled. His chest was smooth and firm. Parker had a great body, six-pack abs, and a torso he definitely waxed. He covered my furry pecs with his hands, flicking his thumbs over my nipples while I laved and sucked his.

"This is so stupid," he said breathlessly.

"You're so fucking pretty…look at you, dying for me. Jesus, you're beautiful and being so good for me. How can it be stupid—making such a good boy come?"

"Oh fuck." He thrust against me, dug his blunt nails into my chest. "Jesus, that gets me going. Why do I like that so much?"

There was an edge of worry to his voice I wanted to soothe. "Because pretty boys should always be told how good they are. Because you deserve it. All those other men were fucking idiots for not telling you how perfect you are."

I was rambling, hoping I was saying the right words. I liked making Parker feel good, liked telling him these things and feeling the way they made him react to me. It was a high I'd never known and couldn't have expected I'd crave so much.

When he kissed me again, his teeth dug into my lip, a sharp, sexy pain piercing me.

"Sorry. Fuck. Didn't mean to bite you." He said it like he'd been so consumed with his desire for me that he lost his head.

"Mmm. None of that. Don't apologize for being a good boy who wants me so much, you can't control yourself. You feel what you do to me?" I thrust against him so he could feel how hard I was for him. "I could probably bust a nut in my pants, just kissing you."

"Make me come…damn it, Elliott, make me come."

I growled into the kiss when my mouth slammed down on his again. I grabbed him, flipped us so Parker was on his back on the couch. I kissed my way down his smooth chest, abs, until I got to his jeans. "Oh look…a present. Should I open it and see what you made for me?" I rubbed my palm against his bulge.

"Please." Parker arched up into it.

"Please what?"

"Do something…anything. Take my dick out."

"Good boys say please."

"I already did." He laughed, and shit, had he?

"Look how you make me lose my head. Say it again."

"Please, Elliott."

I opened his jeans, tugged them and his underwear down. Parker's pubes were neat and trimmed, his balls heavy and full, cock long, thick, and leaking against his belly. "So pretty...so perfect. I used to wonder what you looked like naked. I'd imagine it when I jerked off. What would such a pretty, perfect boy look like without clothes on?" I spit in my hand, wrapped it around his shaft, and gave him a slow, firm stroke. "Now I know, and every time I take myself in hand...or fill my ass with my toys...I'll picture this..." More slow strokes, and he shook beneath me, precum pearling at his slit. I wiped it with my thumb and tasted it.

"I want to see you too." He went for my pants, but I shook my head.

"Be patient."

I stood, then slowly took my clothes off. My dick was so fucking hard, I wasn't sure it would ever go down again. I stood beside the couch, stroking myself. I didn't tell him no when he touched my thighs, danced his fingers up and down them.

"I love thick, hairy thighs."

"What about cock? Do you love that?"

"Fuck yes."

I was on a short fuse, surprised I hadn't already shot my load. I lay over him, kissing him and rutting against him. I wished I had lube down here. I wanted to fuck him...suck him...wanted him to take a turn on me too, but I knew we both needed this release before we self-combusted.

I positioned myself so I could suck his dick to the back of my throat. Parker cried out, pumping into me twice. When I pulled off, he groaned, but then I spit into my hand again, slicking myself up too before I took his mouth again. "Fuck, I'm addicted to kissing you. You taste incredible."

We thrust against each other, rutted together. We were both so turned on, so needy for each other that when my tongue pushed past his lips again, our groins still frotting, we both tensed. My full balls let loose, drew up as I shot my release between us, his joining mine, our cum mixing with our sweat.

I fell against him, breathing heavy. I kissed his chest, licked his nipples again, while we came down from our high. "Fuck, that was good. I needed that."

Parker's response was soft but firm, "That was a mistake."

# CHAPTER FOURTEEN
## *Parker*

ELLIOTT STIFFENED, LOOKING up at me from where he'd been...well, honestly, worshipping me. There was a hint of fear in his eyes, mixed with uncertainty.

"I didn't misread what just happened, did I?"

"Oh shit. Not like that. You didn't do anything I didn't want. I asked you to make me come. I just meant that we shouldn't have done that. Fuck. I can't believe I went back on the commitment I made to myself not to hook up with anyone. Especially not you."

Elliott moved off me, sat up, and laid my legs across his thighs. "You're lucky I don't get my feelings hurt easily."

God, I was fucking this up. I wasn't trying to be a dick. I liked Elliott, even if that wasn't something I wanted to admit. He was a nice guy. He'd proved that more than once, and after watching him with his family, I couldn't deny it any longer. But that made him even more dangerous to fuck around with. I'd fallen for nice guys before, and I either realized it was all a facade, or those guys were good men but just didn't want me. I couldn't let myself fall into familiar habits in this marriage. It was one thing to lose a boyfriend or someone I was dating, but a whole other ball game if I got feelings for the person I was married to when I knew we were going to walk away.

"Are we going to talk about this?" Elliott asked when I'd gotten lost in my head.

"Yeah, sorry. We can't do that again. In fact, let's scrub the last hour from our memories? Deal? Perfect. Thanks. Good night!"

I tried to stand up, but a chuckling Elliott placed his hand on my cum-sticky stomach and held me down. Damn it. I wished I could have tasted him... *No, stop. Bad.* I wasn't supposed to be thinking those things.

"Hear me out," he said, and I sighed.

"Can I sit up?"

"No, you'll run away."

I huffed but couldn't say he was wrong. My gaze flicked to him. Fuck, he was really sexy naked. I took a moment to appreciate the view—the dusting of fur across his pecs and stomach, the way his soft cock rested in a nest of dark hair at his groin. I really, *really* wanted to explore his body, preferably with my hands *and* tongue. I blamed the fact that it had been a while since I'd had sex because of my man break.

"What am I hearing out?"

"You totally want to fuck me right now."

"I do not!" I tried to get up again, but he still didn't allow it, laughing while we wrestled naked on his couch. There was a small chance I let Elliott win, and he ended up lying between my legs, his chest against my dick, which I was willing *not* to get hard again. "Shut up. You know you're sexy. It's a physical response, and it's been a while for me, but again, this is a bad idea. We can be friends, but we can't let the lines get blurry on what this is. We're married in name only, and in a few months we're separating. You're not looking to settle down—I am. You don't know if you'll ever want to get married—news flash: that one is a moot point because *hello*." I held up my hand with the wedding ring on it.

"You don't want to fall in love."

"No, I said I'm not sure if I'm cut out for love. That I've never felt romantic love before. I don't seem to have it in me. I've dated some really great people, but I just didn't feel anything more than affection for them."

Did he think this was helping? Because it wasn't. "You're not making an argument for why we should fuck around, if that's what you're trying to do," I said as we lay there, naked and stuck together with our loads. *Good job, Park!*

"You haven't let me talk much. What I was trying to say is…date me."

I waited for the punchline, for him to laugh or continue, but he didn't say anything else. "Are you out of your mind? I can't date you! We're married! Plus, did you miss what I just said about us wanting completely different things?"

"That's not true. We just have a different reality. You know what you want. I'm not *looking* for love or know if that's in the cards for me. There's a risk, of course. The last thing I want is to hurt you. Jesus, that would fucking kill me, beautiful, but dating is *always* a risk. We risk our hearts in everything we do, and you're never going to find what you're looking for if you don't take that risk."

"And you think that could be you? What happens if it is and you don't want the same?"

"I'm not saying it could be me, and that's where honesty and communication come in. Plus, let's not pretend people can't get hurt by falling for someone they aren't dating. You hear that every week on your show. People in love with their best friend, coworker, neighbor. It happens. But we're in this now, so shouldn't we at least try not to be miserable?"

"You're already miserable? From what everyone says, that's the sign of a real marriage."

"That's not what I meant. But…we're clearly sexually

attracted to each other. I don't think I'll get the sound of you begging me to make you come out of my head for a long time."

I covered his face with my hand. Elliott laughed and licked it. "I didn't *beg*." I asked politely.

"Yes, you did, beautiful, and damned if I don't want to make you do it again." His voice dropped an octave, and it was already low and sexy. My stupid dick twitched between us.

"I'm tired. Can you finish making your point?"

"We'll be together for months, we're attracted to each other, we have a good time together—and don't try to pretend we don't. It's because we enjoy each other so much and somehow manage to let go when we're together that we're in this position in the first place. I have to admit, something about you has its hooks in me... I've been obsessed with you since that first night in the bar."

"Should I be worried you're stalking me?"

"Yes," he deadpanned. "Really, you intrigue me, and I think that's mutual. And I date. It's not like I don't. Emotional intimacy interests me, maybe because I've never had it, and I'm curious if I could feel those things..."

"So this is an experiment?"

He groaned, clearly exhausted by me. "I want to date you, gorgeous. I want to learn more about you. I want to find all the ways I can to make you come *and* to make you laugh. It makes me feel...fuck, I don't know...powerful, yeah, but also important, like I'm doing something good. Even more than that, because making you laugh makes me feel good. It's weird as fuck."

My pulse throbbed against my skin, the beat of my heart echoing through my ears. That was both really self-important and...sweet. Ugh. Why was Elliott Delgado Weaver so sweet?

He continued, "All I'm saying is, let's enjoy this. Let's just…let go and have fun and see what happens. Why shouldn't we have a good time while we're in this marriage? Have some orgasms and go on some dates and have a good time? That's a better option than suffering through it. I've been trying to get you to date me for a damn year. You're my husband. Can't I get you to give it a try now?"

"You've been trying to get me to have sex with you for a year." I had to admit, though, what he'd said sounded strikingly similar to what I'd thought myself at his parents' house tonight—wanting to let go, make the best of this, just enjoy it. Maybe going into it knowing the rules would keep my heart from getting involved. I wasn't stupid. I didn't expect the man who liked being single and wasn't looking to settle down to fall for me. I would have to make sure I didn't fall for him, while also having really hot sex and spending time with someone who was annoyingly entertaining to be with.

"Yes and no," Elliott replied. "I can't pretend I don't want to fuck you, but like I said, you intrigue me too. If not, I would have lost interest a long time ago."

And if he didn't intrigue *me*, I would have told him to stop and leave me alone a long time ago, but I never did, even though Elliott had said that was all I had to do.

"We'll go into this with the caveat that we're one hundred percent honest with each other. If we don't want to date anymore, or if one of us starts to feel something more, we talk about it. We're adults. We can handle that."

"Funny how only one of us acts like an adult," I teased.

"Thank you." He grinned.

"Not you!" I laughed. Why, why, why could he make me laugh so easily? "I need to think about this. I'm not making a decision with post-orgasm syndrome."

Elliott chuckled. "Deal." He reached up and cupped my

face. "Why do I enjoy you so much?" he asked softly, as if to himself.

"I'd say it's my ass, but you haven't had that yet."

"Yet! You said yet!"

"Argh!" I groaned, covering my face this time, and damned if my hand didn't smell like cum…which was hot. "I really do hate you. Now let me up. I need to go to bed. I'll think about your weird-ass idea." He moved, and I sat up.

Elliott said, "I wonder where you'll take me for our first date…"

I noticed how I was the one taking him on this fake date. "I'm ignoring you." And I was also trying not to look at him because then I might jump him again.

"Don't worry, I'll clean up our clothes," he said as I walked naked toward the stairs.

"That's what husbands are for," I teased, hurried to my room, and fell against the closed door.

Oh God. I wanted to use Elliott's ridiculous logic as an excuse to date him. I was screwed.

★ ★ ★

"*DEAR VERS, I don't have a personal question for you today. I'm just curious how married life is treating Parker. I've been listening to you guys since your very first podcast. Parker and I have a lot in common, and when I was struggling to figure out how to move forward with a guy I was interested in, I messaged and got advice. We've been together for almost two years now, and while we're not married like Parker, I'm so happy for him to have met his person too. Sincerely, Benjamin.*" Corbin looked up at me. "Aww, that's so sweet! We're so happy for you, Benjamin. And yes, how is married life, Park? We're all *dying* to talk about your super sexy husband."

Have you ever loved people and thought they were assholes at the same time? That's how I'd been feeling about my friends since this whole marriage thing started. They were either busting my balls about Elliott or fawning over me like they were afraid I was going to get hurt, which I wasn't. Getting hurt would require feelings for my husband, something I refused to allow to happen. Nope. I wasn't at risk for that at all.

"Married life is great. I have someone to pick up my dirty clothes for me." The guys laughed, but I continued, "No, really, though…it's amazing, fun, and Elliott is…great…" Wow, how many more adjectives could I pull out of my ass? None of that sounded real at all, so instead of focusing on the marriage and Elliott, I went with his family. "We had dinner at his folks' house yesterday. Elliott taught me how to make fried plantains, which are delicious; all the food was, really. His mom is Cuban. She had me, Elliott, and his dad in the kitchen, helping to make a traditional Cuban meal. Oh my God, it was so good. Afterward, we were all dancing together in the living room. Elliott's been dancing since he was young. I'm not gonna say I was bad compared to them, but I'm not gonna say I was good either. And then…"

I looked up to see my friends watching me with a familiar spark of worry in their eyes. Did they think I couldn't take care of myself? Yes, I had bad luck with men, but that didn't mean I was an idiot.

"Anyway, it was a great day." I was back to the adjectives again.

"Why didn't we get invited to Mama and Daddy Weaver's house for Cuban food?" Corbin asked.

"Agreed," Marcus added.

"What? Why do you agree? You hate people you don't know and would have only gone for me," I countered.

"Because we're us, and who the hell are we if we're not giving each other shit?" Marcus stared at me, and damned if he didn't have a point.

"I liked it better when we focused on Dec's love life."

"Not gonna lie and pretend I'm not enjoying that the attention is off me." Declan's statement was both true and not. He supported the continue-the-marriage idea, but less than Marcus and Corbin because of his worry about me; at the same time, he also hated talking about himself, so it worked. I was still trying to figure out how to tell them about last night…maybe not about the praising and the frottage, but at least about Elliott's stupid proposal. I hadn't figured out what I was going to do about it. Or if I already had and wanted them to talk me out of it.

"My best friend sucks," I joked.

"Pretty well," Corbin said, "if the way I heard Sebastian calling out his name when I showed up unannounced at their house the other day is any indication." Corbin waggled his eyebrows.

"You leave me and my boyfriend out of this."

"Aww"—I squeezed his hand—"I still can't get over hearing you say things like that." Declan had been all alone in the world before he let me into his life. Then Corbin and Marcus had joined our little group, and Declan hadn't ever wanted to expand his circle until Sebastian. That was the thing about love—it had the ability to change you, to complete you. How fucking beautiful was that?

"Let's take another question." Marcus steered us back on track like he was so good at doing.

"Uh-oh, here we go again," Corbin said. *"Dear Vers, are Corbin and Marcus in love with each other?"* he read. It wasn't the first time they'd gotten that and it likely wouldn't be the last either. Before Sebastian, people would ask about Dec and

I too. "You want to take this or should I?" Corbin continued.

"Either way. We're friends, end of discussion. I might kinda like you in the *he's my brother* way but other than that, I'm good." Marcus winked.

"I think people ask because everyone loves a good friends-to-lovers story," I replied.

"Yes, but we'd kill each other." Marcus wasn't wrong. "And we're not in love."

"Marcus is my person, but no, we don't have feelings for each other any more than Dec and Park did. Some relationships go deeper than romantic love and I feel like that's us," Corbin replied. "All of us." Why was Corbin the sweetest ever?

"Agreed," Marcus added, but Corbin clearly wasn't done.

"You're my ride or dies. My brothers from other mothers. My...someone help me. I can't think of anything else."

"Shut up, Corbin," Declan, Marcus, and I all said in unison.

"I don't know why you're all so mean to me." Corbin fake pouted.

We still had another forty or so minutes of the show left, so we continued on, mercilessly teased each other, and had a session of "Mimosas and Man-Talk," which was where we discussed current events, pop culture, and I raved about Taylor Swift. Yes, I was that guy. Sue me.

As soon as we ended the session, three sets of eyes zeroed in on me, but it was Declan who asked, "How's it really going? And Jesus, I can't believe you met his family yesterday and didn't tell us. What was that like?"

It had been hard to keep it to myself. When Dec had met me at Beach Buns that morning, I'd almost told him, but for whatever reason, I hadn't.

"It was... Hell, it was actually perfect in every way other

than the fact that it's not real. I feel horrible that they think we're in love."

"Babe...it's not your fault." Declan wrapped an arm around my shoulder and kissed my temple.

"Yes, it is. I'm the one who messaged Elliott to hang out that night. I'm the one who started getting drunk first. I was there when we got married and when we agreed to lie to everyone about it."

"But you're not lying. You're married to him," Marcus said. "Did you tell them you were in love with him?"

"No."

"Then you're not lying. You're married, and the two of you are dealing with it the best way you know how."

Corbin said, "Except for the part where they lied about dating and all that—*ouch!*" He jerked away when Marcus thumped him on the forehead. "What? I'm keeping it real. Aren't you the realist?" He rubbed the spot while looking at me. "Sorry, Park."

"You don't have to apologize. It's true." Aaaaand, I wasn't going to get a better lead-in to dating than I had right now, so I just went with it. "I kissed Elliott last night, and then we frotted on the couch until we came all over each other, and then he asked me to date him. I'm hungry. I got up early and baked an incredible cappuccino cake but couldn't eat it. Do you have anything?"

I stood and went for the studio door, followed by the sound of three chairs sliding out and three people rushing after me.

"Excuse me, what?" Declan asked.

"Is he a good kisser?" Corbin added.

"What the fuck, Corb?" Marcus cursed, and the two of them began arguing.

When we got to the kitchen, I said, "The plan wasn't to

tell you about the sex, but it just came out because oh my Goooood, we didn't even do much, but it was really fucking good."

"I thought you weren't going to fuck around with him?" Declan watched me while I opened the fridge, making myself at home in Marcus's house.

"I wasn't going to…but he's hot and I was horny and got all wrapped up in the day."

"Sex is one thing," Marcus said, "but did you miss the part where Elliott asked Parker to date him?"

Corbin laughed. "I love you, Park, but only you would get married to someone you don't like and then start dating him afterward."

"Thanks for that. I love you too."

Corbin tapped his chest, then kissed his hand before pointing at me. "I got'chu."

"I'm confused about the dating thing," Dec said.

"Well…we had fun in Vegas…and then we went to the pier the other night and had a good time. After the sex-couch incident, he said he's intrigued by me and thinks we should enjoy this marriage scheme and date, which I guess makes sense in some ways. He's been trying to get into my pants for a year. We're horny and live together and can't fuck anyone else. This isn't like dating someone where I think there's a possibility we're going to fall in love. This is orgasms between married people before we divorce."

"But he didn't just say he wanted to fuck you; he said he wanted to date you." Marcus crossed his arms, the white tank top he wore stretching across the expanse of his darker skin.

I waved that off. "I know he just wants to have sex with me."

"How?"

"Umm…what's with you and all the questions today? Are

you feeling okay?"

Marcus flipped me off.

"He said you intrigue him?" Corbin asked.

"Yes, though I'm sure that's just because I wouldn't hook up or go out with him for the past year. The novelty will wear off."

"What about the emotional stuff?" Declan grabbed lunch meat, cheese, and mayo from the fridge I'd left open and began making me a sandwich.

"There is no emotional stuff. I don't like him that way. Sure, we're friends now, but I don't want to fall for him. He's still weird about love, and if he were to fall, it wouldn't be for me."

"Did that motherfucker say that?" Marcus growled.

"What? No. I did."

The corners of his lips turned down in a frown.

"Why wouldn't he fall for you? He'd be lucky to have you," Corbin said.

"All I'm saying is that it won't happen. Anyway, we said we'll have to be honest and talk to each other, blah, blah, blah." I shrugged. "I think I'm gonna do it."

"Date him or fuck him?" Dec handed my food over.

"Both. Besides, it's not really dating. It's like…sex with a side of friendship and social gatherings."

"While telling the world you're married," Dec summed up.

"Technically, we are married." I held up my hand, reminding him.

Marcus said, "I think you should go for it. You're clearly interested, and you're a grown-ass man who can handle his thoughts and feelings."

"Thanks, Marcus." I smiled. "But I'm not interested."

"Yeah, sure. Okay," Marcus replied.

"I think you should go for it too," Corbin added.

"Because he's hot?"

"No. Contrary to what you three believe, I don't only care about sex and looks." The thing was, I knew he really didn't. I thought maybe Corbin had the lowest self-esteem of us all. "But also because of that, yes." He grinned, hugging me. "I love you, and you deserve to have fun. If you think fucking and dating this guy will be fun, then you should do it."

"I love you too." I kissed his cheek, then gave my attention to Declan.

He groaned, rubbing a hand over his forehead.

"Dec…" I said sweetly, knowing he couldn't deny me. "You know I can't do this without your support."

"Yeah, come on, Dec." Corbin wrapped an arm around him.

Declan sighed. "I'm going on record saying I think this is a bad idea, but I love you, and if you want to date your husband, you should."

I laughed. "This is so weird."

Declan ignored that. "We should officially meet him if you're dating."

"No!" I shook my head. "That makes it more real. This is just another part of our temporary, six-month agreement."

Declan sighed again but didn't argue. He wrapped me in a tight hug, and I burrowed into his chest. Corbin loved hugs, so I wasn't surprised when he joined. He hug-tugged us to Marcus, pulling him into the group, despite his grumbling, "Why does everything end in a hug?"

"You love it," I told him.

"Lies."

"But you do love us," Corbin added.

He couldn't deny that.

# CHAPTER FIFTEEN
## *Elliott*

I SHOULD LEAVE the house. There was no reason to sit around at home all day, but I did. Not because of Parker, though. It was my day off. Relaxing was a good thing. Why did I need to leave when I had everything I needed at home? Sitting around and waiting for a guy wasn't how I worked, and again, it wasn't what I was doing now.

When I heard the doorknob twist, I didn't look up from my laptop, which sat on the table in front of me.

"Oh, you're cooking dinner?" Parker asked when he came inside. Did he live with the podcast guys on Sundays? He'd been there practically all day.

"Yep. You forgot to say *Hi, honey, I'm home.*" I let my gaze wander over to him.

"I didn't mean for me. I meant cooking in general. Smells good!"

I laughed, and Parker gave me a scowl I was pretty sure was supposed to be angry but just adorably squished up his baby face. "I'm cooking for you too, beautiful. I was giving you shit. It just sounded very husbandly when you came in." I leaned back in my chair, watched as he set a box from Beach Buns on the counter. "Go into work after the podcast?" Before *and* after? My baker was a workaholic.

"Yeah, I went with Declan. It's been a bit hectic today.

Paparazzi have been camping outside Driftwood lately, which is frustrating for him. That's his bar. I'm not sure if I told you that. And Corbin was forcing Marcus to go to the indoor driving range with him, but the last time we all tried that, I almost hit Marcus with my golf stick." He grabbed a glass from the cabinet and got himself some ice water.

"Club."

"Am I supposed to care?" He scrunched his face again, and I snickered.

"Nope."

Had he thought about my proposition from last night? I couldn't stop thinking about it. I'd gone to my room, wondering what the fuck I'd been thinking, why I'd asked to date my husband, but then I decided I didn't fucking care. That's what I was trying to get him to do, right? Let go and have fun? I wasn't doing the same thing if I obsessed about the why of it all.

"You're staring at me."

"I know."

"Are you imagining me naked?" He crossed his arms, letting the counter hold him up.

"Well, I am now. Thanks for that." I kissed at the air and he rolled his eyes, something he did around me often.

"What are you making?"

"Baked chicken and rice. What's in the box?"

Were we going to do this all evening? Volleying questions and playing happy husbands? Because I assumed this was what it was like. My parents had always been the type to ask each other how their days went, and when work allowed, if we were all home, we ate at the table together.

"Oh. I made a brownie-bite tray. It's filled with different kinds of brownies."

I smiled. I loved brownies. When I'd go into Beach Buns

to flirt with him, I'd often get one, something he must have remembered because he said, "Shut up."

"I didn't even say anything."

"You didn't have to. I know what you're thinking. Just because I'm a nice person doesn't mean it's because you're irresistible and I've fallen for your tricks."

"You said it, not me." This banter was so much fun. It was addicting. *He* was addicting.

"You're not irresistible."

"Okay." I stood up, walked into the kitchen, and leaned in close to him, reaching for the box on the other side of Parker.

"You could just step around me..."

"Yes, but where's the fun in that?" I plucked a brownie bite with a pink layer on top and popped it into my mouth. "I love raspberry." He really was an incredible baker.

"Me too."

I cocked my head. "You sound breathless. You feeling all right?"

His mouth curled up into a small smile. I thought he was going to talk shit, to give me some smart-ass reply the way he was so good at, but he just said, "Oh my God," while shaking his head, then grabbed the back of mine, tugging me forward until our lips met.

Fuck yes.

I pressed against Parker, pinning his body between mine and the counter. I ground my hips against him, felt myself grow and throb as we attacked each other's mouths...or, to be honest, as he attacked mine.

"My pretty boy wants me," I said when he came up for air and started kissing his way down my throat.

"Not yours, but I like sex. I've always liked sex."

Oh...I'd called him mine, hadn't I? Sex talk, of course.

"You'll like it even more with me." I circled my hips again, our erections rubbing against one another. He pushed me back. I thought he was going to end this, but instead, Parker dropped to his knees. "Oh fuck." I grabbed onto the counter as he worked open my jeans. Parker tugged them and my underwear down to my knees.

"I love cock." He spit in his hand and stroked me. "I remember the first time I had a dick in my mouth. It made me feel fucking invincible."

"Jesus," I gritted out, white-hot need exploding into a meteor shower in my gut.

"I forced myself not to have this for months because I have the worst goddamned luck with men, but I missed it. I guess that's lucky for you."

He grinned up at me, which strangely, resulted in my heart stumbling a few beats.

We stared at each other, gazes holding while Parker slowly, so fucking slowly I thought I would die, took me to the back of his throat—like all the way to the fucking back, swallowing around my head, mouth stretched wide, eyes glassy. He then worked his talented mouth up and down my shaft, still watching. I squeezed the edge of the counter, already feeling the urge to spurt down his throat, but needing to hold off. Parker pulled away, flicked his tongue around my crown, then my slit, before taking me again, fucking his mouth on my cock.

When he eased off the second time, his gaze turned away. "Do I look pretty down here?" he asked softly, making my dick jerk in his hold. He liked it so fucking much when I praised him, but he was embarrassed by it. Damned if I didn't want to tell him all the things he needed to hear over and over again until he believed them.

"So fucking pretty. I'm sorry I forgot to tell you. You've

been such a good boy sucking my dick that I lost my head. I won't ever again forget to tell you how perfect you are."

Parker moaned, deep and throaty, before lavishing my nuts with his tongue. He sucked them, kissed them, nuzzled his nose in my pubes like cock and balls were his most favorite fucking things in the whole world.

"You're so damn sexy. I can't take my eyes off you. You're the best cocksucker I've ever had."

"Fuck my mouth," he said before swallowing me down again.

He didn't have to ask twice. I kept one hand on the counter, the other cupping his face, holding and caressing him while I pulled back and snapped my hips forward. Parker's eyes rolled back, his nails digging into my thighs, the look on his face begging for more.

"Jesus, I'm not gonna get enough of this. I'm so lucky I married you…that you're in my house and I can use your pretty mouth whenever I want. You're so good at this, aren't you? Such a good boy. Mmm, yes, I have the best husband ever." Words fell randomly from my mouth. I didn't know if all of them were true, if we were going to keep this up, but I wasn't exaggerating about how good he was, how beautiful.

I kept speaking while I pumped my hips, thrusting my cock into the hot suction of Parker's perfect lips. His eyes watered, but anytime I tried to pull back some, he held me tighter, and I obeyed, using and praising him like the good boy he was.

My cock was throbbing, thighs tense, my orgasm right there, teetering at the edge and waiting for me to fall over. When I couldn't hold steady anymore, I let myself fly, balls drawing tight and emptying down Parker's throat.

"Christ…Jesus, that's good. Look at you, swallowing it all down because you're so fucking perfect." The thing was, in that moment, I didn't feel like I was just praising him or dirty talking. He *felt* perfect, which was strange and alarming and had to be the afterglow of sex.

Parker fell backward to his ass, sharp breaths pulling from his lungs as he pressed on his groin with his palm, rubbing it before he dropped his head against the cabinet and closed his eyes.

"Did you just…"

"Shut up," he replied without looking at me. Holy fuck, he'd come just from sucking my cock and hearing me tell him how good he was. That was…shit, he talked about feeling invincible on his knees, but speaking to him the way I did, having that effect on him, made me feel the same. I fucking soared.

"Don't be embarrassed, beautiful. That was the hottest thing I've ever seen in my life. Best. Husband. Ever." Aaaaaand, why had I used *husband* so much since he came home?

He opened his eyes and looked up at me with his baby blues, making my stomach flip-flop. "Yes, I'll date you."

I smiled. "Good boy." I traced his bottom lip with my thumb. When I pushed it inside, Parker sucked it like he had my dick moments before.

"But we have to follow the rules you said—complete honesty, have fun and let go. It doesn't mean anything. I'm not like…in love with you…or going to fall in love with you."

"Okay." I nodded, suddenly a little annoyed. I held my hand out, and he took it, letting me pull him to his feet. "Dinner is almost done. I'll finish up while you go clean the jizz out of your underwear. I'm lucky a good boy swallowed mine down." I winked.

He blushed, trying to give me a look that said I was ridiculous, but really, it just told me how much he liked what I said. "You're so annoying."

"Annoyingly handsome?" I tugged my underwear and jeans up but didn't button or zip them.

"Nope." He headed for the stairs.

"Annoyingly charming? Sexy? Addicting?"

"No, no, no!" Parker's back was to me, but somehow, I knew he was smiling.

As I heard his bedroom door close, I realized I was too.

# CHAPTER SIXTEEN
## *Parker*

THERE WERE TIMES when I was younger that I didn't want to be around my dad. It made me feel guilty because I loved him and I knew he loved me. He was a good father, had never been abusive, loved family time and all that, but…he'd just been so sad after Mom died. I had been too, but his was a different kind of sadness, one that oozed off him, not just strangling him, but me too. Eventually he got better, but it often felt like he stopped living with her, like I hadn't been enough for him. That was heavy to be around sometimes.

Which again, made me feel like an asshole.

Real emotions were so damn confusing and nuanced sometimes. People liked to pretend they weren't real, that we didn't all have those kinds of thoughts, but it was hard to lie to yourself.

It had been a while since the thought of being around my dad filled me with a sense of dread, but today was one of those days.

I was going to introduce my dad to my husband…my husband whom I'd just started dating, which was weird and confusing, but I was going with it. We'd spent the rest of the week blowing each other daily. While we hadn't fucked yet, my mouth was now incredibly familiar with Elliott's cock, and my dick definitely had a good time being lavished by his tongue. We hadn't done any dating yet, but honestly, I didn't expect it. I figured it was an excuse for Elliott to get to have sex with me, and I was a horny bastard who missed coming with someone else, so I was conveniently ignoring that.

"You okay?" Elliott asked, startling me.

"Yep. Fine. Just spacing off. You ready?" I stood in the kitchen, and he walked over to me. Elliott touched my hip, then put a hand around my waist and tugged me forward.

"I'm sorry." He pressed a soft kiss to the corner of my mouth, then another and another as he made a trail to my neck. This was something else he'd been doing all week. He touched me all the time, kissed me like we were a real couple, with the same goals and dreams.

"Why are you sorry?" I asked, trying not to let my knees give out and collapse for a quick BJ before we headed out.

"Because this isn't what you hoped for when it came to introducing your dad to your husband...well, I guess you never would've had to introduce him to your husband because he would've met him as your boyfriend. You know what I mean."

True, it wasn't what I'd hoped, but continuing to obsess about it wouldn't change anything. "It's fine."

"It's really not. You'll be perfect today, though. You're so fucking sexy, it's going to be hard to keep my hands off you."

I smiled. Ugh. *Must. Stop. Liking. Being. Praised.* "I'm literally wearing jeans and a Beach Buns hoodie."

"You're literally the sexiest guy I've ever seen." He swatted my ass. Elliott seemed to like doing that. "Let's go, gorgeous. I'll be on my best behavior all day. Your dad will love me. I'm great with parents."

"Have you ever met the parents of a boyfriend?" I asked as we went for the door.

"Nope. Never had a boyfriend. But parents are people, and I'm good with them. Vaughn's parents adore me."

"The best friend you used to fuck?"

He gave me a knowing smirk. "Do I detect a hint of jealousy?"

"No. Absolutely not. Why would I be jealous?" *Yes, I hate him and I shouldn't, especially considering I've never even met him.* Something to file away for later.

We were on the way in my car when Elliott asked, "You've really never hooked up with any of *The Vers* guys?"

"Nope. We don't work that way. They're my family. I mean, when we were teenagers, Marcus gave me and Corbin our first kisses, but it wasn't sexual. It was just because I was a sad, queer boy who wanted to kiss other boys. I was also a little nerdy. It was before my secretly-blow-the-jocks phase."

"All of them?"

"A good portion of them. They were all super masc and not into dudes *at all*—their words, not mine—but a mouth is a mouth, so mine worked fine. I was a kid and just knew I liked cock, so I went with it."

"Men suck."

"Yes, we do." I waggled my eyebrows, pretending we were talking about blowing people instead of what I knew he meant.

"Do you know where any of them live? We should totally egg or toilet-paper their houses or something."

"What!" I swerved, then jerked back into my lane when there was a loud *honk*. "We can't do that."

"Why not?"

"Because it's wrong? Because we're adults? Because…" Why did the idea actually sound fun? "No. Stop it. I'm not a kid anymore. I don't need revenge on high school guys who haven't been on top since they graduated."

**THE ROMANTIC**

Elliott shrugged. "Just an idea."

I was quiet for a moment, before saying, "There was this one guy in particular. He'd been a complete asshole. I've run into him a few times, and he still is. He thinks he's better than everyone else. He made me feel like shit about what we used to do together." Instead of a teenage bully, he was now a thirtysomething bully who'd been horrible to me. "We can't toilet-paper his house, though." Oh my God. Why did I want to do that? I shouldn't even still be talking about this.

"I'm pretty sure we could."

"What if we got caught?"

"Then we'd be very embarrassed?"

"Dude. Stop. We're not harassing my high school nemesis. You really are a troublemaker!"

"Just defending my husband's honor. I hate bullies, and I hate homophobes. Sounds like this guy could be both."

He definitely was, but still. "I'm not talking about this anymore—or entertaining the idea. I'm better than him."

"You are, and you still would be if you toilet-papered his house. Just know the option is on the table."

I smiled. The idea was ridiculous, and I knew I wouldn't really do it. But it was amusing to think about. Sometimes Elliott was so surprising. "How old are you?" I asked, realizing I didn't know.

"Thirty-four."

My first thought was disbelief that he was thirty-four and never had a real boyfriend where he'd met their parents, but then I remembered I was basically the same age and alone too.

"Why?" Elliott asked.

"Just thinking about two guys in their thirties causing mischief, and I realized I didn't know exactly how old you are. I'm thirty-three."

"You don't look it. You have such a pretty baby face." He

ran the back of his hand down said baby face.

"You're such a flirt."

"Just keeping the romance alive in our marriage. I hear it's important."

I laughed because how could I not? Plus, he was doing a good job at keeping my mind off what we were doing today.

We were almost there when I said, "It'll be different from how it was at your house. I mean, it's just my dad, obviously, and he really is great. It's not like we have to worry about him not being accepting, but he's…" Quieter, lonelier…

"Him," Elliott replied. "It'll be fine. Don't worry so much. I'm good at filling in conversation if I need to. And if all else fails, I'll just teach your dad how to dance."

A laugh jumped out of my mouth. "Clearly you don't know my dad. I can't imagine him ever doing something like that." Not anymore.

"That's because he's never met me before."

"You're so cocky."

"I'm honest."

"Oh my God, you're an idiot, is what you are," I countered, but I was still smiling…and I felt better.

The boulder in my gut returned as we pulled into the driveway. It was an older home that had still cost more than it should. My parents had both been incredibly responsible, and though they'd been young, they'd had life-insurance policies. What we'd gotten when she passed away had helped us keep things afloat.

"Hey," Elliott said softly. "You got this. I know you do. We're gonna have a great day. I'll wow your dad, and you're gonna end up making everyone feel good because that's what you do. And then we'll go home and I'll suck a load out of your balls to celebrate. Sound like a plan?"

Well, shit. I didn't know how I could argue with that,

but... "That's what I do? I make everyone feel good?"

"Yeah. You didn't know?" As soon as the words left his mouth, Elliott got out of the car, not giving me time to respond. Not that I knew how I'd respond if given the chance.

I didn't realize I was still sitting there until he knocked on the window on the driver's side. I hadn't even seen him come over. That was embarrassing.

"What do you mean?" I asked when I got out.

"It's pretty self-explanatory." Elliott took my hand, and when I quirked a brow, he said, "We're husbands and in love. Keep up with the program."

"And I make things better."

"Stop trying to get more compliments out of me, you little praise slut," he joked. I couldn't say he was wrong.

"Quit pretending you don't enjoy it."

"I would never do that."

I raised my hand to knock on the door, but surprisingly, it pulled open, and there my dad was. He must have been watching us.

I was tall like he was, but that's mostly where our similarities ended. He was broad, big-boned, and muscular without having to work for it. Where I was naturally thin and finer boned like Mom, he was thicker. His jaw was stubbled where mine was always smooth.

He wore jeans, a long-sleeved shirt, and a baseball cap. He was a sports guy, and while I enjoyed watching them with him, I'd never been good at playing them and frankly had no interest in it. I used to try when I was younger. Not that he made me feel like I had to, but because I'd wanted to, for him. One day he'd sat me down and said, *"You don't want to play ball with me, do you?"* I'd admitted I didn't, and he'd hugged me and told me I never had to lie to him, that I never had to pretend to be someone I wasn't. When the guys started to come around, Declan and Marcus would play with him sometimes, but I noticed he did it less and less.

Dad's gaze flickered from Elliott to me. "Park, it's good to see ya."

"You too, Dad. Sorry it's been a while." I nodded toward Elliott. "Dad...this is Elliott, my husband. Elliott, this is my dad, Roger."

"Nice to meet you." Dad held out his hand, and they shook. Another subtle difference between him and Elliott's parents, who'd both hugged me at least twice that day.

"You too. Parker has told me so much about you. I'm a little nervous, though, because he said you're a Kansas City fan," Elliott said, surprising me. My gaze shot to him.

When I looked at my dad, there was a spark in his hazel eyes. "If you say you're a Raiders fan, we might be in trouble."

"Guilty as charged," Elliott answered.

"Um...what's going on here?" I mean, I knew. The Raiders and the Chiefs were rivals. I'd randomly mentioned Dad liking Kansas City, but I didn't know Elliott had held on to that knowledge, or that he cared about football all that much. Unless he didn't and it was just his way of trying to bond with my dad.

Dad said, "Well, I was about to invite my new son-in-law into my house, but I have to say I'm disappointed you thought it was okay to marry a Raiders fan." Holy shit. My dad was *joking* with Elliott already? This didn't make sense at all. How did Elliott do this to people? There was just something about him.

"Once he told me you're originally from Kansas City, I kept my true identity secret so he didn't break up with me."

"Smart man," Dad teased while I tried to figure out what alternate dimension I'd been dropped into where my dad was joking around with Elliott. "I met his mama in college and moved out here with her afterward," he added, and there it was, the loneliness creeping back into his voice. "Speaking of, I guess I should let you guys come in. Sorry about that." He stepped aside.

Like at Elliott's parents' place, there were photos on the walls, but here they were all pre-mom's death. Elliott looked at them the way I'd done his, holding my hand, which he must have grabbed again at some point and I just didn't notice. "Look how cute you were." He pointed to one of me and my mom on the beach.

Dad said, "That was Mother's Day. She adored the ocean. She was so happy, and loved being a mom so much. She adored Parker, and he adored her. It was beautiful to see them together. Sometimes I'd just sit back and watch them, like they had their own little world that no one else was a part of. They were exactly the same—sweet and all heart. Sensitive and…well, I don't know why I'm describing Parker to you. Clearly you know how incredible he is since you fell in love with him."

Elliott's hand tightened around mine, one of his fingers gently brushing against my skin. My heart thudded. Words stuck in my throat. I'd never heard my dad talk like this before. We'd always known I was more like Mom than him, but did he really think I was incredible? Did he mean he'd felt left out?

When I didn't say anything, Elliott replied, "He is special. I had to work hard to win him over."

Dad chuckled. "Well, looks like you did it. He deserves the best, so you better treat him that way."

"I'll try," Elliott said.

"Dad?" I finally found at least the one word.

"Don't want to bring the mood down. Sorry. You know how I get sometimes. I'm going to put some food on the grill in a bit. Hope that works. I'm not much of a cook." He turned from me to Elliott. "What did Parker say you do again?"

We went into the living room as Elliott told Dad he was a city planner. We sat down, and Dad asked questions, Elliott answering every one of them. He talked to Dad about Dad's job as an electrical engineer. They got along well, the two of them even ganging up to playfully pick on me every once in a while, probably because I was distracted by what Dad had said earlier.

Elliott and I stayed inside when Dad went to put the steaks on the grill. He liked his moments of quiet, so I gave them to him. When he came back in, we talked some more. We were on the subject of my baking, and Elliott said, "I'm pretty sure I've gained at least five pounds since Parker moved in."

"Your body is fine," I replied, and he grinned.

"You say the sweetest things." I stiffened when he leaned over and pressed a kiss to my lips, and oh…a boy had just kissed me in front of my dad. Being in my thirties, one would think that wasn't a big deal, but Dad had never met a man I'd dated, and the last time he saw me with a guy other than my friends was when I got caught with a dick in my mouth.

"You should have seen Parker and his mom baking. They could spend a whole day in the kitchen."

I winced, but I couldn't quite say why.

"Beach Buns is amazing. Parker has created something really special, and so many of his customers come in at least a few times a week. It's like a family. He makes them feel comfortable. I'll see people with a cookie and coffee, sitting there for hours talking to him. It reminds me of something you'd see in a movie about a small town."

Warmth filled my chest because while this might not be

sexual, turned out I really was a praise slut. I liked hearing him say those things. It made me feel like I mattered.

Dad nodded. "Yeah, I couldn't be prouder of him. He's a good man." Dad looked at me. "And I couldn't be happier that you found a good man in Elliott too."

Guilt twisted my insides into knots, but then…Elliott and I were dating now, so in a way he really was mine. "Thank you, Dad. He's… I'm lucky to have him."

Elliott smiled, and damned if it didn't make me happy that it was him I was stuck with in this situation. No matter what happened in the future, he was a great person. He cared about people and wanted to do right by them. I could have gotten tangled up with someone a lot worse.

"Eh, I think I'm the lucky one," he answered, looking at me with a softness in his eyes that if I didn't know better, I would have fallen for. I knew the rules with Elliott. That was one thing I had with him that I didn't with other men I'd dated—no expectation or possibility of more. Maybe that would make it easier.

Dad cleared his throat. "I'll be right back." He slipped outside to check the steaks, but I knew him; he needed a moment.

"He's not as quiet as I expected," Elliott said.

"He's not as quiet as usual. It's a nice surprise." Between my dad meeting my husband in different circumstances than what I'd imagined, talking about my mom, Dad saying he was proud of me and also sounding like he'd felt left out with me and Mom, this evening had me feeling raw, like each moment was cutting me open somewhere different. Nothing dangerous or too deep, just enough to let me know it was there.

"What about you, beautiful? How's my perfect, sexy, gorgeous husband doing?"

My eyes were drawn to him, pulse speeding. "Laying it on

thick, don't you think?"

"You love it."

I did. "Thank you...for everything. I don't know if I've thanked you. I know this situation isn't ideal for either of us, but...well, it could be worse."

"Aww, baby. Is that your way of saying you actually like me?"

"What? No!" I answered playfully.

"It's okay. I think you're all right too." Elliott leaned in and nuzzled my neck, his stubble rough against my skin, ridiculously making my dick take notice. I was clearly a horny, sure thing. "Look at you. I can tell you want me just by the way you tremble. Don't worry, I want you too. I can't wait to make you come. I'll worship your pretty body all fucking night."

"Elliott..." I groaned. "Do *not* give me an erection at my dad's house."

The words had just left my mouth when the sliding glass door opened. I jerked away from Elliott like I was a teenager who'd just gotten caught.

Dad didn't make eye contact, and his cheeks were pink. "It's just about done."

"Sorry," I said, fairly certain I was blushing too.

Dad was quieter through dinner and the time we spent visiting afterward. He did seem to like Elliott, which felt like both a good and a bad thing. They talked about basketball too, and planned for the three of us to get tickets to a Lakers game together.

It was getting late, and Dad went outside to clean up the grill. Elliott had to go to the restroom, so I showed him where it was before I said, "I'm gonna go outside and talk to Dad for a minute."

"Take your time. I'm not going anywhere."

I nodded, then left him, sliding the door closed behind me.

Dad smiled when I got outside. "Your mom would have loved him."

He was right. She was full of personality the way Elliott was, both of them able to be comfortable and fit in, no matter the situation. "Yeah." I grinned. "She would have."

"You seem happy," he added, making my gaze shoot to him. I did? That surprised me. There was no reason I should be. Elliott and I didn't love each other, and we were only dating to pass the time.

"He's fun to be around," I replied because that was the truth. "And his mom cooked with me. She's been texting me all week. It's nice." The second I said it, I wished I could take the words back. Dad looked away and began fiddling with the grill again. "I didn't mean anything by that. I hope I didn't make you sad."

"You shouldn't have to worry about that."

"Why not? A little kindness goes a long way. We should all worry about how we make others feel."

"I'm your dad. You shouldn't have to protect my feelings, and you didn't make me feel sad. I just…wish she was here tonight, is all. I feel better most of the time. I'll always miss her, but I don't sit around thinking about her all day every day. Then things like this happen, and I wish she could see it. She would have wanted to do with Elliott the things his mom is doing with you. We both know I'm not great about that stuff myself. It's just not how I'm built, but you don't have to feel guilty because you get it somewhere else. You deserve it. I…"

"You what?" I asked, voice shaking. Dad didn't open up to me this way. He didn't let me in or share how he felt. While he'd always been family-oriented, he'd been quieter, more subdued in his emotions, even before Mom passed away.

"I'm glad you found someone, is all. I worried that I'd messed up with you somehow. That I wasn't able to be the father you needed. I know you got a lot of what I struggled to provide from Declan, Marcus, and Corbin, and I feel bad about that. Feel bad that I wasn't better, but now you have Elliott too. I don't want you to end up alone like me. I was afraid that because of me, you would."

"What? No. I… You're a great dad. Do you know how many queer kids have their parents walk away from them? I never had to worry about that from you. We might be different, you might not share your feelings the way I do, but we've always stuck together, and I've always known you love me. And if…if I do end up alone, that's not your fault." Because it was a very real possibility. Who really ever knew what the future held?

"Elliott—"

"Nothing is guaranteed, Dad." He nodded. Both of us were quiet for a moment as if we didn't know what to say. "I love you," was what I finally settled on.

He smiled. "I love you too, son. Even if you did bring home a Raiders fan." We laughed, and he hugged me. Usually, it was the other way around, me pulling him into my arms first, but this time it was Dad.

I closed my eyes, thankful for this moment and knowing it was because of my marriage to Elliott.

★ ★ ★

"YOU GOOD?" ELLIOTT asked as we drove home.

"You're always asking me that." I didn't say it in an annoyed way, just an observation. How I was doing and how I felt seemed important to Elliott. Well, I was sure it wasn't just me he was like that with. The more time I spent with him, the more I realized how caring he was.

"Yes. I know. It's...unfamiliar to me."

"I doubt that."

"No, it is. Mostly I think about myself."

I laughed, knowing what he said wasn't true. "And yeah, I'm really good actually." I told him what happened with my dad when we were outside. How unexpected it was and how much I'd needed to hear those things from him. "Strangely enough, I have you to thank for it. When we divorce, I'll have to figure that part out, but for now, I think this—us—somehow gave my dad something he needed."

"You can make me the bad guy."

"What? I'm not doing that." It was the last thing Elliott deserved. "We'll figure it out together like we have everything else."

"We're killin' this whole being-married thing."

"Right?" We were, weren't we? "It'll help that we'll stay friends...we realized we're not in love and we're better off as friends." The words felt heavy for some reason, sticky, like they didn't want to come apart or come out. "Anyway, we don't need to talk about that right now. This night was perfect."

"Just like you," he said, making me grin. I didn't really think Elliott believed that about me. I had flaws like nobody's business, but I still liked hearing it.

"Do I still get my reward?" I tested the waters.

"You do. You were so good tonight, of course you'll get it."

I pressed my foot on the gas pedal. Elliott laughed.

We laughed again together as we raced for the door, hurrying inside. The second it was closed, he went to his knees and drained my balls just as he'd promised, praising me every time he pulled off my cock.

When I sucked him off afterward, I might have told him he was a little great too.

# CHAPTER SEVENTEEN
## *Elliott*

MY DAY AT work had been crazy. I'd had meeting after meeting, trying to make sure every community in the city had everything it needed, which was basically impossible. Right now, I was working on how to get more public facilities, as well as zoning for a park in a low-income area in Baldwin Hills. It felt like every time I thought I made headway, I hit a brick wall, so by the time my workday finished, I was anxious to meet up with Vaughn.

"Where's your husband tonight?" Vaughn asked, sliding into the booth seat across from me.

"Maybe he's at home," I answered, though I knew he wasn't.

It had been a few weeks since our dinner with his dad, and Parker and I had spent quite a bit of time together, whether at home or going out. The more we hung out, the more I enjoyed him and the more I wanted to be with him. *It's because he's hot and funny*, I told myself. We were becoming friends—actually, we already had. Vaughn had been giving me shit, joking about the old ball and chain and dumb stuff like that.

"Then you would be too," Vaughn replied.

"No, I wouldn't. I can do things without him."

He picked up his phone and did something on it before

holding it up, and there Parker was on *The Vers* Instagram page, his head dropped back laughing, while Declan and Marcus each had an arm around him. Sebastian was there too, playfully on Corbin's back. I'd already known how close the *Vers* guys were; that had been clear from the moment I found out who they were. But seeing this, it was also obvious how Sebastian had fit into their group. They'd all accepted him and loved him because they loved Declan.

Would they do the same for me? But then, why should they?

"And?" I asked, trying to ignore the unfamiliar tightness in my chest.

"Nothing. Just making an observation." Vaughn opened his menu. "How's the dating-your-husband thing going?"

I shrugged. This felt like a trap where anything I said, Vaughn was going to take it to mean something else. "We're just having fun."

"Have you fucked him yet?"

"Jesus. He's my husband. Do you have to say it like that?"

A loud burst of laughter fell from Vaughn's lips.

"You asshole." He'd said that just to get a rise out of me, trying to prove whatever point he was trying to prove. The thing was, I didn't know why we hadn't fucked yet. We lived in the same house and were dating and married. We gave each other orgasms on the regular, but neither of us had taken that step. We also didn't sleep in the same bed.

"I'm giving you shit. You know I'm giving you shit."

"Yes, I'm just trying to figure out why I like you."

The waitress came, and we put in our order. I got salmon and a salad because I really was eating like shit ever since Parker had moved in. There were now always sweets around the house. So far, I hadn't been able to say no to any of them.

When she disappeared, Vaughn said, "You know it's okay

if you really start to like this guy, right?"

"I've never really liked anyone before."

"That doesn't mean you won't. Maybe you're demiromantic. Maybe you just never found the right one. Maybe it's him, maybe it's not. I just think you've been weird about Parker from the start, even just from how you pursued him for a whole damn lifetime, trying to get him to go out with you. It's different, and as your best friend in the world, I approve." He grinned. Vaughn could come off a little harsh or uncaring sometimes, but he really was a good man.

"Thank you. I'm glad I have your stamp of approval."

"What are friends for?"

We got off the subject of Parker after that, but the truth was, I couldn't stop thinking about what Vaughn had said. I hadn't ever considered I might be demiromantic, probably because I'd never fallen for anyone. That bond, that something a little different and special had never been there, so it would've never occurred to me. I wasn't saying it was there with Parker, but maybe that was an option for me. Or maybe marriage had fucked with my mind, which seemed the more likely answer because Vaughn had also been right about how I was with Parker.

When I got home that night, Parker wasn't there. I stayed up for a few hours, but he still hadn't returned. Did I text him? As soon as the thought hit me, I wanted to bang my head against the wall. He was an adult. I didn't need to babysit him, and he wasn't my actual husband in the ways that mattered.

I made sure to leave a light on for him so he could see when he got back, then made my way upstairs to my room. Once I was naked and in bed, my cell buzzed, and I breathed out a sigh of relief when I saw Parker's name, which was...over the top? Again, what did I think had happened? He was hanging with his friends. I knew he was okay.

*Parker:* **Hey...hope I don't wake you. I would have messaged earlier, but I lost track of time. We're all staying at Marcus's tonight. Sebastian brought wine *smile emoji***

*Me:* **Is everything okay?**

*Parker:* **Yeah, just some personal stuff with Corbin. I wish he would just shut down his damn social media accounts. He cares too much what other people think.**

I didn't know Corbin, but I'd made it a point to look at the guys' social media after Vaughn told me who they were. Corbin posted photos almost daily—gym shots, shirtless shots, photos of him in his jocks. He had sponsors and promoted exercise apparel.

*Me:* **Shit, that sucks. People can be harsh. Anything I can do?**

Which was a dumb question. What the fuck did I think I could do?

*Parker:* **No, but I appreciate your asking...I'm tired. It's been a long day.**

*Me:* **You're such a good boy...a good friend being there for Corbin, but make sure you take care of yourself too...**

*Parker:* **Ugh, stop. You're getting me hard. I hate that your praise gets to me so much.**

I smiled. I didn't hate it at all. It made me feel like a fucking king.

*Me:* **No you don't, beautiful. You love it. Don't make plans for after work tomorrow. I'm going to spoil you and take you out for being such a good friend. You deserve it.**

I started to worry I'd said something wrong when it took Parker a while to reply. Fifteen minutes had never gone by so slowly, three dots dancing the whole time.

*Parker:* **Okay...thank you, Elliott.**

And somehow, even though they were only four small words, I knew they meant a lot. That he'd agonized over them and maybe considered telling me no, but he didn't because he liked this. He liked what we did as much as me.

I smiled. This was weird and confusing, but I didn't care. I was going to keep doing it as long as Parker allowed it.

★ ★ ★

"A MASSAGE?" PARKER asked when we pulled up at the small building. "But it says closed."

I turned off my car and waggled my brows. "This is a special massage." Parker's eyes nearly popped out of his head, which immediately sparked my laughter. "It's not a sex thing. We have to be good. This is my friend's place of business, but—and this is probably something you should know about me, considering we're married—I'm certified in massage therapy."

"What? No way."

"Yes way. It was a thing I did in college. I was being a brat and told my parents I was dropping out of school to become a massage therapist. Not that there's anything wrong with that, they knew it was just me being an asshole. Anyway, it didn't happen, but I did get licensed, and I keep it up because I never know when I'm going to be lucky enough to worship—I mean, massage—a beautiful man's body."

"Do this often?" he asked, brow cocked.

"Actually, no. This is a first. Hence why Jamie is letting me use her place on a day she's closed."

"Oh." He cocked his head slightly, holding my gaze, looking for answers.

There was fear there too, so I leaned over and kissed him. "Stop stressing. I just want to see you naked."

"Of course. But how is that fair? I want to see you naked too."

"If you're lucky." I winked, and we got out. I heard the door unlock before it pulled open. "Hey, you," I said when Jamie let us inside.

"*Hey, you?* That's all you have to say to me?" She swatted my arm. "You fell in love and got married and I didn't even know! You didn't message me until you wanted to treat your husband to a special day!"

"Ouch. Be nice, woman," I teased. "We wanted to protect this, is all. But he's here now. Parker, this is my friend Jamie—Jamie, this is my husband, Parker." I pressed a hand at the small of Parker's back.

"Oh my God. It's so nice to meet you!" She hugged him. "I can't believe he got someone to agree to marry him."

I rolled my eyes, but Parker grinned. "I think you're my new best friend."

"I think that's a perfect idea."

"Aaaaand time for you to go," I said to Jamie.

"Ugh, fine. Don't do anything that can get me closed down. Be good, have fun, and I'm so, so, so happy for you. I also love that you want to pamper your man. Why can't I find a good guy?"

Parker said, "I hear you. Some of the stuff I've been through…well, before Elliott, of course." He blushed a pretty pink that was both adorable and sexy.

"Wait," I said. "Hold on. I'm gonna pull my phone out to record, and I'd like you to talk more about how awesome I am."

"I didn't say you're awesome," Parker joked.

"Incredible? Perfect? Sexy as fuck?"

He chuckled, then surprised me by putting his arm around my waist and leaning close, letting his head rest against my shoulder like he would if I was really his boyfriend or husband. "You're ridiculous." He looked at Jamie. "He's ridiculous."

"Yes, he is, and you guys are so cute."

"He is, isn't he?" I said.

"Oh my God. Stop. You're embarrassing me."

No I wasn't. He fucking loved it.

Jamie took us to the massage room, showed me everything I needed, gave me the keys and the alarm code, and left us to it. She worked alone, so we didn't have to worry about anyone else showing up. It was a large room, with a couple of chairs, a massage table, and all sorts of oils. The lights were low, just a soft glow. I sat in the corner and said, "Take off your clothes."

"Aren't you supposed to go out of the room for this?"

"Not when my client is my husband."

"I…" Parker started with a slight tremble to his voice. "Should we be doing this?"

"I'd like to do this. If you don't, all you have to do is let me know."

"Stupid, sexy man," he mumbled quietly, pulling off his shirt.

I laughed. "I guess there's my answer."

"Shut up." He unbuttoned his pants next. When he tugged those down, I saw he was wearing a red-and-blue Superman jock.

"Fuck." I pressed my hand against my groin. Why had I thought this was a good idea? I was going to make myself crazy.

"Exactly." He seemed to have forgotten he wore shoes, which he now removed, then took the jeans all the way off. He stood in front of me, long and lean with that thick bulge I loved tasting.

"Beautiful. Now finish up, gorgeous."

"Can't we just go home and have sex?"

I crossed my arms. "I thought you wanted to date. That you didn't want everything to be about sex."

"Well, I'm really fucking horny right now."

"Let me romance my husband. You're the romantic, right?" And damned if pink didn't run the length of him, starting at his head and making a swift journey down his body.

Parker removed his jock. He was hard, his dick pointing up, hair freshly trimmed and neat just how he liked it.

"Pull the sheet back and lie down on your stomach." He nodded and did as told. I went to him and pulled the piece of fabric up, covering the ass I was dying to devour.

"Really?"

"I'm a professional," I teased. My dick was throbbing, but I ignored it. I pulled out my phone and turned on soft music, then made sure the rocks were warming and got the oils ready. "What kind of pressure do you like?"

He frowned. "Medium."

I slicked my hands with the oil and began rubbing it into his shoulders.

"You're really going to give me a massage?"

"Did you think this was just for show?"

"Kinda," he replied, then, "thank you," like he was surprised someone would do something nice for him. Parker had definitely dated assholes in the past, and I was determined not to be that.

"Eh. It's mostly because I'm selfish and I get to touch you and see you naked. Is this pressure good?"

"Perfect."

"Just like you," I praised and watched goose bumps chase each other down his arms. I spent a while rubbing his shoulders before traveling down his back and then up again. I forced myself to take this seriously and avoid his ass. While I did plan to give that some loving too, it wasn't quite time yet.

Parker moaned when I hit certain spots, making delicious noises that just got my dick harder. I used the hot stones on him, working out the places he carried more tension, before massaging him again.

"Would it be all right if I lowered the sheet, sir? If I promise to be a perfect gentleman?" This was a fun game, heat pooling in my gut as I waited for his answer.

"What if I'm shy? I've never had a massage before. Is it normal for a massage therapist to work me out there?"

Fuck yes. He was playing along.

"First of all, I assure you there's no reason to be shy. I'm not supposed to say things like this, but your body is incredible. The best I've ever seen…or touched…" I dug my thumbs into the muscle above his ass. "It's extremely hard to stay professional with such a sexy man beneath my hands…and yes, it's normal as long as there's consent and we keep it appropriate." I let my fingers dip beneath the cover.

"Oh. Yes…I'd like that."

Jesus, my dick throbbed. I wanted to pull myself out and fuck into him, let him suck me or jerk off, anything, but I kept myself in check, slowly sliding the sheet down and then removing it altogether.

"Beautiful," I whispered, letting my fingers dance along the plump curve of his right cheek. Another set of goose bumps followed where I touched him.

"Is it?" he asked breathlessly. "Do you still think I'm the best you've ever seen?"

"Yes. Fuck yes." Christ, my voice was thick with lust, broken with need as I fought the urge to do things to him I had no business doing here. His skin was so smooth and unblemished, a creamy peach, which yes, was how I would describe his ass too.

My hands shook as I added more oil and began to massage his cheeks.

"Oh God," he whispered as I pressed into his muscles, spread him and rubbed him, letting my fingers tease his crease.

"I know it's not professional of me, but I have to say, yours is the best hole I've ever seen. So tight and pink. I wish I knew what it tasted like…how sweet it would be on my tongue."

"Fuck…Elliott."

I brushed his rim as I massaged. "Oops."

"Give me your fingers."

"I can't. I'm sorry. I'd get into trouble."

"Please…" he begged. "Please make me come."

My cock jerked, my teeth grinding together. I wanted so bad to give him what he asked for, but instead, I lowered my mouth to his ear. "It's killing me not to sink into that pretty, perfect little hole. I want it so bad, but you have to be a good boy. Once we finish our date, if you want my cock, I'll give it to you."

"Fuck…I hate you…that's so unfair."

"That's not very nice to say to your husband." I touched him again, massaging his ass, his thighs, his calves, and then back up again.

Parker fidgeted, made needy noises that just turned me on more.

We weren't even done yet, and this was hands down the best date I'd ever had.

# CHAPTER EIGHTEEN
## *Parker*

MY LEGS STILL felt like Jell-O when we left. Elliott hadn't let me help clean up. Oddly, he was sticking to this pampering thing. I couldn't wrap my head around why he was doing it, why he would go to all this trouble for me, but it felt really, really good…even if I was dying to come and he didn't let me.

"You don't have to do this, you know," I said when we got into the car. "All the spoiling. I'm sure it's not your idea of an exciting date. Also, I have blue balls."

He chuckled. "Actually, it strangely is my idea of a great date. Who knew? Plus, you deserve it. I'm doing it because I want to."

"Oh," I replied, quiet for a moment while Elliott began to drive. I wasn't used to this. I was used to ending up in cuckold situations, getting cheated on, or just not being the person someone wanted. Not that Elliott really wanted me—we were having a good time together and I didn't expect it to be anything more—but this was sweet, romantic, the kind of stuff I'd dream about doing for a man I loved or the man I loved doing it for me.

*Stop. Do not pass go. End that line of thinking right this moment!*

I shouldn't even let myself think that word—the *L*

word—when it came to Elliott. I mean, I knew I didn't love him, but I couldn't let myself be open to even the possibility of falling into *like* with him. Enjoy him as a person? Yes. Friend? Yes. Great guy to date? Also yes, but I needed to keep this in the box it belonged in—enjoying our marriage until we divorced. Allowing myself to get hurt again wasn't an option.

"Uh-oh," Elliott said.

"Uh-oh, what?"

"You're making that cute, scowly face. Usually you only do that when I've done something wrong, but I know I haven't." He reached over and brushed his thumb against my temple. "So that means you're all up in that pretty head of yours. Can't you just enjoy this?"

I should. I did enjoy it, but I also didn't know how to turn off my thoughts. "I'm having fun."

"Yes, but you're thinking a lot too. I've noticed it's a thing you do."

"That I think? Is that bad?"

My question earned me another chuckle. "Only sometimes."

"Where are we going now?"

"To dinner at the sushi place you love—Sticky Rice."

Okay...interesting. "How did you know there's a sushi place I love?"

"I've been listening to old episodes of *The Vers*. To learn more about my husband."

I smiled. Ugh. Why was I smiling? He was so charming and endearing, something I hadn't expected...or hell, maybe I had. Maybe that's why I didn't tell him to leave me the hell alone months ago. "You've called me that quite a bit tonight."

"It's what you are."

I sighed. "Yes, I guess it is. Wanna hear something funny?"

"Always."

"The only sushi I eat is California rolls. But oh my God, they're my favorite. And Sticky Rice makes the best teriyaki chicken too." My stomach growled in the quiet car.

Elliott laughed. "Clearly you're hungry, so I should hurry."

I grinned, pretending not to feel the butterflies in my gut. *I'm just enjoying this. That's all I'm doing.* "Tell me more about you. I don't have a podcast to learn about all your quirks."

"Hmm. More about me... I too love California rolls, but my sushi palate is more varied than yours."

"Well, aren't you mister cultured," I teased.

"Yes, yes I am."

"What else? Do you read?"

"No, but it's cute to watch you get lost in your romance novels. I don't know if you realize it, but you sigh and swoon a lot. Sometimes I'll glance over and you'll have this dopey grin on your face. Maybe I should download one of them to figure out what the hell I'm doing wrong." He winked.

"Oh my God. Shut up. I don't do that."

"You totally do."

"I'm never reading around you again. Also, I'll give you titles."

"How-to guides on wooing Parker Hansley. Sign me up."

I rolled my eyes. "You don't really want to woo me."

"I do too. What do you think I've been doing? Who doesn't want to woo the guy they're dating?"

The thing was, Elliott was very good at it. He was already sweeter than any guy I'd dated. "Can I ask you something?"

"Sure. Can't promise I'll answer, but you're free to ask."

"You've really never been in love?"

"Nope."

"Never wanted more from someone? Felt that...pull to

them, something different inside you when you look at them, talk to them, or think about them?" Elliott was quiet, and I worried I'd overstepped or offended him. "I'm not judging you. I promise. I'm just curious. I'll never admit this again, but you're very good at dating. You pay attention, and that's rare. I'm just surprised that someone who puts in so much effort has never felt something more for someone."

"I didn't take offense. And I think it's a combination of things. I've never been in love, or felt close to it. I've never wanted more with someone, and I've always been okay with that. I never had romance and a family as one of my goals. But I didn't spend my life actively trying not to make it happen either. In my head, it was just a thing people did one day and eventually I'd probably do it too, but I wasn't in a hurry to find that person. I enjoy my life. Occasionally I do wonder if it'll ever happen for me. According to the strange set of rules we seem to have as a society, I know that at my age, I should have already found someone I'm at least interested in pursuing more. I just never have. I guess we're all different."

"Yeah, I guess." My chest was tighter all of a sudden. I didn't want Elliott to be alone, which maybe made me a dick if he did want to be. Everyone's idea of a happily ever after was different, but...I wanted more for him. "Well, just so you know, you'd be very good at it. If you do ever find that person, he'll be lucky to have you."

He pulled into the parking lot and glanced my way. "You like me."

"Ew." But I did, more and more. "Also, just because we're here, I hope you don't think you get to stop talking about yourself now."

He steered the car into a spot, then looked at me. "I love talking about myself, beautiful. And I'm gonna win you over eventually."

I didn't tell him that in some ways, he'd already won me over.

★ ★ ★

WE STAYED AT the restaurant long after we finished eating. When Elliott said he liked talking about himself, he meant it. That didn't come as a surprise, but what did was that where before I'd thought he was full of himself, I realized it wasn't that. Okay, it wasn't completely that. He was cocky, and that was okay, but there was more to him.

Elliott cared about people. He wanted to put good into the world. He was funny, which I already knew, and he was a motocross fan, which I hadn't. He loved camping and going to Big Bear, and he always had to sleep on the right side of the bed, even if he wasn't home.

And now he was telling me more about how he and his family did a lot of work for domestic-violence survivors because Malcolm's mother had been a victim, as had Cat's sister.

"Mom does a charity dinner event every year. It's in about a month, and I'm hoping my husband will attend with me."

"Oh, she did mention that a couple of times. Yeah. Of course I'll be there."

"Good. You know how I like attention. It'll help to walk in with the sexiest date."

I couldn't help but bite my bottom lip, my stomach light and fluttery. He was so good at making that happen. "Stop trying to get me hard."

"Is it working?" He licked his lips, and there was definitely something stirring down there.

"Yes. This has been an awesome date, but can we go home now so you can do what you told me you'd do?"

"But I had more pampering to do."

*Yes, please* was the first thought that went through my head, but that was more dangerous than sex. That's what would play tricks on my heart. If I planned to come out of this unscathed, I needed to keep things in check.

"I promise I'm worth it. It's been a long time since I've had someone inside me. It should probably be my husband."

"Check, please!" he called out, making me laugh.

We laughed most of the way home, both of us joking and teasing about how horny we were. "When was the last time for you?" he asked.

"Oh God. Well, I was dating this guy, and it turned out to be a disaster. It was right around the time when I was considering going on my break from men and sex. I hadn't told the guys yet, and I didn't share this part with them afterward, so I'll kick your ass if you tell them."

"Oooh, I get to know something the Beach Bums don't," he teased.

"It's embarrassing, but I'm going to trust you anyway. I was sad over the jerk I was dating, and I ended up at this ice cream bar where you could pile on all sorts of shit. It wasn't my finest moment."

Elliott smirked.

"You haven't heard the worst of it. This really hot guy was watching me, and I was like, fuck it. I'm just gonna screw anyone I want and not care about dating…so…when he approached me and sat down to talk to me, it was clear what was on his mind, but we still chatted while we stuffed our faces."

"As one does before sex…"

"Good point. I should have known he was playing me."

"Beautiful, if he was playing you, he's an idiot because you're irresistible."

"Thank you, but not to him." I covered my face. What had gotten into me? I couldn't believe I was telling him this. "He asked for my phone. He was going to put his number in and said we could meet up later. I gave it over, and it took him forever. I don't know why I didn't realize what was happening, but…long story short…he didn't add his number. He'd Venmo'd himself money from my phone."

Elliott whipped his head in my direction. "Shut the fuck up! No way."

"I swear. Why would I make up something so embarrassing? That was it. That was when I knew it was time to take a break."

"Their loss, my gain." He winked, and I maybe melted inside.

The moment we got out of the car, Elliott kissed me, his arms surrounding me as we both tried to stay on our feet and make our way to the door at the same time.

"I'll meet you in your room," I said, thinking it was better to do this there than in mine. That way I could go back to my space afterward. I also wanted to do some freshening up first.

"Okay." Elliott nodded. "Race you upstairs."

I ran before I agreed to race. Elliott called me a cheater but was right behind me. Our shoes banged against the floor, sounding like a herd of elephants on the stairs. The second we hit the landing, his arm wrapped around my waist and he backed me against the wall. "Not fair," he said before his mouth slammed down on mine again. My cock was already hard. I wanted him so bad, wanted to let him suck me and then suck him, but Christ, we'd been doing this for a while now and we hadn't fucked yet.

"Stop. I want this inside me." I palmed his swollen shaft.

"You're killin' me, beautiful. Hurry. Be a good boy and don't make me wait too long."

"Fuck. Yes. I'm going." I raced to my room, stripping out of my clothes as I went. I knew my body fairly well, and there was a good chance we'd be okay, but I didn't want to risk any accidents. I hurriedly cleaned up, not pausing to think about tonight or Elliott and risk my good sense telling me to stop this.

I was naked when I made my way back to his room and... What. The. Fuck. He was sleeping?

Elliott was nude too, on his back, eyes closed. My whole body deflated because how bad could he want me if he'd passed out that quickly, but then...wait, was there a small smile on his lips? "Oh my God. You asshole!"

He exploded with laughter as I launched myself at him and straddled him on the bed. "You're a jerk. I thought I was gonna have to resort to my dildo or Fleshlight...again."

"Fuuuuuck. Me too. I've been getting myself off every night."

"You should let me watch."

"Gladly. Now bring that sexy mouth down here and kiss me."

Elliott didn't have to ask twice. I slid my tongue between his lips, caressing his with mine. My dick flooded with heat, getting hard and plump in what felt like seconds flat.

We rutted together, making out, hard body against hard body. As good as this felt, though, I needed more. "You promised if I was good, I'd get your cock." Shit, I couldn't believe he got me to talk that way. It wasn't something I'd ever done with anyone else.

Elliott slid his hand around my ass, between my cheeks. I lifted up some to give him better access. "Do you have a hungry little hole?" he asked, making my dick twitch.

"Yes. Fuck yes."

"Good because I've been dying to have it. You made me

wait so long for what I know is going to be my favorite ass. I might not want to stop fucking it, might sleep with my dick inside you, and every time I wake up, just start fucking you again."

Hello, dirty talk. He was a pro at this.

"Tell me you want me," Elliott said.

"I want you…fuck, I want your cock inside me. Wanna show you how good my hole really is. Wanna be good for you."

Elliott growled and flipped us. The second he had me on my back, he began kissing his way down my body. "Look at you…so fucking needy for me, so fucking perfect." He wrapped a hand around my cock and stroked. "Mmm…you have a pretty cock too…so thick. Are you going to fuck me with it one day? I want it, want this perfect cock in my ass."

"Yes…God yes."

"Good boy. I love tight balls." He nuzzled mine. "Turn over for me. I want this sexy ass in the air so I can eat my favorite hole before I fuck it."

My body vibrated, heart thudding so hard I really thought I was going to suffer an attack. I'd never been this turned on in my life, never felt as desired and craved as Elliott made me feel.

He knelt, and I did as he said, got onto my hands and knees, back arched, legs spread for him. "Do I look pretty?" It was so embarrassing, what his words did to me, the way they twisted me inside out while making me feel whole.

"So fucking pretty. Gorgeous. I can't believe you're mine." He spread my cheeks, then leaned down and pressed a kiss to my rim. "This too… I've never seen such a pink, tight hole."

I cried out when Elliott lashed his tongue over it. I fisted my hand in his duvet, his stubble scratching against my crease in the most delicious way as he licked me, softening me up, working to press his tongue inside.

"I think I found my new favorite meal." There was a smile in his voice, which made me smile too as I pushed back, silently begging for more.

Elliott ate my ass, then pushed a finger inside, fucking me with it, rubbing my prostate, then using his tongue on me again. "So awesome...don't stop."

"Why would I stop tasting something so good?"

I swear he used his tongue on me longer than any man had, like it really was a feast and he couldn't get his fill. I leaked on the bed, wanting his cock and his tongue and just everything at the same fucking time.

"Don't stop," fell from my lips when he pulled back.

"Shh. I'm not going anywhere, beautiful. Just gonna get the lube and a condom so my dick can finally feel the world's best hole."

I stayed where I was, trying to arch prettily for him. Elliott tossed the condom to the bed, then slicked his fingers and pushed two inside.

"You should see this, the way you're sucking me in. You really are hungry for it, aren't you? Your ass is begging for my cock."

"Fuck me," was all I could manage to say.

Two fingers became three before I was empty, stroking my cock and so damn needy for release.

He sheathed himself and pressed the head of his dick against me. "Do you want it?"

"You know I do."

"Ask me. Ask me to fuck your pretty hole with my cock."

Jesus, this guy. "Please, Elliott, fuck my pretty hole with your cock."

"Gladly," he replied before thrusting in.

The feeling of fullness, the slight burn and stretch, was exactly what I needed. Elliott held my hips, fucking into me hard and quick. I loved the sound of our bodies as they smacked together, the scent of sex and sweat in the room. I would lick him clean when we were done if he'd let me.

My dick bounced against my stomach as I took him, pushing back against him and needing more.

"You're too good... I hate to break it to you, gorgeous, but I'm not gonna last long."

"I guess it's a good thing I'm not either."

Elliott swatted my hand away when I tried to stroke myself. "This is my cock."

He wrapped a fist around me, tugging my dick in unison with his thrusts. Each time he rubbed against my prostate I cried out, until I couldn't hold back anymore. My whole body felt like it splintered apart, bursting from the pressure of pleasure filling me up. I shot over his hand and the bed, pulse after pulse of sticky cum until Elliott was saying my name, his erection jerking inside me as he emptied his balls into the condom.

He kissed my back, licked my spine, and I knew he was tasting my sweat.

I fell to the bed, breathing heavy.

He climbed off the mattress, and an unfamiliar panic flooded me. "Where are you going?"

"Just getting rid of the condom."

Well, shit. Now I felt dumb. Why did I feel so clingy, like I needed him close? "Okay."

He came back, then licked my cum off my stomach before using a washcloth to wipe me clean. It felt so good, like I mattered to him, like he got as much out of pampering me as I did.

"Give me a minute, and I'll go back to my room."

"No," he replied. "Part of spoiling you is holding you the rest of the night. Don't go."

My eyes snapped to his, my chest full and strange. "Okay," I said, while telling myself my answer should be no.

Elliott pulled the blanket from under me, then covered me up. He hit the lights next, then climbed into bed beside me and tucked me into his arms. "You fit well here."

*It's not real, it's not real, it's not real.* It was part of this game we played.

"Feels good."

"I'm glad." He kissed my shoulder.

"Have you done this before? The praising thing?"

"No. Am I good at it?"

I chuckled. "You know you are."

"I like it."

"I do too." My admission was gentle, unsure.

"I guess that's a good thing, then. Go to sleep, gorgeous."

I closed my eyes and did as Elliott said, telling myself my heart wasn't softening. That it was still intact.

# CHAPTER NINETEEN
## *Elliott*

THE NEXT FEW weeks sped by. Parker and I continued to spend a lot of time together. I'd brought him coffee in bed the morning after our massage night, and he'd lit up as if I'd handed him the world. Evidently, none of the assholes he'd dated had done this for him, but then, had I ever woken a man up with their morning caffeine? I hadn't, but I couldn't imagine not wanting to do it for Parker. Not that I had another chance to do it since. He hadn't slept in my bed again.

When I was on my own, I kept working my way through episodes of *The Vers*. Well, until I got stuck on one and hadn't been able to make myself listen anymore.

It was from last summer. A listener had written in to ask which one of the guys they would sleep with if they had to choose one, and I couldn't get past Parker's answer. He'd chosen Marcus, which didn't bother me. But...the rest of his answer did. When Declan had been surprised it wasn't him, Parker had explained that because of their particular friendship, the lines could easily get blurred, basically saying that if it was just a sex thing, he wouldn't choose Declan because he was worried his feelings could get involved and he wouldn't want to get hurt or ruin their friendship.

That made me think about us. Clearly, he didn't have the

same reservations with me. Parker wanted that happily ever after, but he wasn't worried he would ever want that from me. We were just fucking and dating to pass the time, and he didn't truly fear his heart getting involved. He could easily fuck me because I wasn't the kind of guy he would want, and while that shouldn't bother me, it did. Or at least, it felt weird. Too many strange feelings had been plaguing me since this whole marriage with Parker, and I didn't like it at all.

"What's wrong?" Mama asked as we sat in her kitchen. Dad was in DC, Parker at work, and Vaughn off with some guy he was fucking, so I'd come over to spend some time with her.

"Nothing's wrong. Why do you ask?"

"Because I know my son."

Yes, she did, and something *was* off with me, but it wasn't like I could tell her what it was. That my marriage had been a drunken mistake, that I wondered if I was demiromantic and why I'd never felt a romantic connection to anyone. How Parker felt new and exciting in a way nothing ever had, so I was confused as fuck about it.

Those weren't things I could ever say to my mom.

"Just been busy, is all. How are the plans going for the fundraiser? Do you need any help?"

It was the perfect distraction. Mom went off, telling me about an issue with the flowers and about her sponsorship troubles. I listened and offered opinions, but I also kept thinking about Parker. What was it that made me obsess about him so damn much?

When Mom looked at her phone and smiled, I asked, "Dad?"

"No. It's Parker. I texted him earlier, and he's just getting back to me. Says he has a surprise for you."

That made me smile. I knew they were talking, but it was

also nice to see. Plus, I loved surprises.

"You should see the look on your face right now. I've never seen it before. You don't know how good it feels to know you're happy."

I *was* happy. Not in the way she thought, but I was happy. "We have fun together. I like making him feel good."

Mom reached over the counter and squeezed my hand. "That's because you're a good man. When you love someone, it's always the best feeling to do nice things for them. It feels like nice things for yourself too."

Part of that was right. Treating Parker special did feel like something special for myself, but I wasn't in love with him—I couldn't be. Though I wasn't sure *why* I couldn't be. Fuck, emotions were confusing.

"Did he say what it is?" I reached for her phone, but she jerked it back.

"You can't cheat! Go see your husband. He's at home. I won't be a part of your evil ways." She grinned, and I laughed.

"I think you might be taking it a little too far." I was already standing, though, excitement shooting through me. Parker had done something nice for me, and it was killing me not to know what it was. "I'll see you later, Mom." I kissed her cheek and tried to walk away.

"Elliott?" she said, holding my hand.

"Yeah?"

"I just… I know I already said this, but it's good to see you happy. When I first heard about the marriage, I was hurt and angry. When you said you had feelings for him, I thought it was just you covering your ass. I'm not proud of that, but it's true. Seeing the two of you together, though, and the way you look when you talk about him…well, I was wrong, and it's clear you absolutely adore him. I can't say I'm not still a bit upset that I didn't get to see you two get married, but the most important thing is that my son found his person, and that's priceless."

My throat tightened. My tongue felt like it was swelling while my gut twisted and turned. I didn't know how to respond. I felt like the biggest piece of shit in the world. "Mom—"

*Buzz!* Her phone went off again. "Oh. It looks perfect!" She hid the screen from me. "Go see Parker." She pushed me toward the door.

I went with a heavy heart, thinking about her the whole drive home.

The second I stepped into the house, I smelled sugar, cinnamon, lime, and coconut mixed with other sweet, spicy, and delicious scents. "What is this?" I asked, seeing all the plates and bowls laid out on the kitchen counter. Parker stood beside it.

"I wasn't really just hanging out with the Beach Bums today," he said as I approached. When I reached the counter, I saw numerous Cuban desserts: arroz con leche, shortbread cookies, pastelitos de guayaba, Cuban churros and capuchinos, and a rum cake. "I was playing around with different treats. I remembered you telling me Cuban desserts are your favorites. I…well, I'm sure they could use some work, and I probably didn't get them right, but you always do nice things for me, so I wanted to do something nice for you."

The heaviness in my chest gave way to a light, floaty feeling that spread down into my stomach, exploding in a kaleidoscope of…fuck, I didn't even know… Joy? Gratitude? Warm and fuzzies? It felt like all those things. Parker had put a lot of thought into this. He'd looked up recipes and bought ingredients and had then made all these things for me because he knew I liked them. And that felt…indescribable. All I knew was an echoey feeling in my head and giddiness flittering through me. I'd had nice things done for me, I'd had people tell me I was attractive, and I'd done well at a million things in my life. None of them felt as special, as perfect, as the thought of Parker doing all this for me.

"It's okay if you don't like it...if I crossed some line I didn't know was there. I wanted to show you I appreciate you. I thought we could watch a movie tonight and have a Cuban desserts party—though if you don't like something, you're not allowed to tell me. I figured it could be a date. You said we are dating, and—"

I silenced Parker with my mouth. God, what was wrong with me? I wanted to melt into him, wanted to hold him and thank him and tell him this was the kindest, sweetest, most incredible thing anyone had ever done for me. I couldn't make sense of why I was so fucking emotional over this, but as my tongue dipped into his mouth, exploring and tasting the familiarity of him, my heart punching at my chest like it wanted to break out and burrow into his, I...well, honestly, I thought about running, changing my name and disappearing because this was scary and impossible and something I never thought would ever happen.

This wasn't just a crush. This wasn't just attraction.

I *liked* my husband.

I wanted *more* with my husband.

How in the fuck had this happened, and what the hell did I do about it?

We settled on the couch together, food on the coffee table, cuddling, eating, talking, and then watching movies. This marriage thing wasn't so bad at all.

★ ★ ★

I'D NEVER BEEN insecure about myself. I knew what I wanted,

and I went for it. I didn't stress about things or overthink them. However, ever since I discovered I was in real *like* with my husband, it was all I seemed to be able to do.

Sure, it had only been a few days, but I thought about him all the time. Cute little things he did that would make me mushy inside. For absolutely no reason I would sit around and watch him, something he noticed. He'd say, *What?* And I'd be like, *Nothing* or *Can't I look at you, gorgeous?* And then he'd visibly get weak in the knees or flush the way he did when he was feeling some kind of something because of my praise, and he'd forget I was a creepy weirdo who wouldn't stop staring at him.

I couldn't help it, though. It was a weird-ass feeling to want more with someone for the first time. To feel that connection, that spark I'd never experienced. It was addicting. On the one hand, I got what people were talking about—it made me feel good, like I was lit up from the inside. On the other hand, it was annoying and made me feel dumb, and I wanted it to go away.

This was a fucking disaster.

And yet I didn't do anything to make it go away, instead spending even more time with him, and now I'd invited Vaughn over to meet him.

"I made a cake for tonight," Parker said when he got home from Beach Buns. He took his shoes off right in front of the door, and I put them on the rack before following him over to the kitchen counter.

"What kind?"

"Just a chocolate whiskey cake with salted caramel drizzle."

I cocked a brow. "Oh, just that, huh?"

He set the cake down, pulled his jacket off, and tossed it on a barstool. I immediately grabbed it.

"Shit. Sorry. I suck."

"Quite well, something I hope you'll do tonight," I teased. We'd only slept in the same bed that one night. He never invited me to his and always left mine afterward. It wasn't ideal, but my super romantic husband wasn't in... In *like*? Whatever it was, he wasn't in that with me.

"It's fine," I told him. "I'm used to your messy ways. I got you a laundry basket for your bathroom!"

He grinned. "Romance totally isn't dead."

I kissed his smile. "No, it's not." I smacked his ass. "Now go get ready. Vaughn will be here soon."

"Is there something wrong with what I'm wearing?"

"Nope, absolutely not, but I also know you, and no way you wouldn't want to shower and change. That's not how you work."

Surprise flared in his eyes. "I...well, yes, but..."

I laughed. "See? I pay attention. I'm a great husband, beautiful." Leaning closer, I brushed my lips over his ear. "But not as much as my good boy, who only has to walk into the room to get me hard. See?" I rubbed my erection against Parker, making him whimper.

"Oh God. Don't get me horny before Vaughn gets here."

"We have time for a quickie."

"No, we don't!"

He ran for the stairs, and I playfully chased him. We played these silly games all the time, and they were so much fun. I didn't remember doing things like this with other men I'd dated, and if I did, it didn't have the same effect.

"Help, my husband won't leave me alone!" Parker joked as his feet pounded up the stairs. I stayed at the bottom, laughing at him.

"We should play predator and prey!" I called after him.

"Oh my God! So hot!" Parker replied before I heard the

bathroom door close.

I hung his coat up, rearranged things that didn't need rearranging, and some fifteen minutes later when Vaughn arrived, I was still smiling.

"Hey, man. How's it going?" Vaughn asked.

"Good. Parker has cake." Vaughn waggled his brows, smirking, which made me realize how that sounded. "He made a cake, you asshole." I hadn't planned on a meal, and just had some finger food and a charcuterie board prepared.

"Interesting…" Vaughn said as he went into the living room.

"What's interesting?"

"The fact that your husband is the first thing you mentioned."

I rolled my eyes. "Just because you're here to get to know him." But really, why did Vaughn have to get to know him? We might be dating, but as far as Parker was concerned—and okay, if you went by what I'd said in the beginning—we'd still be divorcing anyway, so why should it matter? Dating didn't mean we planned to stay married.

"Where is your man?"

"Upstairs, getting ready." Though he should have been down here by now. I was surprised he wasn't. It didn't usually take him this long. The last time it had was the day he met my parents. Shit. "Grab a drink. I'm gonna go up and check on him."

"Okay, but just so you know, if it takes too long, I'm coming up. No hanky-panky without me."

"Did you really just say hanky-panky?" I teased.

"It gets the point across."

I went upstairs. Parker was out of the shower, the bathroom door open, and his clothes in the basket I'd put there for him. Of all the stupid things that could make me grin, that shouldn't be on the list, but it was.

I knocked softly on his door.

"No one's home!" he called out, making me chuckle. I opened the door just as Parker came out of the closet, wearing nothing but a jockstrap—my favorite one that was red and not only made his ass look great, but his bulge too. We'd been playing this little game lately where he only wore a jock when we were home and I'd tell him how hot he was and how much I wanted him. "I don't have anything to wear."

"I can send Vaughn home, and you can wear that."

"Ha-ha. Very funny."

"Who's joking?" I went and wrapped an arm around him, rubbed his right ass cheek. "Best ass I've ever seen. I'd much rather spend the day watching it..."

"Is that all you'd do with it?" Parker asked.

"Nope...I'd kiss it...lick it...use it as a pillow." He snickered. "And I'd fuck it. You know I'd fuck your pretty hole. I can hardly keep my cock out of it." While I'd said I wanted Parker to fuck me, he hadn't yet, though I'd definitely ridden his ass hard a few more times since that first time. "It doesn't matter what you wear, gorgeous. You're the prettiest man in every room regardless."

"God, I hate you," he said breathlessly.

"Aww. You're so sweet." I kissed him. "I'll show you my favorite jeans of yours. They're the ones you were wearing the first night we met. Fucking great for your ass."

"You remember that?" Parker's forehead was all bunched up in surprise.

"Gorgeous...have you seen your butt in those pants? It's impossible to forget." I kissed his cheek. "Now, I'm gonna grab the clothes, and you're gonna get dressed and come down with me. Vaughn is gonna love you, so you don't need to be nervous. Actually, he's gonna be jealous as fuck that you're mine. I'm gonna spend the evening looking at you and touching you, and I want you to show off for me, flaunt how pretty you are and how much you know it. And tonight, when he leaves, I'm gonna show you just how fucking perfect you are...how much I want you, when I make this ass mine."

He gulped, hands shaking as he reached out and held on to me. "Jesus, you're good at this."

"Only for you, baby. Only for you." I winked.

# CHAPTER TWENTY
## *Parker*

*IT'S NOT REAL, it's not real, it's not real,* I told myself over and over while Elliott got the jeans from my drawer and a baby-blue V-neck tee from my closet. He said the color looked good with my eyes.

It was silly that I was so nervous about spending time with Vaughn. What did it matter if he liked me or not? But I knew he was important to Elliott, and Elliott was my friend now, right? So of course it would be important for us to get along. That's all this was.

And Elliott was just being Elliott. He got off on this stuff.

He stayed with me while I got dressed. After running a hand through my hair a few times, I said, "Okay, let's do this." It startled me when he took my hand, but I let him.

When we got downstairs, Vaughn was sitting at the kitchen counter, a glass in front of him, looking at his phone.

"About time, you slow asses," he teased, which immediately made me relax some. It was the kind of thing Declan, Marcus, or Corbin would say, and damned if I didn't wish they were here with me. What would they think about Elliott? Well, outside of being worried about me and not trusting him. If they allowed themselves to get to know the real Elliott, the Elliott who'd begun to reveal himself to me. It was so strange having this whole part of my life they weren't privy to.

We'd never had that before. Well, to a degree, I guess we did with Declan when he got with Sebastian, but Dec had brought Sebastian around, and it had been clear from the start, even before we met him, that Declan and Sebastian had feelings for each other. Allowing my friends to get close to Elliott...that made me worry this would feel even more real to me.

"Are you always this impatient?" I joked, hoping he realized I wasn't being serious.

"He is," Elliott answered.

"Oh great. Now I won't just have my best friend busting my balls, I'm gonna have his husband doing it too," Vaughn replied, making the rest of the tension ease out of my body.

"What's the point in being married if we don't get to gang up on people together?"

Vaughn grinned at my response, and I didn't have to look at Elliott to know he was doing the same. Strangely, I was at this weird point where I felt like I could read him most of the time, could tell when he was annoyed or having a good day. I guessed it was just a part of being around someone so much.

"Best. Husband. Ever," Elliott said. "Hottest too."

Yep, there it went. My face got hot...but in a good way. I fucking loved this, loved that he would say that about me to his best friend.

"He likes that," Vaughn noticed.

"He does and he's mine," Elliott warned.

"I would never... Unless the two of you wanted...?"

"We don't." Elliott brushed his thumb over my hand where he held it.

"Didn't you go on a date once and they were in a cuckold relationship?" Vaughn asked me. "I was dying when you told that story on *The Vers*—not that there's anything wrong with cuckolding, but..."

"Surprise cuckolding shouldn't be a thing! He should have told me. Oh my God! The boyfriend came in while my date was fucking me, and he kept saying that his boyfriend was never going to get his cock again. I don't kink-shame, whatever floats your boat, but all parties should consent, and I hadn't agreed to being watched. I grabbed my shit and ran out of there. The second I got into the hallway in their building, I ran into an ex-boyfriend who must have moved there. He had his new partner with him. I was half naked. It was a disaster."

We all laughed.

"Jesus, beautiful. You really had some bad dates," Elliott said.

"I have the worst luck with men."

"Not anymore." He winked.

*It's not real, it's not real, it's not real.*

But the ice was effectively broken. We spent the rest of the night laughing and talking with Vaughn, whom I really did like. It was a little uncomfortable that he'd slept with my husband, but such is life.

When Vaughn said goodbye, I was surprised he hugged me. "I've never seen him like this. Thank you," he said softly.

I didn't know how to respond to that, but my heart beat harder. My chest felt like there wasn't as much space in it as there had been before.

*Nooooo. No, no, no, no.* I couldn't do this. I couldn't fall for Elliott. I couldn't fall for my husband.

*It's not real, it's not real, it's not real.*

Vaughn pulled away, ribbing Elliott the way my friends and I did, giving me an excuse not to respond.

After he left, Elliott kissed me, and everything else melted away. He took me upstairs and did as he'd promised—made my ass his.

"Stay," he whispered afterward, making my breath hitch

and my heart feel like it grew even more.

"I can't. I...I can't."

When I was alone in my bed, I wished I'd had the balls to stay with him.

★ ★ ★

*"HOW LONG SHOULD you wait from first date to spending your first night together?"* I read the question from a listener.

All four of us were quiet for a moment as we looked at each other.

"Shut up. Read the real question," Corbin said, and I swear I had to bite my cheek to keep from laughing.

"You're a fool," Marcus told him. "That is the real question."

"I knew that. I was kidding." Corbin mouthed to us, *"Totally didn't know that was the real question!"*

My stomach cramped, I fought so hard to hold back my chuckling. Jesus, leave it to Corb, but also, how in the hell were we supposed to answer that?

Declan said, "I don't think that's something anyone can answer for another person. It all depends on what the two—"

"Or more," Marcus interrupted.

"Yeah, or more. It really depends on what the people on the date want."

"I agree," I added. "There's nothing wrong with having sex on the first date. It doesn't mean the relationship can't turn into more, if that's what you're after."

Corbin said, "You also shouldn't feel forced to fuck just because it's a thing that happens a lot. Sex is great, but that doesn't mean everyone wants to have it, or wants to have it on the first date."

"Who are you and what did you do with Corbin?" Declan

asked playfully.

"I'm deep. I know that just because I like to hook up and have no issues with sex, even with men I don't know, and despite liking to tease you guys, not everyone is the same." Corbin gave Declan a look that said, *What's up now?* like he was proud of his answer and showed Declan how serious he could be.

Marcus put an arm around Corbin, then ruffled his hair. "You're all right sometimes, you know that?"

"I'm incredible all the time," Corbin responded.

"And now your annoying ass ruined it," Marcus grumbled but still tugged Corbin closer, kissing his temple. "Love you, kid."

"Aww! Marcus just got sweet!" I teased. "*Vers* listeners, you know how we love it when that happens. Marcus has the biggest heart of us all, but he also tries to hide it the most."

"*Buzz, buzz*...bad reception. Oops, the podcast broke," Marcus joked, resulting in all of us laughing. "That was my one sweet thing for the month. Now, can we all forget that happened? Who's reading the next question?"

For once, we didn't continue to tease each other, and Corbin took the tablet from me to read the next listener question. "*I'm dating this guy I really like. This is a first for me. What's your idea of a perfect date?*"

Three sets of eyes turned my direction. "What? I'm the only one who can answer this? I'm sure Dec has some ideas since he's got a swoony boyfriend." Sebastian was there with us at Marcus's, but he was in the living room, working on his screenplay while we were recording.

Dec grinned. "Yeah, but you're the romantic, babe. This one's on you."

"I hate you." But really, I loved this. No way could I show I loved it, though. "I don't know... It all depends on the person. You have to think about who you're dating and what they like. Elliott took me on a perfect date a few weeks ago where he basically just spoiled me the whole time. It might sound ridiculous, and maybe a little selfish for me to say, but it feels really fucking good. And he knows I think it feels really fucking good, so that's what he did. It meant a lot to me because I knew he'd put thought into what he knew would make me happy. Sometimes it matters less what you do than how you do it…I mean, in general, Elliott is really good at dates. Sometimes we don't even do much, but it's fun and romantic just because we enjoy each other's company and…" Oh shit. *Oh shit!* What the fuck was I saying, and why was all of it about Elliott?

*Abort! Abort! Abort!*

But if I stopped now, the guys would know something was up. I could do this. I could find a way to play it off. I could keep this going and pretend it was all in the plan, and then I'd freak out later. "Also, Elliott mentioned once that he loves Cuban desserts, so I made a bunch of them. And though we didn't do anything other than watch movies all night and stuff our faces, I could tell how much it meant to him. So I guess my answer would be that the perfect date is whatever is perfect for the person you're dating."

No one said anything for a minute, all of them watching me—Corbin with mischief, Declan with concern, and Marcus with curiosity.

I cleared my throat. "Okay, come on. I can't be the only one to answer this question."

They managed to snap themselves out of it. Marcus went on about our sponsors and new products, promoted our merch, and then we ended the show.

"I did that on purpose." I stood and walked out of the room, hoping this conversation would be over. They all followed me, stumbling over each other.

"What's going on?" Sebastian asked when we got to the living room.

Corbin said, "Someone asked about dates, and Parker rambled on about how perfect Elliott is and how much he spoils him. It made my heart go pitter-patter. That's never happened before, so I'm curious."

"Your heart didn't pitter-patter!" I said too loudly.

"How do you know? It's not your heart."

"Um...can we get on topic here?" Declan interrupted. "Do you have feelings for Elliott?"

"No! No. Totally not. I said I wasn't going to do that. I told you guys we are dating, and it's not like I could have answered that question about anyone else, seeing as I'm married to the guy and everyone thinks it's for real."

"The marriage is, legally speaking," Marcus said.

"Not helping," I told my friend. "I don't *like* Elliott. Not that way." But holy shit, it was getting hard to breathe because I hadn't done that on purpose.

"Maybe this is a good thing," Sebastian said. "Think how cool a love story that would be: The Romantic, who had bad luck with men before, finds his own happily ever after *after* accidentally getting married. That's like a romance novel. The story practically writes itself."

"Thank you!" I said before realizing what I was saying. "I mean, not thank you because I like Elliott or I think it's real, but thank you because it's not a big deal." Though he hadn't said that, had he? I fell onto the couch. "Oh God. What if I like Elliott? What is wrong with me? Why am I so broken?"

"Babe..." Declan sat beside me. I covered my face, refusing to look at him. "Babe," he said again.

"Sebastian, control your man," I said from beneath my hands.

Sebastian chuckled. "He might be my man, but he's your best friend and this has nothing to do with me."

I spread two fingers and peeked through them. "Traitor!"

Bastian smiled at me. He was great and fit in with us so well.

Declan rubbed my back. "You're not broken. You have a big heart with a lot of love to give. And when you find the right person, they're going to be so fucking lucky to be on the receiving end of that. If you fall for him, I just don't want you to get hurt."

"Believe me, I don't want to get hurt either." I sat up straighter, determined not to let this happen. "I won't. It's sex and dates and…marriage, but that last one is beside the point. I'm not going to let my heart get involved." Even to my own ears, I sounded uncertain.

"Maybe you should trust yourself," Marcus said.

"Huh?" Why the fuck would I do that? I made terrible decisions.

"I'm not saying I trust Elliott, but I do trust you. If you like him, maybe he deserves it. You've never had anyone plan a whole date around spoiling your ass before."

"Everyone wants to fuck me," I said, trying to turn it into a joke, like Marcus was talking about spoiling me by treating my hole real nice.

"I'm not playin'," Marcus replied. "I'm just saying, protect yourself. Sebastian is right. Maybe this is more than you thought."

I…was at a loss for words. That wasn't typically how Marcus spoke. He sure as shit wasn't a cheerleader for relationships and feelings. Still, I couldn't let myself consider what he was saying. It was a recipe for disaster, and I was tired of being a walking mess when it came to relationships.

"I don't like him that way," I assured the group.

Now I just had to make myself believe it.

# CHAPTER TWENTY-ONE
## *Elliott*

"ELLIOTT! THERE'S A stain on my shirt. How in the fuck is there a stain on my shirt! Oh shit. Never mind. It's a shadow."

I laughed, walking into the closet where Parker was standing in a pink jockstrap while he slid his white shirt on. "You're freaking out."

"I am not."

"You thought a shadow was a stain."

"I was testing you!" He began buttoning.

Fuck, he was really sexy…and sweet. I got closer to him, swatted his hands away, and began helping with his shirt because I enjoyed doing things like this for him.

"This is our first big event as husbands, Elliott. A lot of really important people are going to be there, and this is so important to Cat. I just don't want anything to go wrong."

I kissed the tip of his nose. "It won't."

"There will literally be senators there!"

"Only one. He and Dad are friends. But they're people too. Tonight is about helping people. That's all that matters. Well, that and showing off my sexy husband."

"Oh."

"Praise slut." I swatted his ass. "As much as I'm going to miss the view, you should put your slacks on."

Parker had been a little subdued lately. It started not long after Vaughn came over. Sometimes he would be fine, laughing and talking and cuddling with me, and then it would be like he wasn't sure if he should do that and would suddenly shut down and pull away. I had no idea what had caused the change, but I didn't fucking like it. I wanted my husband back. And I was getting way too comfortable using that word…

"I could fake sick."

"You love this kind of thing."

"I really wish you hadn't listened to old episodes of *The Vers*."

"I didn't hear that on *The Vers*. You mentioned it once." I made it a point not to listen to the podcast anymore, not after the Declan-versus-Marcus debate. All that shit would do was get into my head, so I'd made the decision to stay away from it.

"Oh," he said again, then smiled.

"Always love being the center of attention." I kissed him. "Finish getting dressed, beautiful. We gotta go soon."

"You're good at that—making me feel listened to. Most men I've dated haven't been this way."

I winked. "Other men aren't as good as me."

"There's the cocky husband I know and…know."

"Know and know?"

"Go away so I can get dressed!" He pushed me out of the closet.

I went easily, laughing.

A half hour later we were in my car, driving to the hotel where the event was being held.

Parker went back and forth between fidgeting and texting on his phone. "Who are you talking to?"

"Declan. He's kinda my person. He helps with stuff like

this." *I'm not jealous, I'm not jealous, I'm not jealous.* "Not like you do. It's different."

Was he saying I helped too? I *knew* this, so why did I suddenly feel too hot?

My stupid, annoying heart got that twitchy feeling again. God, this was torture. Why did something so small make me feel like I was going to dissolve into mush?

"What's wrong?"

"Nothing. I'm here for you, ya know? Whatever you need tonight, I want to help too."

Even without looking, I knew he was smiling. "You're a good man. I don't think I tell you that enough."

"You should tell me again...and again and again and again," I joked. Kind of. I loved hearing it.

He laughed. "Never." Then more softly, "You're a good man."

"So are you, gorgeous."

"Obviously."

"Who's the cocky one now?"

"Still you. Always you." But then Parker put his phone away, reached over, and placed his hand on my thigh.

It felt much more special than it should.

★ ★ ★

"MR. AND MRS. Leigh, this is my husband, Parker." They were about ten years older than my parents, and not our favorite people. Honestly, they were a bit judgy, but they were very wealthy philanthropists who donated tons of money. As much as it sucked, sometimes you had to play the game.

"It's so nice to meet you." Parker held out his hand, shaking each of theirs. I'd been introducing him this way all night. I couldn't even remember how many times I'd called him my husband.

"It's so nice to meet you too," Mary Leigh said. "We couldn't believe the news when we heard it. We never thought Elliott would settle down." Unfortunately, that was something we'd heard often tonight. I was pretty sure everyone at the event had made it their life's mission to make Parker want to divorce me, or at least never to trust me.

"So I've heard," Parker snipped, which was different from how he'd responded before. Uh-oh. My hand was at the small of his back, and I brushed against it with my thumb, as Parker said, "Though for the life of me, I can't understand why everyone is telling me this. My guess is he'd never settled down because he hadn't met me yet. And now he's mine."

I smiled a ridiculously and likely comically large smile. The Leighs' mouths dropped open. I probably shouldn't enjoy this as much as I did, but that ship had sailed. "Yes, I am," I replied, glancing at Parker in time to see that he looked like he might get sick. That put a bit of a ding in my excitement.

It was awkward after, and the Leighs didn't stay long, making their excuses. The second they were gone, Parker rushed out, "Oh my God. I'm so sorry! Was that rude? I didn't mean it to be, but Jesus, how many times do people have to say that to us? Yes, I get it, no one thinks this is real, but you're my husband. Can't they have a little respect?" I laughed—not the best reaction, which was proven when Parker gave me his angry scowl. "Be nice to me!"

I wrapped my arms around him and pulled him close. "I'm sorry. I like seeing you get defensive on our behalf. It's giving me a bit of a chub if I'm being honest."

"Don't get hard," he said quietly. "We're at your mom's charity event!"

"I can't help it. You get inside my head, beautiful. And I like hearing you call me yours."

He stiffened against me but didn't pull back or let go. "Your mom is going to hate me."

"My mom hates *them*. She's not going to hate you." I had to admit, I loved that he cared. "In fact, she might like you more than she does me."

"No. She adores you. It's so sweet. Every time she texts me, we end up talking about how wonderful you are—well, let me rephrase. *She* talks about how wonderful you are while I pretend not to gag."

I chuckled, running my hands up and down his back. Parker wrapped his around my neck, and we rocked together to the music in the background. "She adores you too."

His eyes darted away. His voice was low when he asked, "Do you think she'll still like me when we divorce? I mean, that's probably a stupid question. Why would she even have anything to do with me?"

God, he was so fucking sweet. He had this big, throbbing heart that just longed to be loved. "Hey," I said. When he didn't look at me, I hooked my thumb beneath his chin and tilted his head up. "She's not the type of person who will cut ties with you. We'll still be friends when this is over, and she'll still adore you. I promise, beautiful. I don't think you realize how special you are."

The past four months had flown by. We only had two more before Parker would be off searching for the man who would really sweep him off his feet, the man he would love and want his happily ever after with.

"Can I tell you a secret?" Parker asked, resting his cheek against my heart.

"You can tell me anything." I wanted him to tell me everything, wanted to be that person for him.

"I didn't want to let myself see that you're special, but how could I not?"

My heart thumped against my chest, against his cheek, and I wondered if he could feel it. "Oh, beautiful, you ain't seen nothing yet. Wait until I really turn on the charm."

He laughed, his body vibrating against mine, and eventually we were both doing the same.

We held hands the rest of the night. Every time I saw Mom or Dad, they would smile. Everyone else, as if knowing not to fuck with us, kept to themselves any snide comments.

And the way he held on to me, laughed with me and touched me…it almost felt like he wanted this to be real.

# CHAPTER TWENTY-TWO
## *Parker*

THIS NIGHT HAD felt like a dream—being with Elliott, holding Elliott's hand, Elliott telling everyone I was his husband; dancing with him and talking and laughing with his parents like we were a real family. This was exactly what I'd imagined being married would be like—having my person, growing my family.

And it was going to end in two months. My marriage came with an expiration date because of my bad decision.

Elliott was Elliott: funny and annoyingly charming, but I was just... I felt really fucking sad, and I hated that.

I figured he wanted to have sex, but I wasn't sure I was in the mood, so when we got home, before he could bring it up, I said, "I'm gonna take a shower and hit the sack."

He frowned, rubbed a hand over his scruff. "Oh. Okay. Good night, beautiful." And then he kissed me on the cheek like this was a first date or something. It made my pulse go crazy, and I had to fight to slow it down.

I spent too long in the shower, letting the hot water rain over my body, and all I could think about was Elliott. My dick betrayed me too because it was hard and aching. It was a lot easier to focus on that than the tapestry of confused feelings weaving together in my chest.

Elliott made me feel beautiful and strong. Like he enjoyed

my company. Like I wasn't just a warm mouth or someone to pass the time with. But how could I trust myself when it came to my heart when it had played tricks on me before? The truth was, in two short months, Elliott and I were going to file for an amicable divorce, and then he'd have his freedom back.

But right now? Right now Elliott was my husband, and I wanted my husband tonight.

I turned off the shower, then almost slipped while getting out. I couldn't help laughing at myself, at how urgent I felt while drying off, at how my whole body tingled and felt alive at just the thought of going to Elliott's room and telling him I wanted him.

He loved me in jocks, and I'd always had a fetish for wearing them myself. I found the blue ones that matched my eyes, stomach nervous for reasons I refused to think about or let slow me down.

His door was ajar. I knocked, then slid it open. Elliott was standing in his room, with a towel around his waist while drying his hair. His gaze shot to mine, and damned if my knees didn't go weak. He was so fucking gorgeous—short, messy hair, the fur on his chest… I loved the way it felt against my skin and how his stubble scratched when he kissed me.

"Hi," I said dumbly.

"I was trying to talk myself out of going to your room."

"I didn't try," I replied, and he grinned.

"Good." He tossed the towel he'd been using on his hair. "Come here, gorgeous. Let me see that beautiful body of yours." I went, feeling like I was floating. When I stopped in front of him, Elliott brushed his thumbs over my nipples, making me hiss. "I won't ever get enough of this body. Turn around. Let me see my favorite ass."

I did as he said, goose bumps running the length of me.

"Fuck...look at these curves...so round and perfect."

My skin heated as he rubbed his hands over my ass cheeks, spreading them open while he kissed his way down my spine...one knot, then the next and the next. I trembled; I needed him so fucking bad.

Elliott kept going until he got to the band of my jock, which he bit, pulling it and then letting go so it popped against my skin. "Fuuuuuck." Why did that feel so amazing?

"I love peaches." He kissed each cheek.

I laughed. "You're an idiot."

"You married me," he replied simply, and my stomach tumbled in a way that felt both exciting and scary as hell. "But as I was saying, as much as I fucking love this incredible ass, it's not what I want tonight." Elliott reached around me and palmed my erection that was trying to break free from my jock. "I want this pretty cock. Will you give it to me? Will you fuck me until I come with your dick so goddamned deep inside me? I bet you're so good at fucking. I bet it'll be the best cock I've ever had."

"Yes. God, yes."

Elliott stood up straight, and I turned around and slammed my mouth down on his. He tasted like a mixture of toothpaste and laughter. I wanted to drown in it, in him. I pushed my tongue into his mouth, nipped his lip so he could tell how hungry I was for him.

His large hands held my ass, massaging my cheeks and pulling me closer so we ground against each other. I wanted to taste him everywhere, felt like this was our first time touching rather than just my first time getting a shot at his ass.

My mouth trailed down his neck. I bit his earlobe, shoved his arm up, kissing, licking, and nuzzling one of his soap-scented armpits before moving to the other.

"Fuck, cariño. That's so good," Elliott said with a rough

voice.

I rubbed my face over his pecs and the hair there, sucking his skin into my mouth, hoping to leave a mark on him.

Elliott let me devour him, taste him, mark him, let his rough hair burn against my skin before I dropped down to my knees, watching a bead of precum slide down his thick erection. His hair was thicker at his groin, dark and fucking perfect. I breathed it in, let it leave its scent on my body while I nuzzled into him.

I loved his cock, his big heavy balls full of his load. I licked his sac as his hand fisted in my hair. Elliott used his other hand to hold the base of his erection, pushing it past my lips. "Prettiest thing I've ever seen…you on your knees with my dick in your mouth. Can't tell you how many times I've pictured this in my head, how many times I've lain here thinking about it until I came all over my hand, then licked it up, pretending it was you."

My cock was throbbing. He fucked my mouth for a moment and I took it, wanting more, wanting his cum down my throat. I pulled off instead and said, "Turn around. I want to get your ass ready for me."

He grinned cockily but with something else there too, something that looked like…admiration? Adoration? No, that couldn't be right.

Elliott did as I said, spreading his legs the way I did his cheeks. He looked so tight, with this perfect, wrinkled hole I'd get to taste and then fuck.

I kissed one cheek, then the other before lashing my tongue over his rim. Elliott moaned, a delicious sound I wanted to pull out of him over and over again. I didn't hold back. I pressed my face into his crack and devoured him like I'd been waiting my whole life for this, like I'd been starving for him.

Elliott tasted like soap and man. He pushed back against me, practically rode my face, and damned if it wasn't the best ass I'd ever eaten.

"Jesus, your tongue. Why is everything about you so fucking perfect? Best ass…best mouth…best tongue. I might die when I'm riding your dick."

"Please don't," I said before licking him again. I pulled back, sucked my finger, then watched him open up for me, watched as my digit slid into his hot, tight body.

"Fuck yes," Elliott said while I finger-fucked him, first with one, then two fingers.

My heart slammed against my chest, all the blood in my body rushing to my groin. This was fucking incredible, but it wasn't enough. I needed inside him, needed to feel Elliott…my husband…that way.

"Get on the bed." I smacked his ass before standing and pulling my jock off. My dick had never been so hard, never leaked so much, dying to feel him wrapped around me.

I reached for his nightstand drawer, and just as I pulled it open, Elliott said, "We're both on PrEP, and I've been tested. I'm negative."

"Me too. It was before you that I was tested last, but I haven't been with anyone since."

"I want it if you do…wanna feel you come inside me."

God, could we do this? I'd never done this.

"It's okay if you don't want to. It was just a thought."

It was one of those rare moments when Elliott let his vulnerability show, looking bashful and unsure. I'd wanted what he offered before, but that look only made me crave it more.

"I want my cum in you…" I circled his rim with my thumb. "I want to give it to you…not that it's only for you and I'm not gonna love the fuck out of it, but you know what

I mean."

He chuckled. "I've never..."

"Me neither."

"Let's do it."

I skipped the condom and just grabbed the lube.

Elliott knelt on his hands and knees, his sexy ass in the air. Once my fingers were slick, I pushed two inside him, then worked in three, watching his hole stretch to take me. I loved seeing him like this, loved knowing he was giving himself to me; that Elliott wanted me as bad as I wanted him, even if we weren't permanent.

"Fuck, beautiful. That's enough. Give me that thick cock of yours. I can't wait to have your load inside me."

When he said it like that, how could I refuse?

I positioned him so Elliott lay on his side. I was on my knees, straddling his bottom leg. I lifted the top leg so it went over my shoulder. After pumping lube into my hand, I slicked up my cock while looking down at him, unable to believe we were there, that he was giving me this, how honored I was.

"Do it, cariño. Give me your cock. Never had something so fucking perfect inside me."

Aaaaaaand, that was really hot. I grinned, and it felt like it took over my whole face. No one had ever made me feel like this, like I was so damn important to them. I knew it was just the praise kink he'd discovered in me, but sometimes...sometimes it felt like more than that.

I pressed into him, felt his ass stretch and open up for me. His body was so hot, his hole so tight, his eyes so intense on me that it felt like Elliott could see inside me.

"Fuck yes. So good. I knew your cock would fill me just right."

I loved how much Elliott talked during sex, loved how much it got to me. I pushed into him more, kept going until I was buried deep. I watched him, never took my gaze off his as I pulled back, then thrust forward again. I fucked him like that, savored the feel of his ass squeezing my dick.

Elliott slicked his hand and began to jerk himself off. He told me how good I felt, how much he wanted me, that it had never been like this before, which made me lose my rhythm.

*Sex talk, it's only sex talk.*
*Not real, not real, not real.*

"I can't even explain what it's like being inside you raw… I might never want to stop fucking you," I admitted, feeling freer in this space.

"Who said you have to, beautiful?" he asked, which made my balls draw up. I fought off my orgasm for as long as I could, thrusting into him over and over. The second his hole contracted around me, when Elliott arched, cum spurting up his chest, I gave in, releasing my balls inside him.

I lay between his legs afterward, needing to see. "Can I?" Elliott knew what I wanted, so he rolled to his back and opened his legs. I lifted his balls, saw my cum slide out of his puffy, swollen hole. It was the sexiest thing I'd ever seen. "Can I just lie here for a while?"

"You can lie there all night if you want."

He laid his legs out flat, and I rested my cheek on his thigh, face close to his groin. Elliott played with my hair, the two of us just lying there breathing.

"What does it mean? Cariño?"

"It's comparable to sweetheart or dear one."

That was…special. I didn't know why it felt different from other nicknames.

"The jock in school, the one I used to sneak around with, the one I said was worse than the others? Well, basically he hid me, wanted me to suck him off, made me think he cared about me. It turned out bad, the way shit like that always does. My friends know about that part, but they never knew what he said to me."

"What did he say?" Elliott asked, his voice thick, like the question had been hard for him to ask, maybe because he was afraid of the answer.

I hesitated. "Fuck, this is hard to repeat."

Elliott caressed my cheek, gave me space and time before he said, "You don't have to tell me if you don't want, but you *can* tell me anything."

In that moment, I believed him, and I wanted to share with him, wanted to unburden myself because I knew Elliott would make me feel better. "He told me that no one would ever really want me. That I was nice for a good time, but it wouldn't ever be more than that. He was so hateful. I don't know why he was so mean to me. In some ways, I know it was just him and his issues, but how do you forget those words? How do you *un*hear them? Especially when you've had the kind of luck I have." My face was wet, my eyes blurry. I swiped at the tears. "Shit. I don't know why I said that."

"I really, really want to fucking kill that guy," Elliott said. "Tell me you know he's an idiot piece of shit and doesn't know what the fuck he's talking about."

"Sometimes." Some days were better than others. Being alive was difficult and nuanced.

"You gotta know by now that I'm crazy about you, beautiful."

"I'm crazy about you too. It's annoying as shit."

Elliott chuckled. "You took the words right out of my mouth." He began playing with my hair again. This was so complicated. So maybe we liked each other and were dating, but we didn't love each other...and we were married. We couldn't stay married because there was a crush—and that was only if what Elliott was feeling was even true. Maybe he just liked the sex and would eventually be over it. Regardless, we couldn't keep up this marriage shenanigan forever. "We'll figure it out."

"Okay," I replied.

He pulled me up and kissed me, and I let myself rest on him, lying on his chest.

Elliott said, "Tell me fun stuff, happy stuff about you and your friends...and about you and your family before you lost your mom."

I smiled into his chest, rubbed my cheek on it.

We stayed up all night talking, trading stories, sharing our history. It was one of the best nights of my life.

# CHAPTER TWENTY-THREE
## Elliott

WE SPENT A lot of time together over the next couple of weeks. We didn't talk about what we were doing, and frankly, I tried not to think about it.

Parker moved from where he'd been curled up on the other end of the couch, reading, to lie on top of me. He nuzzled his face into my throat. "I like the way you smell."

"I think that's the cinnamon from your baking." I wrapped my arms around him. He made me feel like a marshmallow. Like I was nothing but gooey softness inside. I was probably supposed to hate it more than I did.

"You don't smell like my apple cake."

"You love apples and anything apple flavored."

He peeked up at me. "How do you know that?"

"You seem to forget I stalked you for a year before I married you." He rolled his eyes but smiled in that sweet way he did. He fucking loved it, and I loved saying and doing things to make him look at me the way he did now. "I pay attention." I fingered a lock of his short hair that rested on his forehead. "I like knowing stuff about you, filing it away so I can find new ways to do nice things for you." It made me feel good, like nothing in my life ever had. There was a whole lot I enjoyed before Parker, but it hadn't made me feel the way he did.

"You really like spoiling your lovers, don't you?"

I shook my head. "I like spoiling *you*. This is very much a Parker thing."

Something in his body language changed, like a stiffness settled into his bones. Small worry lines formed around his eyes.

"Okay...call me crazy, but that should have scored me some points. That was really fucking sweet and romantic. You like that romantic shit. What's wrong?" I slid my hand down to his bare ass. He was only wearing one of his jocks, and it was nearly impossible not to touch him.

"Don't hurt me, Elliott."

I didn't respond straight away because I wasn't sure what I could say. Hurting Parker was the last thing I would ever want to do. I'd work my ass off to make sure that never happened, but didn't he know I was scared too? That I didn't want to be hurt either? And that I had no idea what the fuck I was doing?

"I'm not feeling real confident with the delay here," he said, and damned if that didn't make me smile.

"What would a proper romance hero say? *Your wish is my command?*"

"I read gay romance, so you're supposed to be like, *I would burn down the whole fucking world for you!* And then we'd screw each other for the rest of the day."

I grinned. "I'd burn down the world for you, husband. Now come here so I can fuck that pretty hole."

"Swoon!" he replied, then let me do exactly as I'd said, over the back of the couch and minus the rubbers, which we were no longer using.

We were sweaty and breathing heavy afterward, and I kissed his throat and said, "I don't ever want to hurt you." *Don't hurt me either. Say it. Why couldn't I say it?*

"Thank you for not making promises you can't keep.

None of us can."

"I'm very good at husbanding."

"I'll give you an eight out of ten," he joked.

"Lies." I kissed him. "Let's take a shower."

When I tried to walk toward the stairs, Parker held me back. "Tomorrow there's a party at Sebastian and Declan's. Dec doesn't really do parties, but Bastian likes that kind of thing, so Declan planned it for him. Bastian will be starting promo soon for the last movie he shot, *Bound and Determined*. They're having a get-together at their place. I know it's last minute, but would you want to go with me?"

I smiled.

"What?"

"You really do like me. You're asking me to meet your friends."

"Ew. Gross. I do not."

"*Parker has a crush on me, Parker has a crush on me,*" I sang playfully.

"If I did before, I don't now." He smiled, but then his gaze darted away. "Go with me."

"I would love to accompany you to the ball."

"You're doing fairy tales again. Who knew romance hero was so hard?"

I tried to look smoldering when I replied, "There's nowhere I wouldn't follow you…"

"Okay, now you really sound like a stalker."

"Yes, Parker. I'd love to go with you. It might be hard to keep my hands off you all night, though." I grabbed his ass, slid my finger into his crease, and felt my load there.

"Totally just nailed the romance hero," Parker replied with a laugh. I couldn't help doing the same.

★ ★ ★

"I'M GOING TO Sebastian Cole's house today," I said quietly through the phone while Parker was in the shower. I'd known for more than twenty-four hours, yet it was only now sinking in.

"Sucks to be you. If you don't wanna go, I'll take one for the team," Vaughn replied.

"You're the worst best friend ever."

"Would you rather I told you that hanging out at a celebrity's house isn't really a big deal for you, and what you're really freaking out over is the fact that the husband you're not supposed to be madly in love with but are, asked you to spend time with his people? I mean, I can say that if you want."

"I... That's not what this is about." Was it? Sure, I'd introduced Parker to Vaughn ages ago and hoped he would do the same for me, but that wasn't why my pulse was skyrocketing. Said pulse went faster. "Oh shit." That's totally why I was stressing out. "I'm not in love with him." I was in *deep like*, but I'd keep that to myself.

"Yeah, sure, whatever. You're on lockdown. You're the old ball and chain. You're—"

"Annoyed with you. Can you please shut up?"

Vaughn laughed. "It'll be fine. They'll love you. Everyone does."

It was not a fun time that I'd actually needed to hear that. Feelings screwed with everything. "Thanks, man." I turned around and saw Parker standing in my bedroom doorway. "Gotta go. I'll talk to you soon."

We ended the call, Parker standing there watching me for a moment. He had an unreadable look on his face, and honestly, I had a sinking feeling he was going to call it off and tell me never mind, but instead, he said, "We should go."

"Okay, but first, can I tell you how hot you look?" Because he did, he always did. He'd chosen my favorite jeans and a light-purple Henley that looked good against his skin. I was pretty sure the shirt had been in a ball on the floor, but he must've thrown it in the dryer to get the wrinkles out. It was clean, but Parker was still messy, so clothes ended up everywhere.

"Of course you can," he replied cheekily.

I went to him, letting my gaze travel the length of his body. "You look so fucking hot, cariño. It really is going to be hard for me to keep my hands off you tonight. I love that I'll be there with the sexiest man in the room."

He bit his bottom lip, then leaned in and kissed me. He still didn't look like himself. I imagined he was unsure about my meeting his friends. It was a big step. But then the uncertain look melted away and he turned flirty. "I think I'm gonna be the one with the sexiest man in the room."

"We'll be the hottest couple."

"I like the sound of that."

We took Parker's car to Sebastian's place. I wasn't one to get impressed easily, but I had to admit, it was kinda cool. He lived in a Mediterranean-style home in the North of Montana neighborhood. There was a gate with an intercom, which Parker pulled up to.

"Hello?" a voice said when Park pressed a button. I was pretty sure it was Declan.

"Let us in, dumbass."

"What's the magic word?" another voice added.

"Shut up, Corbin," Parker and Declan said in unison.

I laughed.

"Wait," Corbin said. "Who is that? Is Parker's husband here? Dude, I watched you—" The intercom shut off, and the door opened.

"He watched me what?" I cocked a brow.

"Exactly what you're thinking. He googled you after we

got married. I'm sorry. He doesn't mean any harm. He's just…Corb."

It was clear in the way he spoke about him that Parker loved Corbin. He loved all of them. "I listened to some of *The Vers*, so I know. Feels like a bit of an act sometimes with him."

"He's deeper than most people take the time to see…but I'm also a little annoyed that he saw you naked."

I laughed, my heart swelling. "I like jealous husbands."

"You're getting the hang of this romance-hero thing!"

We laughed together. He was so fucking great.

There were cars already there. He parked, and we headed for the house. Sebastian Cole answered the door, which totally blew my mind.

"Hey, you," he said, giving Parker a hug. His brown curls were styled and neat.

"Elliott, it's good to meet you. I didn't get to talk to you in Vegas." Sebastian shook my hand.

"That's because my husband hated me then," I joked, just as Declan approached.

"You probably shouldn't have married him, then," Declan said.

"Dec," both Parker and Sebastian said.

"I'm being good." He leaned in and kissed Parker's cheek. "Hey, babe."

That jealousy I'd just mentioned twisted my gut. I knew they didn't have feelings for each other, but…yeah, he didn't like me and clearly didn't want me with Parker.

When Declan pulled back, he wrapped his arms around Sebastian from behind. Sebastian nuzzled their faces together, and damned if my jealousy didn't grow. They were comforting each other, having a silent conversation, and fuck if I didn't want that with Parker.

"So, are you going to let us in or what?" Parker asked.

They stepped aside. The other *Vers* guys were in the living room, along with a few people I didn't recognize.

"Jesus, Declan. Is everyone you hang out with hot?" a younger twink with short, dark hair and warm brown skin asked. He looked in his midtwenties. His tee was so tight, I could tell his nipples were pierced, and he had a short, groomed goatee around his mouth and along his chin.

"That's Parker's husband," Declan said at the same time with Parker's, "He's my husband." I smiled hearing it from him and appreciated that even though Declan wasn't sure what he thought about me, he was supporting us.

"I'm just stating a fact," the guy told Declan. "Your boyfriend is hot too." Then to me, "Hey. I'm Kai. I work at Declan's bar. What are your intentions with Declan's best friend?"

I laughed. The kid was funny. Not that he was a kid.

"I already put a ring on it. Doesn't that tell you what you need to know?"

"Good point." He turned to Parker. "He's gorgeous, but the important thing here is Marcus. I want him. Declan won't help, so I'm coming to you."

Parker's mouth dropped open, but before he could reply, the man in question approached.

"Hey, baby. Miss me?" Kai winked at him.

"You're playing with fire, little one. Be careful you don't get burned," Marcus warned, his voice dark and smoky.

Kai fanned himself.

Declan groaned. "Please stop. What's happening here? Don't flirt with my friends." Then to Marcus, "Don't flirt with my employees."

"You act like this is a surprise," Kai said.

I would definitely fit in with these people if they allowed it. On instinct, I reached over and interlaced my fingers with

Parker's. His head snapped up, eyes trained on me. I shrugged, and damned if he didn't smile.

And he didn't let go.

Corbin joined us a few minutes later, jumping in and ribbing the guys. It was something they did a lot, and when Marcus joked around with Parker, I wrapped my arms around him and playfully said, "Leave my husband out of it. I got your back, beautiful."

What I didn't expect was the silence that immediately followed. There were other people at the house, and I was sure they still spoke and time moved on in the background, but Parker's friends were silent. Parker's spine was stiff as he buried his face in my pec.

"I have a feeling something's going on that I missed," Kai's voice pierced the silence.

It seemed to be the icebreaker people needed.

Corbin let out a long, "*Awwww!*"

Sebastian freaking Cole, who I still couldn't believe was standing close to me, nudged Declan. "Why don't you defend my honor like that?"

"I do," Declan replied, pulling Sebastian close, but his gaze snagged on me, like he couldn't look away if he tried. It wasn't an angry expression; it was a curious one, like he was trying to figure me out.

"I'm jealous," Corbin said. "Love me until my date arrives. I feel so left out." He hugged Marcus.

He'd spoken teasingly, but Marcus kissed his head. "You know I love you, kid."

"Um...can I squeeze in the middle of you two?" Kai asked, and another round of laughter broke out.

We chatted for a while. The whole time, I held Parker's hand or kept mine at the small of his back. I liked touching him, wanted him to know I was close and that I liked everyone there to know he was mine. It was an unexpected rush I knew he felt too.

Eventually, one by one, they began to trickle away. Parker said he had to go to the restroom but looked concerned about leaving me. "I'll be fine. I'll do some exploring. I might go outside for some fresh air. Just hurry your gorgeous ass back to me," I teased.

He rolled his eyes, then kissed me before sneaking away.

I made my way through the living room and went out the French back doors. There was a pool with a slide, an outdoor kitchen, a workout area, and basically everything you could ever need back there.

So far, today had gone better than expected. Marcus and Corbin had both spent some time talking to me. They were all even funnier in person than on *The Vers*.

When I heard the door open behind me, I assumed it was Parker, but looked back to see Sebastian.

"Needed to breathe a little?" he asked, coming to stand beside me by the pool.

"Yeah, Parker had to use the restroom, and I figured he might want some time with his friends. Is it okay to admit I'm freaking out talking to you?"

He chuckled, then sat down on one of the chairs. I did the same.

"No need to be. I'm just me." We were both quiet for a moment, and then Sebastian said, "Their friendship is incredible, isn't it? They all love each other so much. I was a little jealous at first."

"Can't say I blame you, but hey, at least Declan's best friend didn't hate you." It struck me that in my case, said best friend was Sebastian's boyfriend. "Shit. Sorry. Can we forget I said that?"

"Declan doesn't hate you. He's protective of Parker. They

have a special bond. Parker has been there for Dec in more ways than I can say."

Tension I didn't realize I'd been carrying drained from my chest. "You don't think Declan hates me?"

"I know he doesn't." He picked at the arm of the Adirondack chair. "You care about Parker."

"Yes," I answered honestly.

"You really want to be with him."

"He's my husband."

"Yes, but you know that's not what I mean."

I fell back against the chair and groaned. "Yes. God yes. This is so weird for me. I've never wanted more from someone before. I'm scared it's a fluke, that I'll fuck up and hurt him. I'm scared he doesn't want me. I'm freaked out more than I've ever been in my life. This conversation is proof. I'm talking to Sebastian Cole about all my insecurities about my husband."

He laughed. "I get it. Loving someone is hard and frightening. So many things can go wrong…"

"Is this supposed to help?"

He smiled. "But so many things can go right too. The most important question is whether he's worth it. If he is, that's all that matters."

And he was. So fucking worth it. Despite what I'd said to Vaughn on the phone earlier, I wasn't even sure I wanted to argue about Sebastian's use of the word *love* because…because I knew I loved Parker. And strangely, that made everything easier, made some of the fear lessen. Sebastian shouldn't be the first person I told, though. Instead, I asked, "Does it get easier?"

"Yeah, in a lot of ways, but it's life, so there's always something to stress about. I'll be leaving in a few weeks to promote *Bound and Determined*. It'll be the first time I'm away from Declan. He's coming with me to red-carpet premieres, but I know he doesn't like things like that. I'm worried he'll be miserable or change his mind about me. Deep down, I know he loves me and he won't, but...love is hard. Beautiful and incredible, but hard."

"Still not feeling better."

"But then there are those moments when he just looks at you, or you make him laugh, or he whispers in your ear or does something nice for you, and they feel like your whole reason for being alive. They inspire you. I just finished writing my first screenplay, and the only reason I even had the balls to write it is because of Declan. Really, that's all that matters. Those times are worth the worries because the prize is them."

Sebastian's words fit inside me, helped break down my fears.

"If you're worried about the Beach Bums, they'll love you because Parker does. That's how they work."

Yeah, but that was him assuming Parker had feelings for me.

"Thank you...for this. Talking to me."

"No worries. We'll trade cell numbers."

"I'd like that." I already knew I wanted to be part of Parker's life, but talking to Sebastian made me realize how much I wanted to be a part of every aspect of his life.

# CHAPTER TWENTY-FOUR
## *Parker*

***Elliott:*** **Do you wanna hear the craziest shit?**

I smiled at the midmorning text. We were both at work, but messaging throughout the day was something we'd been doing for a while now.

***Me:*** **Of course. Work drama?**

***Elliott:*** **LOL. No. Just something I discovered today, and I thought you would get a kick out of it. So...I was talking to this guy at work. I can't even remember how we got on the subject, but did you know that when you say frown, to people in other countries that's something you do with your forehead? WTF? I don't get it. How do you frown with your forehead?**

The funny thing was, I could imagine the scandalized look on Elliott's face as he was texting me this. And he was correct in that I did, in fact, find this interesting.

***Me:*** **I don't get it either... What's a forehead frown?**

***Elliott:*** **I think when you furrow your brows? I have no idea. I'm going to ask him.**

***Me:*** **And also, what about the saying "turn that frown upside down"? Do they turn their head upside down? I'm sooooo confused!**

***Elliott:*** **Same! Maybe they don't use that expression? I'll ask those questions and get back to you.**

Okay, so our conversation was slightly adorable. It definitely wasn't something I would have ever thought Elliott would say to me before we started all this.

**Elliott: Funny thing...he's texting his friends and having the same conversation. They're all shocked that we think you frown with your mouth. They're just as confused as we are.**

**Me: LOL. That makes sense. It depends on what you've grown up knowing. Neither side is right, but it's still weird.**

We messaged throughout the day. We'd been ignoring the fact that our time was officially coming to an end soon. Elliott and I were together, we liked each other, but marriage wasn't about like; it was about love. I'd heard him tell Vaughn on the phone that he wasn't in love with me.

And...I wanted my husband to love me. That was the dream, not just a marriage for the sake of being married.

But the thought of walking away... It made my throat feel like it was tightening and made my stomach cramp. Elliott made me feel...fuck, he made me *feel* loved. And I wanted to do the same for him.

And I knew just the person to ask.

**Hey, Cat. I hope I'm not bothering you.**
**You're my son-in-law. You're never bothering me.**

My heart squeezed at those words. I wanted to lock them inside me, hold them there so I would always remember what this moment felt like.

*We're supposed to get divorced soon...*

**Thank you... I... Thank you.**

Ugh. I was an idiot. Why did I type the exact words that came to mind? I could have at least tried to make it sound like I wasn't being strange.

I dropped my phone when it rang, Cat's name on the screen. Why was she calling me? Fumbling with it, I plucked the cell from the counter. "Hello?"

"What's wrong?" she asked.

Oh God. *Was* something wrong? I was all up in my head today for whatever reason. Okay, so I knew the reason, but I didn't want to admit it out loud, afraid saying it would jinx me and I'd lose it. Once I admitted how I maybe felt, it was all over for me. "Nothing. Just one of those days. Listen…I want to do something special for Elliott. He's always so good to me." To the point I wasn't sure I deserved him, but I kept that tidbit to myself. "Do you have any ideas?"

But as soon as I asked the question, I didn't need her thoughts. The perfect idea hit me, and I knew it was something Elliott would love.

"Actually, I think I know what I want to do."

"I'm all ears," Cat replied.

As I told her what I wanted to do for Elliott, I forgot that this wasn't real—I felt as though Elliott and I got married because we were in love…that our time wasn't running short.

★ ★ ★

"ELLIOTT…" I KISSED his pec, his throat, rubbed my cheek against the hair on his chest. "Wake up, Elliott."

He groaned before wrapping his arms around me. "Is it morning already? Someone was a very good boy last night…keeping me up doing all sorts of dirty things." His voice was thick with sleep, raspy and sexy.

"Yes, it's morning. You can stay in bed if you want, but if you do, you won't get my surprise for you."

His eyes jerked open, because of course they did. "Surprise?"

I laughed. "I might be a praise slut, but you're totally an attention slut. And yes, I was going to keep it a secret, but then you'd have to be blindfolded the whole way."

He cocked a brow. "The whole way? Color me intrigued."

"I worked it out at Beach Buns so I'm off today and tomorrow. It's only a short trip, but we're going to spend the night in a cabin in Big Bear—and I don't like wilderness, so you're welcome."

He smiled so big, it took over his face. There was something special about seeing a man like Elliott so happy and knowing I was the one who gave it to him. There was nothing like it. I would miss this, miss seeing how joyful he could be over the smallest things.

"You're taking me to Big Bear?"

"Yep."

"God, you're the best." He flipped us so he was lying on top of me.

He buried his face in my throat, kissing me before his hands slid beneath my arms and… "Oh my God. Stop!" I laughed, trying to wiggle out from beneath him as Elliott tickled me. "I hate you. I take it back. We're not going anywhere."

He was laughing too, the two of us wrestling around on the bed before Elliott suddenly stopped, looking down at me, his brown eyes dark and intense. "Thank you for this. I love it."

"But we haven't gone yet."

"I still love it. It'll be nice to have some time together before…"

Before this ended. Before we went our separate ways. Would we go our separate ways? Would we still date? Had he gotten his fill and it was time to move on?

*Ask him. Ask Elliott what he wants.*

The thought of putting myself out there locked my throat tight. My gut sank. My chest felt heavy. When he didn't say anything else, I forced myself to nod, trying to ignore the taste of bile in my throat. "Yeah, it'll be nice."

But really, it hurt already. I couldn't imagine how it would feel when we walked away.

# CHAPTER TWENTY-FIVE
## *Elliott*

WE SHOWERED TOGETHER, packed a small bag, jumped into Parker's car, and then were on our way to Big Bear. I couldn't believe he'd done this—that he'd taken the day off and planned a trip for us. This fucking man tied me in knots in ways no one else ever had, and he didn't even know it.

I wondered what the plan was for *The Vers*. They recorded on Sundays, so either they rescheduled, or Parker was missing an episode. Well, I guessed they could record after we got home from our trip tomorrow, but he usually went there before noon.

"Let's play road-trip games," I said when we were on the road.

"No."

"Yes," I countered.

"Sometimes you're like a big child."

"Don't pretend you don't love it. I'm endearing. You also know I won't stop until I get my way. So you might as well give in now."

"You're gonna harass me to play road-trip games with you for a year?"

I was aware that it didn't really make sense, especially considering we would be divorced by then. I nodded. "Yep, absolutely."

He gave a playful, dramatic sigh. But still, he played with me. It was only a two-hour drive to Big Bear, but we hit traffic, which made it closer to three. We laughed the whole time, singing songs and searching for certain color cars and trying to get semis to honk at us, the way I used to do as a child.

By the time we pulled up at the small cabin, it was already my favorite day ever.

"It's cute," I said when he parked. There were other houses, but they were off in the distance. The cabin was tucked in an area with trees as far as the eye could see, and a porch ran the length of it, with a swing at the end.

"Are you sure you don't want to stay in a hotel?" Parker asked, making me laugh.

"I'm very, very sure. But if you'd like, we don't have to leave the cabin at all. I'm telling you, though, I'll expect you to be naked."

"Will you now? Aren't you bossy."

"You fucking love it. You'd walk around naked all day, flaunting that perfect ass just like you do at home with your jocks. You revel in driving me wild." And I adored that he liked it, so it totally worked.

"Ugh. What the fuck, I'm hard," he said, making me laugh. "How the fuck do you do that shit just by talking to me!"

"Because I'm good, cariño. Now let's go." We got out of the car, I plucked our bag from the back seat, then followed a grumbling Parker to the door. Summer was on the horizon, so the temperature in Big Bear this time of year was high sixties to low seventies, which was basically perfect. He used a code to get into a lockbox, then let us inside.

It really was small, the cabin a studio with the living

room, kitchen, and bedroom all in a large space. There was a fireplace surrounded by brick, but everything else was made from wood, all dark earth tones.

I dropped the bag and wrapped my arms around him from behind. "Mmm. I can't wait to fuck you here…or you can have my ass. I'm not picky. I just want to come with you."

"You always want to come with me." Still, as he spoke, he was pushing his ass against my groin.

"Can you blame me?"

"Nope."

"And why is that?" I kissed his nape, let my lips press a trail across his skin. He sucked in a sharp breath. He knew what I wanted, and I wouldn't give up until I got it. "Tell me, beautiful. Why is that?"

"Because my ass is your favorite," he said breathlessly.

"And?"

"It's perfect."

"And…"

"So is my mouth…and you think I'm sexy and pretty, and no one turns you on the way I do." He was still pushing against me, basically humping himself on my cock, if only the damned clothes weren't in the way.

"Yes, exactly…good boy. You know how fucking perfect you are."

He dropped his head back against my shoulder, arching his torso. I ran my hands up and down it, under his shirt, then down to cup his bulge. "Save this for me for later. We're going to go have some fun."

"What!" he complained when I pulled away, and I laughed. "You're mean, Elliott. I don't like you anymore."

The truth was, I didn't want Parker just to like me. I wanted him to love me.

# CHAPTER TWENTY-SIX
## *Parker*

WHEN I SAID that Elliott was like a big kid sometimes, I hadn't been exaggerating. The thing was, he'd also been right. It was one of my favorite things about him. He made even the smallest things more fun. He made me want to try activities I wouldn't want to try without him, and he made me curious about the world in new and exciting ways.

While I really didn't love the outdoors, I also didn't hate it as much as I made it sound, but we both delighted in the back-and-forth teasing. Since it was a short trip, he wanted to jump in right away, and I pretended to want to rest while he dragged me out of the house.

We'd left Santa Monica early, but only having one day would seriously limit what we were able to do. We'd brought towels, swimming trunks, and things like that, so I assumed he would want to head to the lake right away. Still, I asked, "Where to?"

He looked at me and grinned. "The zoo."

"The zoo?"

"You heard me."

I...hadn't expected that, but I kinda loved it. "Did you choose that for me or for you? Because this trip is supposed to be all about Elliott."

"*All about Elliott* are probably three of my favorite words, and I love the zoo here. They only take in wounded or orphaned animals, or ones who can't live in the wild on their own. They work to rehabilitate them where they can and, if possible, eventually reintroduce them to their natural habitat."

I hadn't known that, but the fact that Elliott did and that he cared so much gave me all the warm and fuzzies. Ugh. This man. "Okay. Let's do it."

I looked up the address and let the navigation lead us there. It was fairly busy, but we didn't have any trouble getting in right away. Elliott didn't argue when I paid for us. He entwined his fingers with mine as we made our way along the path, stopping at every habitat.

They had multiple species of bear, as well as wolves, mountain lions, badgers, leopards, and more, but by far, my favorite were the flying squirrels. "Oh my God. We should totally get one!" I said as if that was a real possibility.

"Oh, so I can spend the rest of my life cleaning up after you *and* a flying squirrel?"

"We're both cute." I grinned, and he did the same.

"You're cuter." He gave me an adorable, wrinkled-nose look that made me melt inside.

"I'll reward you for saying that later, Mr. Weaver."

"I like the sound of that."

After the zoo, we grabbed fast food for lunch so we didn't waste time at a sit-down restaurant.

Elliott said, "We should head to the lake. Next time we come, I want to take you hiking up Castle Rock Trail. It's only just over a mile, but it's a pretty tough hike. Worth it, though. The view is incredible."

Next time. He said these things as if we would have more days like today, more weekends away together, as if we were a real couple and not two men who were supposed to get divorced soon. "Okay."

*Don't get your hopes up, don't get your hopes up, don't get your hopes up.*

My whole life, I'd never talked to myself as much as I had since I'd married Elliott.

The lake was busy as hell. We definitely should have come earlier in the day, and I hated that I felt like I'd robbed Elliott of the place he enjoyed with such a short trip. I wanted more for him, wished I could make him feel the way he did me, even if it was just a sexy game we played together.

But it didn't seem like just a game to me. Not anymore.

We changed in the restrooms, which were honestly a little gross. When I came out of my stall, Elliott was there in—"Board shorts?"

He turned, his eyes taking me in from head to toe. Hunger crackled in his gaze, making me vibrate with need of my own. "I like yours much, much better." Mine weren't quite a Speedo, but they weren't fucking board shorts either. Not that he didn't look hot as fuck in them because Elliott looked hot in anything, but still, I felt underdressed with my very short, short swimming trunks. Elliott said, "Think we can sneak—"

"No. Be good." Though the thought of being bad with him sounded a lot more fun. "There are families here!"

"Totally should have chosen somewhere more secluded instead of the lake," he grumbled.

"Your mistake," I joked.

"Come on…I want to have fun with you." He nodded toward the door, took my hand, and we went outside.

The beach was filled with families, but there were also couples and groups of friends. I noticed a gay couple kiss before running for the water together.

We found a spot and laid our towels out. I was surprised when Elliott sat down instead of heading straight for the lake. Still, I did the same.

"What was your favorite vacation spot with your parents before your mom passed?" he asked, and God, I loved that question.

I smiled. "We liked winter trips. There's so much sunshine in California that we liked snow destinations. Mom was a great skier. We only got to do that once, in Colorado. We skied, played in the snow, drank hot chocolate by the fire. She was so happy that it just made me and Dad happy too, ya know? She had that ability with people."

"You got it from her, then," Elliott replied, making my heart race.

"No I didn't," I argued.

He rolled his eyes. "Yes you did, beautiful. Come on, you gotta know that."

No, no I didn't. Jesus, how would I divorce him? How could I survive it? It was going to break me if I let it, and I refused to allow that to happen.

"Race you to the water!" I shoved to my feet and ran for the lake.

Elliott was right behind me.

We played in the water for hours. There was a mom there with a little boy. Dads were picking up their kids and tossing them into the water, and I heard the little boy ask his mom if she could, but she said, "I'm sorry. You're too much of a big boy. I can't."

"El…" I said, wanting to help.

"Come on."

We befriended them, playing water games with them as if they were our family. Elliott was great with him, just like he'd been when he'd done magic tricks for Samantha all those months ago.

He would be a good dad…

I shook those thoughts from my head and focused on

making this day perfect.

They left before we did, Elliott and I lounging around in the water.

He hugged me...kissed me...made me feel treasured.

As evening broke, he said, "We should probably go."

We hadn't had dinner yet, but I just wanted to go back to the cabin and be with him all night.

"Okay." I took a step, then another, and suddenly pain shot through my foot. "Ouch. Fuck."

"What happened?" Elliott frowned.

"I stepped on something." I lifted my foot, and sure enough, there was a little cut there. Luckily, it wasn't bad, and the pain was just a slight sting.

"Get on my back."

"I can walk."

"Shut up and get on my back."

"Oh my God." I feigned annoyance, but I fucking loved this. I did as Elliott said, wrapping my legs around his waist and my arms around his neck.

He carried me toward our things, saying, "I'm a fucking great husband."

We laughed, but all I could think about was how right he was.

# CHAPTER TWENTY-SEVEN
## Elliott

I SAT DOWN on the couch and said, "Take off your clothes." We'd come back to the cabin after the lake, cleaned Parker's wound, showered, and changed before going into town again. We'd had dinner, then walked around town, looking into shops, before heading back.

This day had been…well, really fucking incredible, but now I just wanted to be naked with my husband.

"Excuse me?" Parker said, but I saw it, the blue fire igniting in his eyes, the flames so hot, I felt the heat of it against my skin.

"You heard me. Take off your clothes."

He blushed, then smiled, and I knew he would do exactly as I said.

Parker pulled off his shirt and tossed it to the floor.

"Always so messy," I teased.

"Is that what you're thinking about right now?"

"No…I'm thinking about my beautiful husband and all the things I'm gonna do to him tonight."

Parker shivered. I saw his body vibrate from ten feet away where he stood.

I leaned against the back of the couch, legs spread, watching…waiting.

His fingers were shaking as he unbuttoned his jeans, then

pulled the zipper down. I didn't speak, didn't look away even for a second while he slid them down his legs, revealing his pale skin and the dusting of dark hair on his thighs. He tossed his jeans away, now standing in front of me in a black jockstrap. Fuck, he was so damn sexy. My cock was already rock hard.

"Are you planning on staying dressed while I'm naked?"

"For a little while. You want me to see my pretty boy, don't you?"

"Fuck…Elliott." He hooked his fingers in the band of his jock.

"Wait," I rushed out. "Keep those on. Turn around and let me see you."

"I…" he started, but then did as I said, showing me the smooth skin of his back, the arch of his curvy ass, the perfectly plump cheeks I loved to have my face in or my cock between.

"Christ, cariño. You're so goddamned beautiful. You're fucking perfect. Now I want to see your pretty little hole too. Will you show it to me?"

"Jesus, El. You're killing me here." But still, he bent forward.

"No, no. You're too far away, gorgeous. I need you to come closer."

He did, taking slow steps backward until he was right in front of me, standing between my spread thighs. I leaned up, just as he bent forward. His cheeks spread, but then he used his hands to part them farther.

"Fuck yes. Look at how sexy my little pink hole is. Prettiest thing I've ever seen." I circled my finger around his wrinkled pucker. Shivers ran the length of Parker's body, and he moaned. "You like it when I touch my hole?" I asked, because it was mine. For as long as he would let me have it, I wanted him to belong to me.

"You know I do."

"Tell me, then. Tell me you like it when I touch my hole."

"I fucking love it when you touch your hole, Elliott."

Hearing him say that made my dick throb. I pulled my hand back and spit on his rim, then massaged it before pushing the tip of my finger inside him.

"I've never seen anything sexier than you standing here in a jock in front of me, spreading your ass for me, watching my finger pressing into your cute pucker."

I slid it in, then all the way out, watching it close again. Jesus, I wanted him so fucking much. I was trembling not to take him right away, but I wanted to play, wanted to savor him and try to make him come from more than just fucking.

I leaned forward, lashed my tongue over his entrance, smiled into the crease of his ass when he gasped, and then I sat back again.

"Will you show me how pretty you look on your knees for me?"

"Yes. God yes." Parker turned, then immediately lowered, looking at me with so much naked want, it stole my breath. "Do you…do you like it? Do I look pretty?"

"So fucking beautiful, cariño." I caressed his cheek. "Help me take off my shirt." He did, tugging my tee off. "Now my pants."

"You're lucky I want you so much," he teased, which made my cock twitch.

Parker opened my pants. I lifted my hips for him to tug them and my underwear down. He had to scoot over so he could get them off before settling between my legs again.

I wasn't sure my balls had ever been so full or my cock so hard. It pulsed and leaked against my belly, dying for his touch.

"See something you like?" I wrapped a hand around the base of my shaft.

"You know I do."

"Wanna kiss it?"

He grinned up at me. "You know I do, you cocky bastard."

"Tsk, tsk. Such a mouth on you." I cupped the back of his head and pushed him down so his face was in my groin. Parker read what I wanted and kissed my erection, then my balls, not licking or sucking me.

"Fuck, you smell good." He nuzzled my sac, kissed it. I was dizzy with lust, like I might come or die or lose my mind at any second.

"I like you down there. Maybe we can spend a whole day with you on your knees, nursing my cock. Every time I want to see something pretty, I'll just look down at my gorgeous husband with his sexy lips around my dick."

"Oh fuuuuuck." He shoved his hand down between his legs, and I knew he was trying to keep himself from blowing his load.

"Someone likes that idea."

"Like you don't."

"Yeah, but I would never deny it. I always say how I feel." But then, that wasn't true, was it? Before Parker, maybe, but now there were stakes. I wanted forever, and that held me at bay. When there was something to lose, it was so much harder to take the gamble. "Wrap those lips around my cock."

He didn't have to be told twice. Parker immediately took me to the back of his throat, bobbing his head, swallowing around my dick, hitting the back of his throat. The hot suction of his mouth went straight to my head. "Best cocksucker I've ever had." I tangled my hand in his hair. "Best everything I've ever had…my sexy, sweet husband."

He moaned, dick in his mouth, and looked up at me, his eyes slightly watery, what almost looked like sadness in his gaze.

"Hey, what's the matter? Did I do something wrong?"

He shook his head, with my dick still inside him, which was sexy as fuck. He pulled off to say, "No, I just want you so much."

I growled in response, on a hair trigger, need fueling every one of my movements. I stood, tugging him to his feet. I lifted Parker, his long legs wrapping around my waist. Our mouths crashed together in a flurry of hungry tongues and tasting lips.

I carried him to the bed, almost tripping, and then we were laughing and kissing before I dropped him to the mattress.

I tugged his jock off, brought it to my face and breathed in the scent of the pouch. Parker's erection twitched against his belly, his balls big and full with the load I couldn't wait to work out of him.

"Such a pretty, pretty cock." I let my finger drift up from his nuts to the crown.

"Fuck me," Parker begged.

"Be patient," I replied, as if I wasn't dying myself. "Get your head on the pillows."

I grabbed the lube while Parker moved over to lie in the center of the bed. He was on his back, legs spread, stroking his erection.

"Hands off." I swatted them away, kneeling close to him. I pulled his legs over my thighs, resting my ass on my heels. He wrapped his legs around me, half on my lap, half on the bed, his cock right there for the taking...well, his ass too.

Once my hands were slicked up, I used one to wrap around his hot length, the other to push two fingers inside his tight ass.

"Fuck, Elliott. Why does this feel different with you? Why is everything so fucking different?"

Hope grew roots in my chest. Maybe this could work out. Maybe he could want us too. Maybe I could treat him right and wouldn't hurt him.

"It's all you, cariño," I told him, fucking him and stroking him. His cock was red and leaking, his balls growing tighter by the second. Every time he looked close to orgasm, I'd let go, pull off, remove my fingers from inside him, and he would growl in response.

"Make me come!" he begged.

"So cute when you're needy."

"Aren't I cute all the time?"

"Fuck yes." I jerked him again, worked two fingers inside him, watched him writhe and heard him pant beneath me. Again, just when I thought he would lose himself to the pleasure, I pulled back.

"Please, Elliott...please make me come."

"That's not what I want you to call me right now. Who am I?" Jesus, I needed to hear him say it tonight. He had me so entranced with him, so entangled with him, and I didn't ever want to become unwound.

"Husband...please make me come, husband."

How could I deny him that?

My hands actually shook when I lubed myself up. I grabbed his waist, helped him arch up just a little more before I slid into him in one long, slow thrust.

We both groaned together, the feel of his hot body shooting me to the fucking moon. I gave him a second to adjust to my cock before fucking up and into him.

His dick bounced against his stomach, leaking precum on his abs. My fingers dug into his hips as I took his ass, letting my cock make a home in his hole, wishing I never had to leave it.

When Parker reached for his dick again, I shook my head. "No. Do you think I can make you come hands-free? Do you think I can make my pretty husband blow his load without even touching his cock?" I slammed into him again, making more precum leak from him.

"Yes, fuck yes. I'm close, so goddamned close already."

Our bodies slapped together, my thighs against the back of his. His torso was still arched, me helping hold him up while I railed into his ass.

"Fuck, I love being inside my hole. Love knowing that the best ass belongs to me. My husband is so pretty and perfect. I want the world to know you're mine."

Parker cried out, my dick shoving hard into him again. When it did, his ass tightened, pulsed around me as his prick twitched and he shot over and over and over again. Every time I pumped my hips, he'd spurt again, cum all over his chest and neck, one shot even hitting his face.

I didn't think I'd ever seen anyone come so hard. I basically roared in triumph before my balls drew up, cum pulsing inside him, filling him.

I pulled out slowly, and he moaned. I'd gone at his ass hard, and I knew he had to be sensitive.

"What do you need?" I asked. There wasn't anything I wouldn't give him.

His pupils blew wide, like he was surprised at the question. Not that it was me who asked, but I didn't think anyone had ever asked him that kind of question before me.

"Just you," Parker replied.

"I can do that." I lay beside him, pulled him into my arms, and almost let myself ask him to stay.

## CHAPTER TWENTY-EIGHT
## *Parker*

WE WERE BOTH fairly quiet the next day. We left early, the air and tension around us hot and thick. I couldn't say why, really, at least not for him, but for me it was because I couldn't deny my truth anymore.

I loved Elliott.

I was *in love* with him. I wanted to stay married to him. And wanting that scared the shit out of me. Because as much as I'd thought I'd been hurt in the past, as hard as it was when a relationship hadn't gone as planned or a man hadn't turned out to be the person I thought he was, nothing would compare to losing Elliott.

I glanced over at him in the passenger seat. He was looking out the window, watching the scenery go by. What was he thinking? Did he sense it too? That things were different and this was more than dating for me?

A million thoughts kept popping into my head. It felt like one of those whack-a-mole games, only I missed every single one when it emerged, and they kept coming, more and faster.

"Do you have any plans this afternoon?" I asked.

"I think I'll go see my mom."

Go see his mom? I knew they were close, but it sounded like an excuse. Oh God, it was an excuse, and he wanted to get away from me. He knew I loved him, and he needed space. I fought to swallow around the lump in my throat. "Nice." Did that sound strange? Why was my voice so raspy? "I'm going to see the guys." We weren't recording *The Vers* until the following evening because I hadn't been sure what time Elliott and I would be home, but I didn't have another excuse.

Home. His home wouldn't be mine anymore. I would be moving back into my apartment, which I'd always loved, but now the thought of being there alone, being without him, without sleeping in the same bed as Elliott every night, left me feeling cold and empty.

"You guys always have fun together."

We fell into silence again as I finished the drive back to Santa Monica. I was surprised when we got there that Elliott didn't even head to the door, instead tugging his keys out of his pocket. "I'm gonna go ahead and run. I'll be back this evening."

"Okay." *Talk to me. What's wrong?*

Elliott watched me for a moment before he gave a simple nod, walked to his car, and left.

*He regrets this, regrets us.*

Fuck, why couldn't I stop these stupid voices in my head telling me no one would ever want me?

Instead of getting back into the car, I went for the house. My heart thundered, my hands were shaking, my breathing hard and sharp.

I was so stupid. Why the fuck was I so stupid? I never should have let myself fall for him. Hell, I never should have dated or fucked him. We should have kept it as a stupid business transaction, the way we'd planned from the start because...fuck, this *hurt*.

I curled up on the couch. Hugging myself into a tight ball would surely make things feel better, would make me feel less alone.

I didn't know how long I lay there before my cell rang. I tugged it out of my pocket to see Declan's name on the screen.

"Hello?" I answered.

"Hey, babe. Just checking in on you after your night away."

I didn't answer right away because what could I say? That he was right and I would get hurt?

"Park..." Declan said, his voice soft and knowing.

"I'm so stupid."

Declan sighed, knowing where this was going. "Did he say he didn't feel the same?"

"No. I didn't tell him. I'm not an idiot. I just... No one ever wants me, Dec."

"Shit." He cursed. "Are you alone?"

"Yes. Elliott is at his mom's. He said he wouldn't be back until this evening—oh God. I'm going to lose his mom too. Cat's going to hate me. I don't want to lose them, Declan."

"Babe, calm down, okay? Text me Elliott's address. We'll be right there."

When Declan hung up, I texted him the address. The truth was, I needed them. We all needed each other, and there was no shame in that.

# CHAPTER TWENTY-NINE
## *Elliott*

I DIDN'T GO see my mom. If I did, I'd spill the whole truth. I'd tell her I was in love with Parker and that it scared me. Which would confuse her since we were married, so why would I have just figured out I was in love with my husband? I'd have to tell her what we did, that it was a drunken mistake, and if I was truly honest with myself, what also scared me was that Parker wouldn't return my feelings.

Love was the absolute worst. Why in the fuck would anyone want to feel this? It was terrible. I'd never been so insecure in my life.

But I needed to talk to someone, and as much as I loved Vaughn, he wasn't the person I contacted.

"Hey, Elliott. How are you?" Sebastian answered. I still couldn't get over the fact that I had *the* Sebastian Cole's phone number.

"I'm in love with Parker and scared out of my mind." God, what was wrong with me? I couldn't believe I'd just said that. "Ugh! This is torture. Can you pretend this never happened?"

He chuckled. "I don't think I can. Where are you?"

"At the pier."

"Okay, well, we're going to need somewhere a little less public, unless we want to be followed around by the paparazzi.

Declan is with Marcus and Corbin. He thought Parker was with you. Do you want to come over?"

*No, say no.* I didn't need to burden him with my drama. Still, I said, "Yeah, that'd be great."

"What are friends for?"

Damn, he really was a good guy.

I drove to his house, and he buzzed me in. He was waiting on the front porch when I walked up, a knowing look on his face. "I called it."

"You knew I would be an absolute mess and afraid of losing something for the first time in my life?"

"That's what love does to us. It rips us open, bares all our fears and insecurities, but there's nothing more beautiful either because it heals us too. It makes us less alone."

We went into the house, Sebastian closing the door behind him.

"But what if you're scared you'll suck at love? What if you screw up?"

"Then you're human. None of us are perfect, Elliott. We're flawed, and we all make mistakes. You do your best. You love them in the best way you can. There's always a possibility we might do or say the wrong thing, and when that happens, you fix it, you work through it because love is imperfect. Sometimes I think that's what makes it even more incredible."

I was speechless. "Wow. You're good at this."

"I'm trying," he teased.

I sat down on his couch, making myself at home in a major movie star's house. "I didn't think I could… I mean, I'm not gonna say I wanted to fall in love or get serious, but sometimes I wondered if I wasn't cut out for it, like maybe I wasn't built for romantic emotions. But him…fuck, how could I not love Parker?"

"Damn. You're better at this than you think." He chuckled, then shrugged. "So maybe you're demiromantic. Maybe you're not. How important is the label to you? Does it change anything? You're still in love with Parker, and that's what matters."

He was right. I didn't need labels. Demiromantic might fit me, but in the end, whether that was me or not, I loved him.

That wasn't all that weighed me down, though, and this second point mattered a lot more. "What if he doesn't feel the same? Parker wants the fairy tale, and I'm not that—or at least, he doesn't look at me and see that. I'm not an idiot. I know he likes me, but…"

"Parker loves you."

My gaze snapped to him. "How do you know? Did he tell Declan?"

"Okay, well, I don't know, but that's what I think."

"You suck at this!" I dropped my head against the back of the couch and groaned. "He didn't even tell me he doesn't want me, yet I'm freaking the fuck out about losing him. This is the worst feeling ever. I don't know if I can do this."

Sebastian clamped a hand on my shoulder. "You can. You told me before that Parker is worth it. You're worth the risk too."

"I…" Holy shit, did I not think I was worth it? I wanted to be. I wanted Parker. But the only way to get him was to tell him how I felt, to take a chance and put my heart on the line. I'd never been afraid to go after what I wanted, and I sure as shit wouldn't start now. "Thank you."

"You're welcome. What's the plan?"

The plan was to come clean. I'd flirted with Parker, asked to date him, was open with him in all the ways I should be except one. That changed today. "I'm going to tell Parker I love him. He's mine, and I'm not willing to walk away without at least telling him how I feel."

Sebastian's genuine smile told me he really was happy for me, that he really was my friend. "These Beach Bums...they're something else, aren't they? There's something addicting about them."

"There is...holy shit...I'm in love for the first time in my life." It hit me again, what all this meant. I'd never fallen in love before, but I'd never had Parker before, and now I did, and he was my whole damn heart.

"No big deal, right?" Sebastian teased.

"It's scary as fuck, but that's okay."

"What can I do? How can I help?"

"Nothing...not yet, but I appreciate your offer."

Suddenly, he wasn't Sebastian Cole anymore. He was just Sebastian, my friend, and now I was going to get my man.

# CHAPTER THIRTY
## *Parker*

I WENT TO the door the second I heard the knock. As soon as I pulled it open, my family was there, my best friends, my brothers.

Declan hugged me, and then the four of us talked nonstop. About Elliott, about me...well, I'd been talking. Rambling and losing my mind more like, but they were listening.

"You plan on giving us a turn to speak, or are we just supposed to listen to you the whole time?" Marcus quirked a dark brow.

I paced the room, unable to sit still. "You're not allowed to be mean to me today. I'm in love...*really* in love. All those other times I had feelings for other men were nothing like this. I'm very close to having a panic attack, Marcus, because this isn't what I thought it would be—at all!"

I saw it in Declan first, the way he bit his cheek and tried not to laugh. When my gaze found Corbin, he was doing the same. Once I settled my stare on Marcus again, he smiled at me, a teasing, confident, bossy smile. I couldn't help chuckling before collapsing onto the couch. "You guys are the worst friends ever."

"Pretty sure you mean best." Corbin reached over and placed a hand on my thigh. He was right, of course, because strangely, them laughing at me was exactly what I needed. It always was. "So...you've fallen in love with your husband..."

"Yes."

Corbin covered his mouth and spoke very quickly. "Pretty sure we told you that would happen."

Like we were all so good at doing, I ignored him.

Dec added, "And you took him on an overnight trip to the mountains, which is a place he loves. It was really romantic, and then he fucked you like you've never been fucked before, and you realized you're in love with him."

"Yes. Maybe you guys could try to keep up. You're just repeating everything I already told you." I huffed. "Also, it wasn't the sex that made me realize it, but the way he looked at me, the way he made me feel inside. I've never... I've wanted this my whole life, and I never knew it could feel this way. It's terrible and wonderful and a dream come true, but also the most frightening thing that's ever happened to me."

I was flanked by Declan and Corbin, Marcus sitting in front of us on the coffee table, which, now that I thought about it, was kinda his thing. Dec shrugged, then leaned over and kissed my cheek. "Sounds like love, babe. You wanted it, and now you have it. I thought I was going to self-combust when I realized I was in love with Sebastian."

"Yes, but Sebastian loved you back." Why didn't they understand that part?

Marcus said, "And you know Elliott doesn't love you because...you asked him? He told you?" He waited for me to respond, and when I didn't, he added, "That's what I thought."

"I hate you."

"You love us," he countered.

Yes, yes I did.

"From the start, he told me he'd never wanted more with

someone before, that he didn't feel like it was something he could do, that he didn't think he was cut out for it."

"Are you explaining Declan before he fell in love with Sebastian, or your man?" Corbin questioned.

I knew where he was going with that. "Just because Dec fell in love doesn't mean Elliott will too. That's not how the world works."

"But he did say you intrigue him…numerous times from what you've said. He also asked you to date him. And he loves to spoil you and take care of you…"

"He praises me," I admitted. "That's a thing we do, and it's really fucking hot."

"I knew it!" Declan shouted. When we all looked at him, he blushed. "Sorry. I had a feeling about that before. Carry on."

"Wait. You did?" I asked, then waved off my question. "Actually, never mind. I don't even want to know. We need to figure out this in-love-with-my-husband situation. Just because I intrigue him and he said he's crazy about me isn't the same as love."

"Imagine loving your husband," Corbin teased, just as Declan asked, "He said he's crazy about you?"

"Why don't you think he loves you again?" Marcus questioned.

"You guys are the ones who warned me away from him. You said he would hurt me, and now I…well, now I can't figure out what you're doing other than kicking me while I'm down." I crossed my arms, knowing they were doing no such thing. They were being them, we were being us, and I loved them for it.

Marcus sighed, then spoke in that deep, thundery voice of his that had been known to bring many men to their knees. "Park, you know me. If I thought that motherfucker was wrong for you, I'd say it. But I watch, I pay attention. I've listened to the things you've said over the past few months. I kept my eyes on him when we were at Dec and Sebastian's. I doubted him at first, but he's feeling some kinda something for you, and he's scared, just like you are. Has he recently told you any of those things he said in the beginning?"

"Well...no. I did hear him tell his friend that he wasn't in love with me."

"How long ago?" Marcus asked. "And what was the context? Maybe he meant the exact opposite." He scooted the table closer so he was right in front of me, my legs between his. He pulled me forward until I was sitting up. "I love you, but I've also gotta keep it real. That's how I roll. You've spent your life going after the worst possible guys for you, ones you knew would fuck up. You might not have felt this way before, but you have sabotaged relationships with decent men in the past, and something inside you is doing the same here. Because as much as you want love and romance, you're scared of having it. I think you're scared you'll lose it like your dad did, and it's easier to tell yourself you can't find the right man or that you have bad luck than it is to really put your heart out there and risk it getting broken. You'd rather be alone than know what it feels like to have someone and then lose them. You deserve more, sweetheart."

I gasped, heart in my throat. My vision went blurry, eyes filled with unshed tears. "I..." That couldn't be the truth, could it? I didn't do that. Why would I do that? I loved romance. I wanted my special person. I didn't sabotage relationships and pick the wrong men.

*He's right. You know he's right.*

And maybe I could deny it if it had been Declan or Corbin who said it, but not Marcus, because Marcus *did* pay attention. Marcus was good at knowing things and looking at the world and dissecting it—well, for everyone but himself.

"No." I shoved to my feet, squeezed around him and began pacing again. "That can't be right." Oh God. He was right. "I love Elliott. I would never try to ruin that. But he doesn't love me."

My friends stood and crowded around me, offering me their support, and I knew that seeing me realize this truth about myself and being in denial about it hurt them as much as it did me.

"Babe..." Declan started.

"No!" I said again. I couldn't... Why would I... "This isn't about love." At least not from Elliott. "It was a dumb drunk marriage that never should have happened. It's fake. It's not real. It's..."

"Elliott?" I froze at the sound of Cat's voice behind me.

No. *No, no, no, no.* I was afraid to turn to the door, afraid to look, but seeing my friends, who were facing the opposite direction, I knew I'd just made the biggest mistake of my life.

"Elliott, is what he's saying true? You lied to us? This isn't real?" Cat asked.

I forced myself to face them. Cat was watching Elliott, who couldn't pull his eyes off me. His stare shredded my heart, ripped it and broke it down until there was nothing but dust.

"Cat, I can explain," I said, but Elliott held up his hand to silence me. I'd already fucked up enough, so I listened.

"Yes, it's true," he said to her without taking his gaze off me.

"I..." she started, but her voice broke. Her hand shook as she covered her mouth. "I've never been so disappointed in you." Cat turned to me. "And I'm disappointed in you too. I love you. You're like a son to me. I thought you loved Elliott. I...I can't."

She turned and walked out of the house.

"Elliott, I didn't mean—"

"Stop," he cut me off. "I can't do this with you right now, beau—Parker. I have to deal with my mom."

And then Elliott walked out too.

When I started to fall, three sets of arms were there to catch me, hugging me, telling me they loved me and that it would be okay.

But it wouldn't. I didn't think it would ever be okay again.

# CHAPTER THIRTY-ONE
## *Elliott*

"*T*HIS ISN'T ABOUT *love. It was a dumb drunk marriage that never should have happened. It's fake. It's not real.*"

"*I've never been so disappointed in you.*"

My hands tightened on the steering wheel as I drove to my parents' house. I couldn't stop replaying Parker's words, or my mom's.

I'd gone home to tell him I was in love with him, that I wanted this to be real and for us to stay together. Only when I got there, I saw Mom had stopped by. We went inside together and... "*This isn't about love. It was a dumb drunk marriage that never should have happened. It's fake. It's not real.*"

Those words were a bullet straight to the heart, pulverizing it and leaving a mess in their wake. I guess there was my answer. Parker didn't love me. My insides had been scooped out, everything good inside me gone and replaced with pain.

And Mom... I hated myself for what I'd done to her. This was so wrong. Why had we kept up this dumb fucking lie? All it did was hurt everyone around us.

Mom was sitting on the couch with Dad beside her when I arrived. He had his arm around her. She'd been crying. Neither spoke, both looking at me as I came closer and sat in an armchair. I was defeated. My body felt like my bones didn't have the strength to hold me up, like I was running off pain because it was the only thing that could fuel me.

"I think we deserve an explanation, son," Dad said.

Yes, they did. They deserved better than what I'd given them.

"I fucked up," I said, because I had. There was more to it than that, but broken down, it's what happened. I pulled an Elliott. I acted without thinking, and those around me got hurt.

"We need a better answer than that." Mom's voice cracked with pain.

"I did meet Parker over a year ago, at a bar, like we said. Something about him grabbed my attention immediately. He's beautiful, of course, but it was more than that. It was just…" How did I describe it? I didn't understand it myself. "It was a spark. I realize now that I'd never felt something like that before, but at the time, I thought it was just me seeing a hot guy and wanting him." When they didn't reply, I continued. "We talked, just an hour or so, but I found him captivating. It felt…different. So after that, I'd go see him at his work, flirt with him, ask him out, and he always said no.

"We ended up running into each other in Vegas, which is a huge coincidence if you think about it. Parker was lonely and messaged to ask me to hang out. I jumped at the chance because…because I liked him and knew he was special. Christ, even back then, I just didn't recognize it for what it was." Attraction had been part of it for sure, but that spark had always been there, and all it did was grow.

"And you got drunk and married him?" Dad asked.

Shame thickened my blood, slowly filling my veins with sludge. "Yes. We woke up the next morning and realized what we'd done, but the consequences were already in effect. Word got out. The idea of letting you down, of again being the reason your name was in the press for negative reasons…

You're the best parents, and I love you both so much. I didn't want to hurt you, and Parker was worried about hurting his dad, so we decided to keep up the facade for six months, and then we'd say it didn't work but that we're still friends, yada, yada. It was my fault. I screwed up, and there's no getting around it. I just didn't think of the fallout." I leaned forward, elbows on my knees, hands in my hair. "Fuck, we were so stupid. *I* was so stupid."

Dad sighed. "I'm angry with you, Elliott, but I'm also hurt that you didn't think you could come to us with this. Haven't we always been there for you? We wanted you to know you could always depend on us."

"What? That's not it. You have. I've let you both down so much in my life that the thought of doing it again..." I shook my head. "I just want to make you proud. I want to be the kind of person you both are."

"Oh, Elliott," Mom said. "You are, and we're always so damn proud of you. You're a good man who cares about others. No one is perfect, but don't think for a moment that I'm not the proudest mom in the world. I look at you, at your compassion and your confidence in who you are, and it makes *me* want to be like *you*."

My vision swam, my parents becoming blurry. Before I could stop myself, I was between them on the couch, the three of us hugging.

"We love you. So much," Dad told me.

"I love you both too." Mom wrapped her arm around me, my head on her shoulder. They didn't speak for a moment, and I didn't either. What else could we say? But then the words were there, rolling from my lips in unrestrained waves. "Sometimes I forgot it wasn't real. The more time I spent with him... He's so fun and doesn't even know it. Making him happy, making him laugh means more to me than my own happiness. It makes me feel like a king. Have you ever experienced that? Like there isn't anything you wouldn't do to make someone smile? He makes me feel like…me. Which is weird and makes no sense, but…"

"You're in love with him," Mom said.

"Yes," I admitted. "I didn't realize it until recently. I knew I wanted to be with him, that I wanted to date him and be able to call him mine. I just didn't know how deep that went. I was going to tell him today, but…well, you heard him."

"Elliott Delgado Weaver, I don't know what the hell it is you're saying right now, but that's not the man I know. Since when do you give up that easily?"

My gaze snapped to Mom's. "Excuse me?"

"You heard me. Mi niño is in love, and I don't take that lightly. You're a fighter. Are you just going to walk away without at least telling Parker how you feel?"

"I'd have to agree with your mother on this one," Dad said.

My gaze went back and forth between them. I was speechless. My parents were…fuck, they were incredible, and I was so damn lucky to have them. "He said this isn't about love."

"We heard one sentence out of what he said. I've seen the way that man looks at you. You should have heard how excited he was when he told me he wanted to do something nice for you. Love is hard. If neither of you is willing to put the work in, then you don't deserve it in the first place, but I don't believe that's the case. I know my son, and I know how determined you are. Tell him how you feel. You'll beat yourself up for the rest of your life if you don't."

I would. She was right, but… "And if he doesn't feel the same?"

"Then it wasn't meant to be," Dad said. "You walk away knowing you told your truth, and that's all you can do."

They were right, but damn, it was hard. I wasn't sure I ever wanted to put myself out there; fucking my way through life was a lot easier than this.

But that wasn't true, was it? Because then I couldn't have Parker, and there was nothing more important than him.

# CHAPTER THIRTY-TWO
## *Parker*

IT WAS EVENING by the time I was sitting in my car in front of Dad's house. After Elliott left, I'd pulled myself together, gone to my apartment with my friends, and then fallen apart again. The guys had been there with me, like they always were, and as much as I loved them, I'd wanted it to be Elliott.

I always wanted it to be Elliott.

And I would never forgive myself for hurting him. Or for hurting Cat and Malcolm, for that matter. I was going to find a way to fix this, but I didn't have it in me tonight. I was so tired, my emotions all over the place, feeling too many things to focus on just one.

For whatever reason, I'd wanted my dad. I was too old for that, and maybe it didn't make much sense, but I needed to talk to him, and I needed to come clean.

Lights were on in the house as I got out of my car. I didn't even know what I planned to say to him, hoping something would come to me.

My arm was heavy as I lifted it to knock on the door, and I was surprised when it pulled open. "Parker? What's wrong?" Dad asked, a tremble in his voice. "I saw you walk up."

"I'm sorry… I don't know… I just wanted…" My dad. I hadn't let myself want my father in so long, not wanting to put more pressure or responsibility on him, not wanting to be a burden, but he was my father, and I loved him.

My eyes welled with stupid tears again. I seemed to have an unending supply. Dad's arms immediately wrapped around me. I collapsed into them, let him hold me and shush me and tell me everything would be okay.

Somehow we got inside and to the couch, where he still kept me in his embrace while I lost it. I felt like I was crying for a million different things, like I couldn't just settle on one.

We'd never done this—not after Mom died. Not ever, really.

"I messed up so bad. I ruined everything with Elliott, and I hurt his mom. I lied to you. God, what is wrong with me? How could I let all this happen?" I swiped at the wetness on my face.

"I'm sure it's not as bad as you think. We can fix it."

We. Because my father was on my team. He didn't know what I'd done wrong, and I'd just told him I'd lied to him, yet he was still on my side. "I don't know if I can. It's big. Elliott loves his parents and…" The look on Cat's face…the look on Elliott's… "I lied to you. Elliott and I, we weren't in love when we got married. I was feeling like shit about myself and lonely, we were drunk, and he was just…he was so much fun, and he made me feel good about myself, even back then."

Because he had, hadn't he? And I'd always enjoyed being around him, soaking up his energy.

"We woke up the next morning, and people had already heard. He was worried about his parents being disappointed, and I didn't want to make you sad. It felt so easy at the time, to just lie about it. That was wrong. The reasons don't matter, and I'm sorry we did it."

He frowned, cocked his head slightly. "You didn't want me to worry about you."

No, I hadn't, but I could have found a better way to deal

with it other than lying. "I'm sorry. You deserve better."

"Parker, don't you know how much I love you? That I just want you to be happy? I know I'm not always the best at saying how I feel, but you shouldn't have had to go through that alone. I should have made sure you always know I'm here for you. I don't want you to ever feel like you have to lie to protect me, or that you can't come to me if you're in trouble."

"Dad…I shouldn't be in this kind of trouble. I'm too old for this shit."

He gave me a small smile I couldn't help but return.

Dad said, "I'm too old for a lot of things I still do too…like living in the past, not fighting for myself and my happiness. I just feel like I don't know how."

Hearing that broke my heart. "You can lean on me too, ya know? If you'll always be there for me, you need to know I'll always be there for you too." We'd done a shit job at communicating. Hell, even the fact that we didn't live that far apart, and yet I went months at a time without seeing him. "We need to do better. We'll both do better."

He took off his Kansas City hat, pushed his hair back, and slid it back on. "I just always felt like you deserved to have her."

"What? No. I wouldn't trade you for Mom. I loved her, God, I loved her so fucking much, but you're my dad and I love you too. I need you."

My father pulled me into his arms again, and this time it was him who cried first, and then I did too. Why hadn't we done this before? Why hadn't we leaned on each other? Mom would have wanted that. If she was out there in the universe somewhere, I knew she was cursing us for being so dumb.

I didn't know how long we sat there together before the tears dried up and Dad said, "Now tell me what happened with Elliott."

"I fell in love with him for real. He's... Dad, he's everything."

"You sound like I did when I spoke about your mother."

I did, and I refused to let myself lose that, refused to walk away out of fear or anything else. Elliott had fought for me even before I realized what he was doing, and I damn sure planned to fight for him.

Elliott was my dream come true, only better.

# CHAPTER THIRTY-THREE
## *Elliott*

I STAYED THE night at my parents' house, then pulled a brokenhearted teenager move and called in sick to work, staying at their place, listening to emo breakup music and scrolling Parker's Instagram like a creepy stalker. I was pathetic and couldn't even find it in myself to care.

Parker and I needed to talk, that much was obvious, but I would rather put it off, to be honest. Couldn't we just go through with the original plan and never speak again? I could pretend not to know he didn't love me, and we could move on. The end.

I didn't really want that, though.

I wanted him.

My phone buzzed. My stupid pulse skyrocketed in a really embarrassing way when I saw Parker's name on the screen.

**Will you meet me at the entrance of Santa Monica Pier at 7:00 p.m.? We need to talk.**

*Nah, I'm good*, was the first thought that came to mind, but instead of texting that, I just stared at his words. Three dots appeared on the screen again.

**Please?**

Ugh. Like I could deny him. There wasn't anything I wouldn't do for Parker.

**Of course I'll be there. You're too spoiled for me not**

**to be.** I immediately started to message again. **Stop smiling.**

Because I knew he was, and damned if my stupid mouth wasn't curled up in a grin of its own before I remembered that he was likely telling me goodbye.

★ ★ ★

I ARRIVED TEN minutes early, and Parker was already there. He leaned against the railing of the pier, wearing my favorite jeans and the blue shirt I thought matched well with his eyes.

My heart jumped, excitement and fear colliding into an explosion of emotions that threatened to overtake me. I wanted him so fucking bad. I was hurt at what I'd heard him say, though he had every right to speak the words. While I was used to getting my way, I couldn't make him love me if he didn't, nor make him *want* to love me.

Still…he was wearing clothes he knew I liked. That had to be a good sign.

Or was this like a movie where he chose to do this in public so I couldn't make a scene? Ugh. Too many ridiculous thoughts were going through my head.

It felt like it took three hundred years to make my way to him. Parker didn't take his gaze off me the whole time. When I reached him, he smiled, his cheeks that pretty shade of pink I liked on him so much. I was maybe feeling a little more optimistic because of it.

"Hey, beautiful." Did my voice shake? Fuck, I couldn't believe my voice was shaking.

"I'm sorry…about yesterday…what I said. I have to get that out before anything else. Your mom never should have found out that way. I'll never forgive myself for hurting both you and her."

Yeah, I was sorry too. But I knew he hadn't done it on

purpose. "We can't go back and change it. I hated lying to them. They deserved better. Now it's out there, and we'll deal with it."

He nodded, but I could still see the insecurity flittering through his eyes. He wasn't sure about this, or about me. Fuck, I didn't even know. I needed him to tell me before I drove myself insane.

"Walk with me for a second?" he asked.

"So you can break up with me? Do we even consider it that? Shit. I can't believe I said that. My head is a mess. You've ruined me, Parker. I'm confident and cocky, not emotional and needy. I know how awesome I am!"

A guy walking by frowned at me, clearly having heard the last sentence. Oops.

"See what you do to me?" I asked. "I'm a disaster."

He smiled. Nice of him to enjoy my torture so much.

"Walk with me, El."

El. I liked that. Even a dumb, stupid nickname from him made me mushy inside. "I guess it couldn't hurt to show off a pretty man on my arm. You do realize that when we're together, we're even more stunning, right? Have you seen two more beautiful men? I haven't. You'll be losing that if you break up with me." *Tell him. Tell him you love him.*

"That would be a tragedy," Parker said as we slowly made our way down the pier.

"It would."

Parker hooked his arm through mine. "I was freaking out yesterday, after our trip. It was…it meant so much to me. I was so scared of losing you, of chasing you away, of not being worthy of you…a million different things, and…"

He let the words linger until I nearly lost my mind. "What are you saying?"

"I'm getting there."

"Maybe try faster," I joked, making him chuckle.

"You're such a jerk...only, you're not. You never were, even from the start."

"I think you're getting sidetracked, and I want to know what you were originally trying to tell me."

"I went to see my dad last night. We talked about a lot of things...me and the guys too. It made me realize some important things."

My stomach dropped. I was a cut-the-cord kind of guy, so I said, "That this isn't about love?"

"That I'm more afraid than I ever realized. There was something about you from the start, El. I felt it deep in the marrow of my bones, even that first night. As soon as I said no to you, I regretted it. I went back to find you, to tell you I changed my mind, and—"

"Shit." I. Was. An idiot. "You saw me with another man." Everything began to make sense now—why Parker had been so insistent on not dating me, why he'd seemed angry with me.

"I was interested in you already. I wanted to get to know you, but then I saw you with him, and I felt...replaceable. Like you could never really want me. Want to fuck me, yes, but you'd never really *want* me."

Like the other men in his life. Like the fuckface from high school. "Beautiful...no, that's not true. I wanted you. I'm sorry you felt that way. I've never wanted anyone the way I want you. I—"

"Shh." He pressed his fingers to my lips. "Let me get this out first. I need to do this."

*Do what?* I wanted to ask, but instead I nodded, waited.

We were standing in the middle of the pier now. My gaze darted away and...was that Vaughn? What the fuck was he doing here? And wait...my parents were standing off to the side too, with Parker's dad...and Sebastian, who was wearing a hat and holding Declan's hand, Corbin and Marcus beside him.

My heart began to *flutter*, which was the only way I could think to describe it. For a moment I worried I should go to the doctor and get that checked. I'd never fluttered in my life, but then, Parker had changed everything, hadn't he?

"What's...?" I turned to look at him. "What are you doing?" But I knew, I fucking *knew*. He was down on one knee, with a box in his hand, looking up at me like I was the whole fucking world. Like his universe couldn't exist without me, the same thing I felt every time I thought of him.

"What do you think I'm doing?" he asked with a cocked brow.

People began to come closer. Mom was crying, as was Parker's dad, and I was pretty sure Corbin was too.

We were the center of attention. It was like something out of a movie, or one of the books Parker read, those romances I teased him about. Fuck, the way I felt right then, I would read one every day if I could recapture it.

Parker said, "My whole life I've dreamed of finding the one. I've chased love only to never catch it. For years I thought that was because I wasn't worthy, but now I know it's because all those other men weren't you. You're... You're *everything*. No one has ever made me feel the way you do, and I know we're already married, but this time I want to do it right, before I spend the rest of my life showing you how thankful I am for you. I'm so fucking in love with you." He opened the box. The ring was a million times better than the ones we had on—black, with a row of embedded diamonds in the middle. "You are the most romantic man I've ever met...you're sweet and kind...the perfect hero. Elliott Delgado Weaver...will you marry me...again?"

Jesus, my cheeks were hurting, I was smiling so big. Parker was *proposing* in a big and very public way. My perfect boy was on one knee for me, asking me to be his.

"You're leaving me hanging here," he said with a grin.

"I just...I didn't think I could feel this way. I didn't understand all the fuss about love until you. I'm crazy in love with you, beautiful, and fuck yes, I'll marry you again."

I tugged Parker to his feet, pulled him into my arms, and took possession of his mouth. Everyone around us was clapping and cheering, but it felt like it was just the two of us, this moment forever ours.

"That was incredible. I can't believe you did this for me." I nuzzled his neck, speaking softer. "Look at you, my perfect boy, making me the happiest man in the world. I can't wait to spend the rest of my life loving you."

"Oh God...don't get me hard. Why do I feel like I'm always saying that to you?"

I laughed. "Because you are."

"Elliott...this is better than I could have ever imagined—*you* are better than I could have ever imagined. Now stay still so I can put another ring on it!"

I laughed, our audience still cheering for us. Parker's hands were shaking as he pulled off our cheap Vegas ring and slid the new one on.

"I can't believe you're really mine." I held his face in my hands before kissing him again.

"Always."

"I can't hold back anymore!" Corbin yelled, running at us. "Beach Bum Hug!"

"Huh? What's that?" I asked, but then Corbin had his arms around Parker, followed by Declan, then Marcus. Just as Sebastian stepped up to my side, Parker reached for me and took my hand. He tugged me close, fingers tangled with mine,

Sebastian and I both joining in on their hug orgy.

It was perfect.

Vaughn was there when we parted. Mom, Dad, and Parker's dad too. People congratulated us as they walked by.

"Everyone want to hang out at our place to celebrate?" Dad asked.

The group agreed, but it was Parker's dad I was looking at. "We'd love for you to come too. I hope you will."

He nodded, before saying to Parker, "I'm so happy for you, son."

"Thank you, Dad. I love you so much."

He turned to me. "Thank you for loving my boy the way he deserves."

I got choked up, my throat full. "I'll always love him."

"We have a wedding to plan!" Mom cut in, and oh fuck, I was getting *married*. Dizziness swept over me. Forget that I already was married; this was…this was something else entirely.

"Oh my God! I know! I can't wait!" Parker replied, and once the panic eased, I realized how much I couldn't wait either.

We all went to my parents' place after that. When we first arrived, Parker asked to speak with me, Mom, and Dad in private. He apologized to them for our lies and to my mom for what she'd heard. "I'm so sorry. You welcomed me into your home and your family and…"

"Shh." Mom pulled him close. "It's in the past and we'll let it stay there."

Parker wiped his tears, clearly grateful before we met up in the living room with everyone else. We stayed for hours, eating, talking, and yes, already wedding-planning. I found a time to talk with Parker's dad to make my apologies for our lies too.

It was late by the time we got home, and now we were naked in bed after we'd made love. We talked more, about why both of us had been so quiet after Big Bear, about what I'd walked in and heard him say, and about the things he and his dad had spoken about.

"El?"

"Yeah?"

"Thank you for loving me."

"Beautiful, you don't have to thank me for doing that. I don't know for sure, or if it really matters to me, but I've been wondering if I might be demiromantic."

He pushed up onto his elbows, looking at me. "Really? How do you feel about that?"

I shrugged. "I don't know. I just know I love you. This…how I feel…I don't know that I had it in me before you. This connection we have, it's deeper. You give me something no one else ever could. It's always been you I was waiting for."

"God, I love you, El. Thank you for never giving up on me."

I couldn't wait to begin my happily ever after with Parker, The Romantic, by my side.

# EPILOGUE
## Parker

*Three Months Later*

"HELLO, BEAUTIFUL PEOPLE. Welcome to *The Vers*, where four best friends who rarely agree on anything give their versatile opinions about everything. I'm Corbin Erickson, The Charmer."

"I'm Parker Hansley-Weaver, The Romantic, and happily married man planning his second wedding to my current and only husband." I loved reminding people that Elliott was mine, but also, *I was planning a wedding!* It was such a dream come true, and I wanted to talk about it all the time.

"And I'm Marcus Alston, The Realist—in case everyone forgot since last week."

"Oooh, Marcus is grumpy today." Corbin nudged him.

"Is there a reason you interrupt before I introduce myself practically every time?" Declan questioned. Sometimes I didn't know how we actually got through the show each week. We were always nitpicking at each other.

"Yes, I love to annoy you. And you are again…?" Corbin teased, earning himself an eye roll from Declan.

"Declan Burns, The Loner."

Corbin winked at him. "Don't sound too excited, Monotone Molly. Oh, I was thinking—"

We all groaned at the same time. Corbin thinking was

always a dangerous thing and usually resulted in something absolutely ridiculous.

"Please don't," Marcus told him.

"Shut up. You're mean. This is fun. We need to come up with a combo name for Parker. The hyphenated one is too long. I vote for Parker Wansley." It was clear he was biting his cheek to keep from laughing.

I looked around for something to throw at him, but when I couldn't find anything, I settled on saying, "You're not calling me Parker Wansley."

"Parker Heaver?" Declan asked.

I punched him in the arm. "Why are you entertaining this idea?"

"Hansley-Weaver is a mouthful," Marcus said.

"Hey! That's what my date last night said about me!" Corbin joked, earning a second round of groans.

God, I loved them—loved us. Every day I woke up unable to believe my life was real. I had the best friends in the world and a husband I absolutely adored. And he felt the same about me, even if I did still leave my clothes all over the house. A secret, though…sometimes I left them there just so he could watch me pick them up and then tell me how good I was. I would always be a praise slut for him.

"I'm sorry, man," Marcus told Corbin when we'd all settled down. "It sucks when someone you're with lies to you."

"Um…you've seen my penis." Corbin looked at us. "Do you guys want to see it too?"

"What! No." Declan shook his head.

"Wait," I said, "why has Marcus seen your penis? And why are we calling it that?"

"Because we're professional adults." Corbin snickered. "You and Dec don't show each other your dicks?"

So much for professional adults. "What? No. I mean, I guess I might have seen his accidentally at some point, but this doesn't sound like the same thing."

Marcus rubbed a hand over his face. "Oh my God. Why the fuck do I hang out with you guys? It wasn't anything sexy. This dumbass let someone put a cock cage on him, and the guy took off with the key. I had to help him get it off, and when I did, well, let's just say Little Corbin got excited to be free."

"Big Corbin, and what the fuck, dude? You said you wouldn't tell anyone."

"You brought it up!" Marcus argued.

"Also…Levi, wherever you are, fuck you." Corbin flipped off the mic as if anyone other than us could see him.

"Wait, you…" I couldn't even finish my sentence without dissolving into laughter.

When Marcus and Declan joined in, Corbin said, "I was experimenting!" before he was cracking up too.

As always, it was Marcus who reeled us in. "All right, let's get back on track."

"Yes, Daddy," Corbin told him.

"I want to go first! Elliott and I finally nailed down a wedding date! We'll get married on the first day of summer next year." I appreciated that no one gave me a hard time about planning the ceremony—at least no one I cared about. There were comments on *The Vers* social media accounts, people wondering why we were having another ceremony and why we were waiting so long. We played the first part off by still letting them believe the first one was for love, but we wanted a ceremony with our family and friends. As for waiting until next summer, I only planned to do this once—well, once other than Vegas—and I wanted our wedding to be exactly what Elliott and I envisioned. Plus, Cat fucking loved this shit. We'd robbed her of the experience the first time, and neither Elliott nor I wanted to do it again. She and I were always talking wedding plans.

"Let me know if you need anything," Marcus said, and I grinned.

"You mean like your house?" I waggled my brows. His place was large enough, and he had private beach access.

"Anything for you, Parker Wansley-Heaver," he teased.

I mouthed a quiet *"Thank you"* to him before we continued with the episode.

It had been an interesting summer, to say the least. Sebastian had been gone for most of it, traveling all over the world to promote *Bound and Determined*. Declan had gone to some events with him. We'd all attended the LA and New York premieres, but Declan joined him for the London one too. They'd done a bit of exploring for a couple of days before Declan had to return home, and they were now planning a trip to Italy next summer.

Sebastian still hadn't taken on any other roles, but he was writing a second screenplay—while still unsure what he wanted to do with the first. I had a feeling the next movie he appeared in would be one of his own.

I tuned back in to the podcast just in time to share our sponsors, and then we finished recording the episode.

When we got out to the living room, Elliott and Sebastian were waiting for us. While they hadn't been able to spend a lot of time together the past few months due to Sebastian's travel, they were close. They spoke often, and I knew how much Sebastian's friendship meant to El.

"Hey, beautiful." Elliott pulled me into his arms and nuzzled my neck.

"Gag," Declan teased.

Corbin said, "I think I want to try this praise thing. It

sounds right up my alley. Try it on me, Elliott. Let me see if I like it." Corbin playfully tried to join our hug.

Elliott put an arm around him too. I loved how easily he'd fit in with the guys now that they didn't think he was going to break my heart. They actually teased me about being the heartbreaker of the two.

"I'm not sure it's praise you need," Elliott told him. "You're affectionate as fuck. You want someone touching you all the time." Wow, that made sense. My husband was good at reading people.

"Are you calling me a cuddle slut?" Corbin asked before his pupils blew wide. "Holy shit. I'm a cuddle slut. So I just need to find guys who want to touch me all the time? Eh...but I'm not typically affectionate in that way with men I'm sleeping with; just with Parker, Declan, and Marcus." When I cocked a brow, he added, "And your partners. Whatever. Same thing."

"Kid, get your ass over here and stop flirting with Parker's husband." Marcus wrapped a hand around Corbin's wrist and tugged him closer.

"Aww, you missed me. You secretly like hugs. I know you do." Corbin buried his face into the rose-and-skull tattoo on Marcus's chest. Marcus rolled his eyes, but still hugged Corbin.

"I'll get the grill going," Declan said. He kissed Sebastian before heading outside.

We all ended up out there together, cooking, chatting, and just hanging out. Our group had grown from four to six, and every day I was thankful for the people sitting around me.

"How's the bar doing?" Corbin asked Declan.

"Good. I'm a little stressed out because I might lose Kai. I give him shit sometimes, but he's really come through for me more times than I can count. His landlord is raising the rent, and his roommate is moving back to San Diego. Kai was already struggling, so there's no way he can afford to live there even if he found someone else to move in. He'll probably have to head back to Riverside, where his family is."

"Damn, to the IE, huh?" Parker asked. Riverside was part of the area known as the Inland Empire or the IE.

Sebastian said, "It sucks because he loves it here. Dec and I wanted to help him out, but he's too proud to let us help him with rent, plus with Dec being his boss and all…"

We got off the subject of Kai a few minutes later. Declan and Sebastian were the first to say they were heading home, followed by Elliott and me.

"Did you talk to your dad about next weekend?" Elliott asked. His parents liked to get us all together at least once a month. Dad had been every time so far. We were both making a point to be more active in each other's lives, and Dad was also trying to get out and do more on his own. I didn't know what it was about me finding Elliott, but I felt like it set something free inside Dad—at least, I hoped so. I wanted him to be as happy as I was.

"Yep. He said he'd be there."

"Good. I really want to take him to a football game this season."

"He would love that. Do I have to go?"

"My pretty boy doesn't want to go with me?" Elliott said in that low, seductive voice of his. There was nothing I wouldn't do when he spoke to me that way.

"Ugh. I hate you. Yes, I'll go."

He laughed. "You love me."

"I do…more than I thought possible."

He pulled into the driveway at home, the porchlight shining into the car. "I love you, beautiful. I'm going to take you inside and show you just how much."

"My Prince Charming is so much hotter than in the movies," I said, making him laugh.

We raced into the house, me pulling off clothes and tossing them as I went. When we fell into bed, Elliott worshipped my body the way only he could, and I knew we would spend the rest of our lives creating our own happily ever after, just like they did in the books.

Want more from *The Vers* crew? Preorder Marcus's story, The Realist!

Find Riley:

Newsletter

Reader's Group
facebook.com/groups/RileysRebels2.0

Facebook
facebook.com/rileyhartwrites

Twitter
twitter.com/RileyHart5

Goodreads
goodreads.com/author/show/7013384.Riley_Hart

Instagram
instagram.com/rileyhartwrites

BookBub
bookbub.com/profile/riley-hart

# Other Books by Riley Hart

**Series by Riley Hart**
Inevitable
Secrets Kept
Briar County
Atlanta Lightning
Blackcreek
Boys In Makeup with Christina Lee
Broken Pieces
Crossroads
Fever Falls with Devon McCormack
Finding
Forbidden Love with Christina Lee
Havenwood
Jared and Kieran
Last Chance
Metropolis with Devon McCormack
Rock Solid Construction
Saint and Lucky
Stumbling Into Love
Wild side

**Standalone books:**
Boyfriend Goals
Strings Attached
Beautiful & Terrible Things
Love Always
Endless Stretch Of Blue

Looking For Trouble
His Truth

**Standalone books with Devon McCormack:**
No Good Mitchell
Beautiful Chaos
Weight Of The World
Up For The Challenge

**Standalone books with Christina Lee:**
Science & Jockstraps
Of Sunlight and Stardust

# About the Author

Riley Hart's love of all things romance shines brightly in everything she writes. Her primary focus is Male/Male romance but under various pen names, her prose has touched practically every part of the spectrum of love and relationships. The common theme that ties them all together is stories told from the heart.

A hopeless romantic herself, Riley is a lover of character-driven plots, many with flawed and relatable characters. She strives to create stories that readers can not only fall in love with, but also see themselves in. Real characters and real love blended together equal the ultimate Riley Hart experience.

When Riley isn't creating her next story, you can find her reading, traveling, or dreaming about reading or traveling, and spending time with her two perfectly snarky kids, and one swoon-inducing husband.

Riley Hart is represented by Jane Dystel at Dystel, Goderich & Bourret Literary Management. She's a 2019 Lambda Literary Award Finalist for *Of Sunlight and Stardust*.

Printed in Great Britain
by Amazon